I0535858

SIXTY-FIFTH-ANNIVERSARY ISSUE

Spring, 1988   All artwork by George Barr

THE DEAD MAN .... Gene Wolfe   9
After a narrow escape, he only wanted to go home . . .
AT THE POINT OF CAPRICORN .... Gene Wolfe   14
Everyone came to the end of the world to hear the old woman's tales!
MARY BEATRICE SMOOT FRIARLY, SPV .... Gene Wolfe   16
Collecting cookbooks can lead to odd acquaintances.
JOHN K. (KINDER) PRICE .... Gene Wolfe   20
His obsession with the grimoire grew beyond reason!
THE BOY WHO HOOKED THE SUN .... Gene Wolfe   21
He went fishing . . . and hooked more than he bargained for.
THE OTHER DEAD MAN .... Gene Wolfe   30
A weird tale of interplanetary doom!
THE UNLAWFUL HUNTER .... Keith Taylor   44
Stealing cattle on Samhain Eve was not a good idea . . .
MENAGE A TROIS .... F. Paul Wilson   54
A caretaker, a maid, and a hag—a recipe for love and death!
THE WONDERFUL WALLSTRETCHER .... Felix C. Gotschalk   74
It was a machine every house should have . . .
BOILED ALIVE .... Ramsey Campbell   80
Just a typical video nasty—until its characters phoned him!
THE MYSTERIES OF THE FACELESS KING .... Darrell Schweitzer   90
He could never remove the mask, never return to what he'd been.
WHAT CAN A CHILD DO? .... Chet Williamson   105
When kindness was no longer enough, only terror remained!
WELL-CONNECTED .... T.E.D. Klein   111
Inevitably, it was time to meet Mr. Hagendorn. There was no escape.
SISTER ABIGAIL'S COLLECTION .... Lloyd Arthur Eshbach   121
He buried his wife with that pendant. So why was it in the pawn shop?
DEATH DANCES .... Tanith Lee   132
Death came at suns' rise. She had appointments to keep . . .

VERSE
JOHN MASON SIDD by Joseph Payne Brennan: 88, IMPROBABLE BESTIARY: THE BIGFOOT by F. Gwynplaine MacIntyre: 89, HAD I APPROACHED MY DISCOVERY IN A MORE NOBLE SPIRIT by Ruth Berman: 110, OLD GODS PROWL by Nancy Springer: 120

FEATURES
THE EYRIE 4
PROFILE: GENE WOLFE .... David G. Hartwell   13
WEIRD TALES™ TALKS WITH GENE WOLFE .... Darrell Schweitzer   23
REVIEWS .... John Gregory Betancourt   141

Published quarterly by the Terminus Publishing Company, Inc., Box 13418, Philadelphia PA 19101-3418. Application to mail at second class postage rates pending at Philadelphia, PA, and additional mailing offices. Single copies, $3.50 (plus $1.00 postage if ordered by mail). *Subscription rates:* Eighteen months (six issues) in the United States, its possessions, and Canada: $18.00; elsewhere, $27.00. The publishers are not responsible for the loss of manuscripts, although reasonable care will be taken of such material while in their possession.
Copyright © 1987 by the Terminus Publishing Company, Inc.; all rights reserved; reproduction prohibited without prior permission. *Weird Tales*™ is a trade mark owned by Weird Tales, Limited.

THE EYRIE

Weird Tales™! The Unique Magazine! We welcome you to the fifth incarnation and the 290th issue of *Weird Tales*™, sometimes jokingly called The Thing That Wouldn't Die. But, while Undying Things will certainly be at home in our pages, we editors wish to be serious for a moment to explain what we intend our *Weird Tales*™ to be.

For generations of fantasy readers, *Weird Tales*™ has had a very special magic. There have been other fantasy magazines, even brilliant ones such as *Unknown*; but somehow *Weird Tales*™ remains the best remembered — a magazine for which the phrase "proud title" was invented, or certainly should have been — and that is why *Weird Tales*™ has been the subject of so many revivals.

We intend to resurrect the magazine, not to exhume it. Our *Weird Tales*™ is to be a living magazine, not a ghostly revenant from the past. *Weird Tales*™ has been a wonderful old title. It has occupied a major place in the weird-fantasy field; it has been a home for almost every important writer of fantastic fiction in the first half of this century: H.P. Lovecraft, Robert E. Howard, Ray Bradbury, Fritz Leiber, Clark Ashton Smith, Robert Bloch, Henry Kuttner, E.F. Benson, Algernon Blackwood, Henry S. Whitehead, Seabury Quinn, Theodore Sturgeon, Edmond Hamilton, Joseph Payne Brennan, H.R. Wakefield, Jack Williamson, August Derleth, plus writers more commonly associated with science fiction — Robert A. Heinlein, Isaac Asimov, Fredric Brown, and Eric Frank Russell, for example

— and even such less likely people as Tennessee Williams, Harry Houdini (though ghosted by H.P. Lovecraft), and the author of *The Phantom of the Opera*, Gaston Le-Roux. We are responsible for living up to that history, but we recognize that nostalgia can be a trap.

Therefore, the new *Weird Tales*™ will try to be what the magazine would have become had it survived, continuously and uninterruptedly up to the present, as a living, changing, viable publication. We think this is what all the people who helped make *Weird Tales*™ great in the past would have wanted. This is the greatest tribute we can give them.

In *Weird Tales*™, then, we will offer the best *new* fiction by the best writers now active in the fantasy and horror field — without limiting our scope entirely to those genres. The magazine will publish fantasy and horror, yes; but it will include an occasional story which doesn't fit *any* classification, as well as the odd science-fiction tale which seems to be a *Weird Tales*™ story first and secondarily a science-fiction one, such as Gene Wolfe's "The Other Dead Man," which appears for the first time anywhere in this issue. Will we use reprints? Well, sort of. The T.E.D. Klein story in this issue is a retitled and revised version of a tale that appeared in a New England hotel magazine. The Ramsey Campbell story was published in England. Some of the Gene Wolfe material has previously appeared in incredibly obscure sources: not even Gene has a copy of that 1965 issue of *Sir!* containing "The Dead Man." So these are reprints, but we don't think you've seen them before. We don't intend to reprint stories from the previous incarnations of *Weird Tales*™ since so many of them have already been reprinted, to the point that a collector of *Weird Tales*™ has a hard time finding an issue whose contents aren't already familiar through various reprintings.

We will be using work by some of the great old *Weird Tales*™ names. Lloyd Arthur Eshbach, whose "Isle of the Undead" was the cover story on the October 1936 issue, has a brand-new story in this issue: "Sister Abigail's Collection." We may also use a few stories by great writers who are now dead, but we make a distinction between posthumous publication and literary necrophilia. If a story is good enough, and its previous publication — if any — was obscure enough, then we may use it; if not, we won't. Printing disastrous rejects or juvenilia by Famous Old-Time Writers is necrophilia. (We have nothing against necrophilia in *Weird Tales*™, but not as an editorial policy.)

This, then, is what we mean by a living magazine. We want *Weird Tales*™ to be known for the strength of the stories, not just for its history. With your help, we think we will succeed.

But that history *is* interesting: *Weird Tales*™ was founded in 1923, three years before *Amazing Stories*®, which was the first all-science-fiction magazine. *Weird Tales*™'s original publishers were John Lansinger and Joseph Henneberger, who started the magazine because there was little outlet for weird and bizarre fiction. Henneberger wanted, as he put it, *"to give the writer free rein to express his innermost feelings in a manner befitting great literature."*

Clearly this was no conventional pulp magazine, for all that much of the contents of the early issues were hardly "great literature." Henneberger and his editor, Edwin Baird, managed to keep going for just one year; but in that year they published early stories by H.P. Lovecraft and Seabury Quinn, who were to become the magazine's mainstays in later times.

In 1924 *Weird Tales*™ was reorganized. Farnsworth Wright was named editor, and

the great era of the magazine began. Wright was a tireless, brilliant editor who persevered, sometimes without salary in the depths of the Depression, because he believed that the magazine had, as its subtitle suggested, something unique to offer to American literature. It was Wright who gave the world Robert E. Howard's Conan the Barbarian, the bulk of Lovecraft's fiction, the early stories of Robert Bloch, and C.L. Moore's wonderful Northwest Smith and Jirel of Joiry adventures. He is remembered very fondly by the writers who worked with him.

Farnsworth Wright edited the magazine through the March 1940 issue, in spite of deteriorating health; he died later that year, having outlived all too many of his major contributors — Lovecraft, Howard, Henry S. Whitehead, and G.G. Pendarves. His successor was Dorothy McIlwraith, a very competent pulp editor, who is less well remembered than she deserves to be. When she took over, *Weird Tales*™ faced serious competition from John Campbell's *Unknown*; many of the magazine's major authors were dead or had, like Clark Ashton Smith, virtually ceased writing; and higher-paying markets were drawing off the best

of the others. She discovered and developed new talents: Ray Bradbury, Fritz Leiber, Joseph Payne Brennan, and others. Much of the material for Bradbury's classic *Dark Carnival* (1947), which Stephen King has called "the *Dubliners* of American horror fiction," appeared in the early McIlwraith issues. She managed to keep the magazine going until 1954.

Almost at once there was talk of reviving *Weird Tales*™. Leo Margulies apparently planned to do so in 1957, but Sam Moskowitz was the first to actually get the project off the ground. Moskowitz edited four issues which appeared in 1973 and 1974. His was a good try; but without an adequate editorial budget Moskowitz could buy only a few new stories, so the contents were mostly public-domain reprints, more rare than genuinely interesting. Truly terrible distribution soon killed the magazine again in any case. The next revival was by Zebra Books: four mass-market paperback anthologies edited by Lin Carter, who assembled an excellent array of new and old material. Although these sold well enough that some issues went back to press, Carter was unable to continue; and the Zebra incarnation ceased.

More recently, *Weird Tales*™ was revived in California, but with very small printings and somewhat confusing circumstances. We do not understand just what happened (at times it seemed like the old Abbott and Costello joke, "Who's on first? No, Who's on second."), and we suspect some of the participants don't either. Two different people claimed to be the sole editor. An issue appeared in 1984 and another in 1985, both edited by Gil Lamont. The first featured a fine story by Harlan Ellison, as well as one by Stephen King. Although that issue was distributed to a few specialized comic-book shops, none of us has seen the second issue on sale anywhere except at science-fiction conventions at prices of $20.00 or more.

Throughout these last two incarnations of the magazine, the title itself has been owned by Robert Weinberg, the author of a fine history of *Weird Tales*™ as well as other books about the pulp-magazine era. Neither he nor we were involved with publication of those previous incarnations:

Weinberg simply leased the title to the publishers.

In March of 1987, at the urging of John Betancourt, we — George H. Scithers, Darrell Schweitzer, and John Betancourt — rented the title from Weinberg; formed the Terminus Publishing Company, Inc., a small, closely-held corporation; and began buying material for the magazine. Our *Weird Tales*™ is going to be as much a continuation of the Baird-Wright-McIlwraith magazine as we can make it, reasonably priced and readily available, by subscription and through specialized bookstores. We have no interest in newsstand distribution. Initial frequency is quarterly, increasing to bi-monthly as soon as circulation permits.

So, watch this space for further, exciting developments.

The Eyrie is the traditional *Weird Tales*™ lettercolumn. We want to see your reactions to this first issue, and we will publish the most interesting of them in the second. But for now, let us share a few interesting letters from the magazine's past, beginning with the most famous *misquotation* in the history of fantasy literature. What H.P. Lovecraft actually wrote, in a letter in the February 1928 *Weird Tales*™, was:

*"All my tales are based on the fundamental premise that common human laws and interests and emotions have no validity or significance in the vast cosmos-at-large. To me there is nothing but puerility in a tale in which the human form — and the local human passions and conditions and standards — are depicted as native to other worlds or other universes. . . . Only the human scenes and characters must have human qualities. These must be handled with unsparing **realism** (not catchpenny **romanticism**), but when we cross the line to the boundless and hideous unknown — the shadow-haunted **Outside** — we must remember to leave our humanity and terrestrialism at the threshold."*

This was later misremembered by August Derleth as the celebrated "quote" justifying *Derleth's* version of the Cthulhu Mythos:

"All my stories, unconnected as they may be, are based on the fundamental lore or legend that this world was inhabited at one time by another race who, in practising

black magic, lost their foothold and were expelled, yet live outside ever ready to take possession of this Earth again."

As a result, the Cthulhu Mythos followed Derleth's ideas, not Lovecraft's, with such concepts as good and evil applied to the cosmos at large, a kind of eldritch shoot-out of Good Gods versus Bad Gods, all of which is quite alien to Lovecraft's aesthetic and philosophical outlook.

On a less serious note, when Conan the Barbarian was appearing in virtually every issue of *Weird Tales*™, then-fan Robert Bloch wrote in the November 1934 issue:

"I am awfully tired of poor Conan the Cluck, who for the past fifteen issues has every month slain a new wizard, tackled a new monster, come to a sudden and violent end that was averted (incredibly enough!) in just the nick of time, and won a new girl-friend, each of whose penchant for nudism won her a place of honor, either on the cover or on the inner illustration. Such has been Conan's history, and from the realms of the Kushites to the lands of Aquilonia, from the shores of the Shemites to the palaces of Dyme-Novell-Bolonia, I cry: 'Enough of this brute and his iron-thewed sword-thrusts — may he be sent to Valhalla to cut out paper dolls.'"

In the February-March 1931 issue, E. Hoffmann Price had commented that the *"epic sweep"* of Howard's work *"makes you hanker for a horse and battle-ax, and about forty men-at-arms to give you something to practise on."* In 1934, editor Wright humorously suggested that readers might want to sharpen their axes for Bloch, whose first published story was about to appear; but the anticipated massacre never came off. Bloch was instantly popular, and expressed real appreciation for some of Howard's work at the time of Howard's death two years later. He never backed down on Conan, but readers forgave him as he went on to contribute such classic chillers as "Yours Truly, Jack the Ripper" (July 1943). For the November 1942 issue he was asked to contribute a brief verbal sketch of himself (during this period "The Eyrie" was not so much a letter column as a "meet the author" feature) and he wrote, in part:

*"... This vicious gossip that I am a fiend in more or less human form is utterly incorrect. I have **never** strangled anyone with my bare hands. Always use gloves, because of fingerprints. The only time I ever tasted human flesh was during a wrestling match when I accidentally chewed off a man's arm. As a matter of fact, I am really a very lovable person, as my friends tell me — or would, if I had any friends. Deep down underneath I have the heart of a small boy. I keep it in a jar, on my desk."*

In the November 1943 issue, Ray Bradbury explained the essential insight which brought him his own early success:

"I don't particularly care about ghosts, vampires, or werewolves; they've been killed by repetition. . . . There are good stories in everyday things. Trains, crowds, motor-cars, submarines, dogs — the wind around a house. I'd like to use them more. There's much good stuff buried in the green leaves of childhood and the heaped dead leaves of old age. I want to get at that too. I want to write about humans; and add an unusual, unsuspected twist."

In the 25th Anniversary issue, March 1948, August Derleth summed up the importance of *Weird Tales*™:

"For a quarter of a century Weird Tales *has given those who delight in the fantastic and macabre the best in the genre, and it has remained the most consistently satisfying outlet of its kind. For all these years authors and readers have looked to this unique magazine as something very special, and, despite a welter of imitators, something very special it has remained. A magazine which brought to the attention of the public the work of such authors as H.P. Lovecraft, Clark Ashton Smith, Henry S. Whitehead, Ray Bradbury, and many another fine writer has justified many times over its sterling reason for being and has earned its right to exist."*

With the current issue, *Weird Tales*™ marks its sixty-fifth anniversary. We can only hope that in your estimation, readers, we have earned the right to *continue.*

Next issue in "The Eyrie": letters from *you!*

— The Editors
∎

THE DEAD MAN
by Gene Wolfe

When the peasant came out of his house in the morning, the Brahman was sitting cross-legged in the sunshine before his own door. The Brahman was old, and emaciated by fasting in the way often seen in wandering fakirs but seldom in settled members of the highest caste. And although the peasant was early abroad to escape the banter of the women (water-carrying being unfit for a man), the Brahman had been about before him, for when he neared the ford he could see floating in the slack water the marigold wreaths the Brahman had cast in to propitiate the river and the magar and the other powers of the waters.

The magar was a crocodile. Nine days ago it had taken the wife of the peasant's half-brother as she waded across the ford, so notifying the villagers that the crossing was unsafe again, as it was said to have been in their grandfathers' time but had not been within living memory.

That same day, his own wife had been bitten on the foot when she kicked a jackal snuffing too near the spot where their son was playing. She had cursed, then laughed at the bloody scratch left by the frightened jackal's teeth; but next morning her foot was hot to the touch and twice its healthy size. Now, after prayers and poultices of dung, it was better. She could hobble on it, though not far, and cook and care for the child; but it would be long yet before she could bring water, and his mother — who had cried, and shrieked that the gods intended the destruction of the wives of all her sons — was too old.

With a pad on his shoulder, he could carry their largest jar easily, for he was a strong man, brown and lean from hard work in the fields of millet and upland rice. Stepping with care so as not to stir the mud, he bent slowly; and where the depth was great enough to take the jar, he filled it with the morning-cool, nearly stagnant water. There was nothing at the ford to disturb the peace of daybreak, though a hundred feet away, where the village stood just above the flood mark, many were stirring into wakefulness.

The magar was not to be seen. The peasant knew well how cleverly a crocodile assumes the very angle and position most natural to a stranded log on a sandbar, and how softly shadow-like it slips through still water without rippling the surface; but it was not there. He shouldered the jar again and began the walk uphill.

He and his fellow villagers, ignorant of the comparative religion of the schools, would cheerfully have killed the magar if they could. Indeed, one of the boatmen had been fishing for it with an iron hook as thick as a man's thumb hidden in the well-rotted haunch of a goat. Still, until the boatman caught it or they found it far enough from water to be slain with axes and spears, they would have been fools not to try to persuade it to be content with homage from their village and, especially, to move on up or downstream. Possibly in the dry season, when the river would dwindle to a trickle, something might be done. The peasant set down the water jar carefully so as not to waken his family. He heard his mother's rasping breath; as the jar made a soft *chunk* on the earthen floor, his wife moaned and moved her arm.

9

was a strong man, taller and bigger of bone than most of his people, he had time for one full-throated scream, and time to draw the breath for another, before the water closed over his nose and mouth.

For a few seconds he resisted before instinct, or reason, or the passivity of India and the East made him swallow, hug his chest with his arms, and submit, feeling the dark, cold fingers of the river loose his rag of turban and tangle his long, black hair. Then, as his heart pounded and his ears swelled and the trapped breath tried to burst past his closed throat and locked lips, he fought again, ignoring the pain already creeping into his numbed leg.

When next he came to know our world — *maya*, that which is not God — it was as a small circle of pale blue far above his eyes. He tried to blink and discovered that he could not, and that his mouth was filled with water and mud (or perhaps with blood) which he could not expel. Even the muscles that controlled the motions of his eyes had forgotten their function, so that he could not direct his gaze to right or left; but he found, in the absence of this ability, that he could treat his field of vision as a window and shift his attention to one side or the other, so as to peer slantwise across his own eyes and examine the edges, where the ghosts of the newly dead and the more material demons flutter away from a man's view.

He was lying in a dark abscess in the earth, on mud, as his shoulders told him. Toward his feet was the carcass of a young blackbuck, its belly stretched by the rapid decomposition that attacks dead ruminants.

To his left (he strained to see, and in straining felt the vertebrae of his neck move ever so slightly, grating one upon another) nearly hidden in shadow, rose the familiar, undulating curves of a young and not unslender woman lying

The second jar was smaller and older than the first, with a chipped place at the lip. He took it up and left the dimness of his home again for the brilliance of the street. The house had smelled of smoke; outside a breeze brought the rank, indescribable early-morning smell of second-growth jungle, a jungle cut fifty years before for timber, now growing up again in hardwoods. By the water, the river-odor of rotten vegetation returned, and the gray warmth of dust under his bare feet changed once more to the cold slipperiness of mud.

This time he was not quite so careful, and one of his feet slid a trifle, sending out a slow cloud of fine black sediment. He took two more steps in the direction of the barely perceptible current before bending to fill his jar.

Without warning, his left calf was struck by steel bars, simultaneously from front and rear. A hip-dislocating wrench sent him sprawling in the shallows while the half-filled jar rocked in the waves of his struggle. Because he on her side — the roundness of the head, the concavity of the neck, the rise of the shoulder declining to the waist, and the strong domination of the child-bearing hips tapering to thighs and knees lost in darkness. A drugged and whirling concourse of surmises rushed through his mind, until simultaneously and without consciousness of contradiction he felt that he lay in the palace of a scaled river-spirit and asleep beside his wife.

His attention was drawn from the woman by an alteration in the light, the passage of some dark object across the disk of blue. It came again, hesitated, and returned by the path it had come. This it did three times in what could have been a hundred breaths; and while he watched it, he became aware of a stench indescribably fetid in the air that stirred sluggishly through his nostrils.

The dark object crossed the light for the fourth time, and he saw it to be a leaf at the tip of a twig. Then he understood that his shadowy vault was the den of the magar, hollowed in the mud of the river bank, where he lay with his face beneath the "chimney" providing the minute ventilation necessary to prevent the den from filling with the gases of putrefaction. When the sun rose higher, it would become an oven in which decay would luxuriate and dead flesh rise like dough until the bodies were soft enough to be dismembered easily. He did not connect this with the crocodile's teeth, which were of piercing shape only, unable to grind or cut; nor with its short front legs, which were unable to reach what its jaws held, although he knew these things.

He knew all these things and the habits of the magar — the rotting-den and the sudden grab at the ford or the rush up from the water — but he was unafraid, though he knew without looking a second time the identity of the woman beside him. After a long while he rose and began working his way out through the chimney, uncertain even as he did whether he laboriously pushed the earth aside to enlarge the hole or merely drifted through, and up like smoke.

The village was quiet now with the emptiness of noon, when the men were in the fields. He heard sobbing from his house as he dragged his injured leg along the village street, and the softer sound of chanted prayers. Sunlight shone brighter than he could recall having seen it ever before, the dazzle from the dust and the sides of the mud houses so great that he scarcely cast a shadow as he stood in the doorway of his home; neither the young woman, nor the old, nor the Brahman saw him

© G. Barr - 1987

11

until he entered the gloom of the interior where they sat, though his son ceased his gurgling and stared with wide brown eyes.

When they saw him at last, he could not speak, but looked from face to face, beginning and ending with his wife, conscious of having come to the close of something. After a moment the Brahman muttered, "Do not address it. It is seldom good to hear what they will say." He took up a handful of saffron powder from the brass bowl beside him and flung it into the air, calling upon a Name that brought dissolution and release. ■

George H. Scithers
Darrell Schweitzer
John Betancourt
Editors & Publishers

Leslie Smith
Karl Würf
Assistant Editors

Yale F. Edeiken
Of Counsel

John M. Ford
Technical Assistant

David J. Williams, III
Computer Consultant

Robert Weinberg
Special Consultant

Advanced Litho, Inc.
Photographer

The Twin Company, Inc.
Typesetter

Malloy Lithographing, Inc.
Printer

SUBMISSIONS?

Like most editors, we get unsolicited manuscripts, *lots* of them. We survive, as do other editors, only by imposing Rules.

Yes, we read unsolicited manuscripts—*if* they are in proper manuscript format. Each must arrive with a return envelope, addressed and stamped, big enough to take that manuscript back to you, or with a business-letter-sized envelope (addressed and stamped) for our reply *and* instructions to dispose of the manuscript if not bought. And no, we will not read manuscripts in unacceptable format.

This proper format is described in many standard reference works. One is the pamphlet "Constructing Scientifiction and Fantasy," available from Dragon Publishing, PO Box 110, Lake Geneva WI, 53147, for $2.00 a copy. Another, *On Writing Science Fiction: The Editors Strike Back!*, by George Scithers, Darrell Schweitzer, and John M. Ford, discusses format—and the whole art and practice of writing and selling fantastic literature; $17.50, postpaid, from Owlswick Press, PO Box 8243, Philadelphia PA 19101 (if you live in Pennsylvania, add $1.05 for sales tax). We also recommend Strunk & White's *The Elements of Style*, Margaret Shertzer's *The Elements of Grammar*, and Arthur Plotnik's *The Elements of Editing*, widely available in inexpensive, hard-cover and paper-bound editions from the Macmillan Publishing Co., Inc.

PROFILE: GENE WOLFE

by David G. Hartwell

Gene Wolfe writes stories of astonishing clarity and complexity, stories that disturb and excite, wonder stories. He does this by applying Arthur C. Clarke's dictum about sufficiently advanced technology to the art of writing—and so his effects are indistinguishable from magic. I can tell you about one of his tricks, though. At the World Fantasy Convention in Chicago several years ago, where he was the guest of honor, he told a joke as part of a panel appearance. He told it well, and when he got to the punch line, everyone laughed—although he never actually uttered the punch line—because everyone understood what it had to be from the telling. He does that on a larger scale in his fiction, embedding information and detail in the text with such art that you can know more than you have been overtly told. I gain much pleasure from reading a Wolfe tale twice because, yes, there is an immediate payoff the first time through; but the story yields more, and at the same time becomes even more suggestive, upon re-reading.

Gene is a friendly, sensitive man given to kidding and pleasant anecdotes on social occasions, open in some ways but quite private and reserved in others. He has the rare social grace of allowing others to expose themselves, encouraging it, and gently undercutting whatever inadequacies emerge. He allows you to feel improved by exposure. Not that he's always that way with me, his editor—I recall with some pain a seven-page letter accusing me of careless skimming when I didn't pick up a detail embedded in a sentence on page 137 that made clear and obvious what was going on 200 pages later in *Free Live Free*. I had read the manuscript twice and must have slipped up on that sentence both times. I believe that I have been partly forgiven. James Joyce spent more than a decade writing *Finnegans Wake* and is reported to have said that one should spend that amount of time reading it to approach a thorough understanding. Gene Wolfe's stories are less demanding than that.

But the effects are still indistinguishable from magic. And he achieves them through concentration and care. As to what his goals are, he once said that he tries to do his absolute best each time out. He loves words and uses a great variety of them with gusto and precision. He knows the mechanics of sentences and wields each one like a craftsman driving an auto he built himself from the finest parts and materials. And like a craftsman proud of his artifice, he wants you to admire and treasure his work, whether he has made a charming cuckoo clock this time, a marvelous automaton from clever gears, or a mighty engine such as *THE BOOK OF THE NEW SUN*.

I'm glad that Gene could choose to retire from his job a few years back, because it has meant that we are seeing more of his fine work, more often; stories and novels of variety and substance heretofore only hoped for, seldom seen. Wolfe, in the 1980s, is tantamount to a one-man New Wave in fantasy, SF, and horror. Last year there was *Soldier of the Mist*, this year *The Urth of the New Sun*, next year *There Are Doors*, and after that *Soldier of Arete* and at least one more entirely different novel, this one about a castle in the Midwest, and all the while a continuous outpouring of short fiction. All of it will be the highest form of entertainment: rich, dense, worth experiencing again.

Wow! ∎

13

AT THE POINT OF CAPRICORN

by Gene Wolfe

The children crouched in a circle around the fire, looking skeptical and attentive as the old woman poked the embers. "It is true that the days have been getting shorter," she said. "But that is no reason to be afraid."

"*I* haven't been scared," the oldest boy announced, and he tossed the bone he had been sucking into the fire. The others stirred and looked at one another sidelong, for they had been afraid and knew that he had been too. The old bone cracked and popped in the heat like green wood.

"That shows how wise you have be-

© G. Barr - 1987

come by listening to my stories," the old woman said, and the oldest boy smiled, then frowned, for she said it so that it cut on every side, like the jagged ice he sometimes threw. A few snowflakes drifted through the mouth of the cave, and the smallest girl, who had been made to sit with her back to it, pulled her wolfskin more tightly about her.

"All the world comes here to the end of the world just to hear my stories," the old woman said, and the children nodded because they had heard her say that many times and knew it was true.

"That is so," the viking confirmed, and the children turned to look at him, for they had not seen him come in.

"Welcome, Knute's son," the old woman said softly.

The viking squatted behind the children, propping his chin on the haft of Legbiter, his sword. "Tell them, old woman," he grumbled. "Tell them why we kindle bonfires in winter to bring back the youth and life of Tyr Odinson the one-handed, who was stolen from us by the Frost Giants of Niflheim."

"That I will not," the old woman said, "since you yourself already have."

A lexicographer who had been listening at the mouth of the cave stepped inside, powdered with snow and looking very dusty. "*Bonfire* has nothing to do with all that," he said. "Such fires take their name from the bones that were burned in them at mid-winter."

Knuteson rose and slashed at him with Legbiter, catching him quite effectively just where the neck joins the shoulder.

14

The children moaned "Oooh!" in chorus, and the old woman spread her hands before the fire. "It does warm old bones," she said. "Tyr's or mine, and that's a fact."

A pastry chef who had been watching from the back of the cave cleared his throat and twisted the left point of his small, black mustache. "Is is for that reason, Chèr Madame, that we call him *le bonfeu* — the good fire, how-you-say. May I inquire of you, since already I am so bold, how far are we here from the fine city of Paris, Texas? I there conduct Le Café de Paris, which perhaps has need of me."

"We are at the end of the world," the old woman said.

A druid entered, combing his white beard with long fingers. He was crowned with mistletoe. "It is now the winter solstice," he told the pastry chef, "When the Sun rises between Sacred Stones Fifty-Five and Fifty-Six. Though He has not done so yet. Quite an important date, really." He looked at Knuteson. "Would it bother anyone if I were to take this chap for a bit of a sacrifice?"

A professor of comparative religion who had entered with him declared, "It is firmly established that the Druids did not practice human sacrifice."

The druid murmured, "Quite so — we really don't *need* the practice now, do we? But it seems such a shame to waste him."

The oldest boy, who had been going through the lexicographer's pockets, told them, "He's already dead, I think."

"Very possibly," the druid admitted. "But since the Sun's still asleep, perhaps He won't notice. Take his ankles will you? There's a good little chap."

When they were gone, the youngest girl asked, "Where is the Sun? Is he really sleeping?"

"He has gone into the south," the old woman said, "following the birds. He will return when he sees the beautiful tree we have made —"

"Yggdrasil," Knuteson explained.

"— for he will know the birds will want to perch on its boughs." Then the old woman began to tell them that story.

The professor grunted. "Another solar myth. It is actually the inclination of the Earth, I believe."

Mother Gaea, one of whose mouths the cave was, rumbled, "It *is* my inclination, and don't you forget it," Several large stones dropped from the roof of the cave.

"Don't make her talk any more," the oldest remaining boy advised the professor.

Just at that moment, the first rays of the new-risen Sun streaked through the mouth of the cave. "It's true!" the youngest girl piped to the old woman. "All the world comes to hear your stories! The Sun has come too."

"He always comes at this time of year," the old woman said. "Still, the Sun comes not to hear my story, but to tell his own, here at the beginning of the world. ∎

MARY BEATRICE SMOOT FRIARLY, SPV

by Gene Wolfe

Born Beatrice Smoot Friarly, Easter Sunday, 1925, in New Canaan, Massachusetts. According to Sister Mary herself, her birth on Easter was due entirely to the efforts of her mother (Martha Smoot Friarly), who would normally have given birth on Holy Saturday, but who contrived by an uncommon effort of will and with considerable pain to delay genesis until the minute hand of the large clock on the wall of the delivery room was well past twelve.

Mrs. Friarly was undoubtedly hoping for a boy. She did not, however, proceed to raise little Beatrice like one, but like nothing on Earth.

When Beatrice was fifteen she appeared (weeping) one fine June morning at the door of Father John O'Murphy, her pastor. She had spent the previous twenty-four hours in prayer and had concluded that her vocation was real. She begged Father O'Murphy to bring her to the attention of some order that might accept her as a postulant. Muttering that it would at least get her out of her mother's house, Father O'Murphy promised to see what he could do.

Approximately a year later (June 17, 1941), Beatrice entered her novitiate with the Sisters of Perpetual Vigilance, an order of nuns intent on saving their oil for the coming of the bridegroom. Upon completion of the vows, she took the religious name of Mary and took over the Fourth Grade at the School of Saint Apollos the Persuasive.

Her collection of cookbooks was begun somewhat late in her life, when the grateful mother of one of her pupils presented her with a tattered volume that had been passed from one generation to the next for nearly eighty years. That evening, Sister Mary spent half an hour looking it over, and was a collector evermore.

As such, she possessed but feeble means; the prices of all but the most humble dealers were far beyond her reach. But she had a considerable amount of time at her disposal, having discovered long ago that reading did her young charges more good that anything she could say; boundless patience; the good will of thousands of men and women now scattered across the face of the world who looked back upon the Fourth Grade as the happiest year in their lives; and a strange, unpresuming suppleness of speech that she attributed (when she was willing to admit that she possessed such a power at all) to nearly fifty years of the most faithful prayer to St. Apollos.

On a sullen summer night not long ago, when black clouds gathered over the Hoosac Hills and the wind stirred like a restless child, Sister Mary completed her evening devotions and retired to bed. It was about nine thirty.

A short time later, as it seemed to her, she heard a knock at the door of the small convent she shared with Sisters Bruno and Evangellica. For a moment or two she lay quiet, waiting for Sister Evangellica, who was much younger, to answer it. Then it came to her (she could not say how) that Sister Evangellica and even Sister Bruno slept on, and would go on sleeping though

16

the knocking continued all night. That they could not hear it and would never hear it.

She rose then, went to the door, and opened it. It was raining, and the rain turned to steam when it struck the cloak of the short, dark man who stood at the doorstep. "Shalom," he said.

"Shalom," Sister Mary replied automatically, and he stepped across the threshold.

"And I mean it," he said. "I come in peace. I'm coming in answer — partly — to your prayers."

"You mean my prayers have only helped to condemn me," said Sister Mary, who had recognized him. "I'd hoped for more. But I'm sure the sentence is just, and I'm ready to obey it."

"So let me explain," the dark man said. "It's not like you think. In fact, I gave up on you a long time ago. Can I sit down?"

"Please do," Sister Mary told him.

"And can I smoke? It won't bother you?"

"Not at all."

He began to smoke, mostly from the groin, but a good deal from the hands and the top of the head. "You've prayed to behold an angel," he said. "Your exact words were 'the least of Your messengers, Lord, would be sufficient for me.' Behold, I'm an angel, and not the least of His messengers."

"Come now," said Sister Mary.

"I'm Lucifer, the Morning Star. A real angel. You haven't read about me? A certain loose liver we both know pretty well said, 'I watched Satan fall from the sky like lightning.' That's nothing to you?"

"All right," Sister Mary said, "you're an angel. But a fallen angel wasn't exactly what I had in mind."

"I'm the archangel in charge of punishments," Lucifer explained. "That's all. Sure, I've had a lot of bad press."

"Please don't say it's a dirty job, but somebody had to do it." Sister Mary gathered her bathrobe more tightly around her, the unconscious legacy of ancestors who had donned armor a thousand years past. "Then you're saying you're not really evil after all?"

"If I were evil, would I come here to ask you to do good?"

"By the way, I didn't know you were Jewish."

"You need time to think, huh? Sure, I'm Jewish. If I weren't, would I cut the kind of deals I do? We're all Jewish. Gabriel, Michael, everybody. Even on Broadway, they know all the best angels are Jewish. Now you'll say I don't look Jewish."

"You don't, more Syrian or Greek. What's this about doing good? I thought you'd come to tempt me."

"I have." Lucifer rubbed his hands, which nearly went out. "I've got for you the one proposition you can't turn down — a chance to help somebody who really doesn't deserve it. Me. And do good at the same time. You've got the greatest cookbook collection in the world. You didn't know that?"

"I've got a very good one," Sister Mary acknowledged. "I've put in shelves in the attic. They're mostly up there."

"The best. I've checked out everybody's. Now in that collection, you've probably got a lot of recipes for what you might call spiritual or mystical dishes, don't you? Like how to make sacramental wine, for instance?"

"You can hardly expect me to tell you that."

"Oh, I know. I was just for-instancing. But you've got it?"

"Certainly," Sister Mary replied with some pride. "I know how manna was baked. Do you want to know the broth simmered in the Cauldron of Cerridwen? I can tell you. And I can give you the recipe for the dish of bitter herbs into which Judas thrust his hand."

"I know him," Lucifer said. "A real

loser, believe me. No, my problem is I've got a dish I don't know how to cook. I've boiled it, I've baked it, and I've roasted it, but nothing helps. Would you have a look at it and see if you can help out? Wait a minute — before you answer, let me say right off you won't find my kitchen an unpleasant place at all. You won't get burned, or anything like that. And what I'm trying to do — this is orders from On Top, you understand. You want to help Him out, don't you?"

"Yes," Sister Mary said.

At once the convent vanished, and she was surrounded by the leaping flames of Hell.

"Hey, don't be so panicky," Lucifer told her. "Didn't I say you wouldn't get hurt?"

"It's just that it was so fast."

"I like running tollgates — a little hobby of mine. Come on, I'll take you to see him. Hey, what's the matter now?"

Sister Mary was looking at herself. "For one thing, I'm nude."

"Everybody is. That's the rule here. For you I'd like to bend it a little, but I can't."

"And for another thing, I seem to be about eighteen again."

"Nice-looking, too. You should be proud, and I'm not saying that just because I'm in the business. See, everybody here looks the right age to give other people the most pain. I'm naked too, you've noticed."

"But you've got more hair than I do, and it's much better positioned. I'm not stirring a step until I get some clothes."

"All right," Lucifer said, "I know I don't have the rep, but I'm really a generous guy. Here's the entire habit the SPV was wearing when you joined. The black skirt, the wimple, the whole schmeer."

For a moment, Sister Mary could see it just as it had once hung in her closet

at the convent. Then the cloth vanished in a flash of fire. The wire hanger melted to something like quicksilver and splashed the smoking stones of Hell. "I've been very foolish to allow you to bring me here," she said.

"Listen, if you could wear that stuff, everybody'd stare. This way, nobody'll notice. You want to get out? Come on."

They walked down a narrow valley where every ledge was occupied by a writhing figure. "I didn't know Hell was this crowded," Sister Mary said sadly.

"For people who don't like crowds, it's crowded. For people that do, lonely. Hey, there he is. We're in luck; sometimes he wanders around."

The man was tall and muscular. His face was expressionless, his skin a dull red.

"So look at him," Lucifer complained. "I've fried, I've chopped, I've boiled, and just look. That's agony?"

"Well, he certainly isn't smiling," Sister Mary said.

"He isn't anything. I work my tush off, but does he give one damn? Hell, no. You're the expert; you're going to tell me what I should do? Go ahead, I'm listening. You think marinating might help? I've tried it. Sulfuric acid."

As if on cue, a dickens appeared. "From Abraham, Isaac, and Jacob, the Chairman says so where is he?" the dickens announced. "It's line seven. Should I tell him out to lunch?"

"Get out of here, you little schmuck." Lucifer made Sister Mary a little bow. "I got to go. Look him over, okay? I'll be right back."

Sister Mary nodded, and he vanished in a puff of evil-smelling smoke. When it had drifted away, she said softly, "He knows what I'm going to do, you know. He knows exactly what I'm going to do.

I find that encouraging, exciting, and disturbing. The universe is not as we thought."

The red-skinned man nodded slow assent.

"Or perhaps this is not the universe at all," she said. "Just the corner of a bad dream. But I know how to end it. Take my left hand."

"My hand burn you," the red-skinned man grunted. He extended it nevertheless; and when she clasped it, it did not. It was a man's hand, living and strong. She held it and knew she had lived her entire life for this moment. And that it had been worth it.

Then she crossed herself.

On the morning she awakened, there appeared in New Canaan a tall, swarthy man whom the people of the town have decided is a Micmac Indian. He does very little work, and sometimes he drinks too much. But he does no harm either (which is much the same as not working), and he is very strong, so they leave him alone. Besides being an Indian, he had another peculiarity, which is that he whistles softly whenever he sees Sister Mary.

Sister Mary no longer looks eighteen, and from time to time she slaps the boys' fingers with her ruler as she has for nearly fifty years; but now she has a peculiarity too. It is that on sullen summer nights when lightning flashes in the west and black clouds gather over the Hoosac Hills, she joins Man-on-Fire, the Micmac Indian, on his park bench and talks with him in tones too low to be overheard. She has told Monsignor O'Murphy, the pastor emeritus, that she is compiling a volume of Indian recipes. ∎

JOHN K. (KINDER) PRICE

by Gene Wolfe

Born in Pottstown, Pennsylvania, April 3, 1873. The family moved to Dalton, Massachusetts in 1878. Price left school in 1889 and took a job in the shoe factory where he worked for 47 years before retiring as a foreman. In 1894, he married Amy (Prescott) Price. A son, James, died in 1895 shortly after birth, Mrs. Price in 1938.

Following her death, Price seemed to be at loose ends and experimented with a number of activities and hobbies; these included building ship models and stamp collecting. In 1939, he announced to a friend that he had discovered a pastime that would hold his interest for the remainder of his life: searching for a book of spells mentioned in a pulp magazine he had happened upon in a barbershop (believed to have been Ray & Bill's in Dalton). When the friend ventured to point out that the book so mentioned might not in fact exist, Price told him he was sure it did not, and it was this certainty of its nonexistence that underlay the charm of the search. Because the book did not exist, he could neither fail nor end the search by discovering a copy.

During the following years, Price became a familiar figure in all the libraries and book stores within a hundred miles of Dalton. He often traveled as far as Adams and was said to go at times to Springfield. Postal employees have reported that he frequently sent mail to (and received mail from) such little-known localities as the Congo Free State, Persia, and Bithynia. The entry of the United States into World War II must have made Price's activities more difficult, but he appears to have continued them.

In 1952, a neighbor reported to the police that she had not seen Price in over a week and that there were no lights in the windows of the Price house in the evening. The door was forced, but no body was discovered. Left vacant, the house was vandalized several times; it burned in 1959. Earlier, in 1957, a retired sole-cutter who had known Price as a foreman had reported seeing him near the Dartmouth campus, and he was said to have been spotted in 1961 and 1962 (and later) at garage sales in and around Boston.

The most recent sighting (1977) was in the stacks of the British Museum Library, from which he vanished before he could be apprehended. It is conjectured that Price has still not discovered the book he seeks; but he appears to have found something. ■

THE BOY WHO HOOKED THE SUN

by Gene Wolfe

On the eighth day a boy cast his line into the sea. The Sun of the eighth day was just rising, making a road of gold that ran from its own broad, blank face all the way to the wild coastline of Atlantis, where the boy sat upon a jutting emerald; the Sun was much younger then and not nearly so wise to the ways of men as it is now. It took the bait.

The boy jerked his pole to set the hook, and grinned, and spat into the sea while he let the line run out. He was not such a boy as you or I have ever seen, for there was a touch of emerald in his hair, and there were flakes of sun-gold in his eyes. His skin was sun-browned, and his fingernails were small and short and a little dirty; so he was

just such a boy as lives down the street from us both. Years ago the boy's father had sailed away to trade the shining stones of Atlantis for the wine and ram skins of the wild barbarians of Hellas, leaving the boy and his mother very poor.

All day the Sun thrashed and rolled and leaped about. Sometimes it sounded, plunging all the Earth into night, and sometimes it leaped high into the sky, throwing up sprays of stars. Sometimes it feigned to be dead, and sometimes it tried to wrap his line around the moon to break it. And the boy let it tire itself, sometimes reeling in and sometimes letting out more line; but through it all he kept a tight grip on the pole.

The richest man in the village, the money-lender, who owned the house where the boy and his mother lived, came to him, saying, "You must cut your line, boy, and let the Sun go. When it runs out, it brings winter and withers all the blossoms in my orchard. When you reel it in, it brings droughty August to dry all the canals that water my barley fields. Cut your line!"

But the boy only laughed at him and pelted him with the shining stones of Atlantis, and at last the richest man in the village went away.

Then the strongest man in the village, the smith, who could meet the charge of a wild ox and wrestle it to the ground, came to the boy, saying, "Cut your line, boy, or I'll break your neck."

But the boy only laughed at him and pelted him with the shining stones of Atlantis, and when the strongest man in the village seized him by the neck, he seized the strongest man in return and threw him into the sea, for the

21

power of the Sun had run down the boy's line and entered into him.

Then the cleverest man in the village, the mayor, who could charm a rabbit into his kitchen — and many a terrified rabbit, and many a pheasant and partridge too, had fluttered and trembled there, when the door shut behind it and it saw the knives — came to the boy saying, "Cut your line, my boy, and come with me! Henceforth, you and I are to rule in Atlantis. I've been conferring with the mayors of all the other villages; we have decided to form an empire, and you — none other! — are to be our king."

But the boy only laughed at him and pelted him with the shining stones of Atlantis, saying, "Oh, really? A king. Who is to be emperor?" And after the cleverest man in the village had talked a great deal more, he went away.

Then the magic woman from the hills, the sorceress, who knew every future save her own, came to the boy, saying, "Little boy, you must cut your line. Sabaoth sweats and trembles in his shrine and will no longer accept my offerings; the feet of Sith, called by the ignorant Kronos, son of Uranus, have broken; and the magic bird Tchataka has flown. The stars riot in the heavens, so that at one moment humankind is to rule them all, and at the next is to perish. Cut your line!"

But the boy only laughed at her and pelted her with the shining stones of Atlantis, with agates and alexandrites, moonstones and onyxes, rubies, sardonyxes, and sapphires; and at last the magic woman from the hills went away muttering.

Then the most foolish man in the village, the idiot, who sang songs without words to the brooks and boasted of bedding the white birch on the hill, came to the boy and tried to say how frightened he was to see the Sun fighting his line in the sky, though he could not find the words.

But the boy only smiled and let him touch the pole and feel the strength of the Sun, and after a time he too went away.

And at last the boy's mother came, saying, "Remember all the fine stories I have told you through the years? Never have I told you the finest one of all. Come to the little house the richest man in the village has given back to us. Put on your crown and tell your general to stand guard; take up the magic feather of the bird Tchataka, who opens its mouth to the sky and drinks wisdom with the dew. Then we shall dip the feather in the blood of a wild ox and write that story on white birch bark, you and I."

The boy asked, "What is that story, Mother?"

And his mother answered, "It is called 'The Boy Who Hooked the Sun'. Now cut your line and promise me you will never fish for the Sun again, so long as we both shall live."

Aha, thought the boy, as he got out his little knife. *I love my mother, who is more beautiful that the white birch tree on the hill and always kind. But do not all the souls wear away at last as they circle on the Wheel? Then the time must come when I live and she does not; and when that time comes, surely I will bait my hook again with the shining stones of Uranus, and we shall rule the stars. Or not.*

And so it is that the Sun swims far from Earth sometimes, thinking of its sore mouth; and we have winter. But now, when the days are very short and we see the boy's line stretched across the sky and powdered with hoarfrost, the Sun recalls Earth and her clever and foolish men and kind and magical women, and then it returns to us.

Or perhaps it is only — as some say — that it remembers the taste of the bait. ∎

WEIRD TALES™ TALKS WITH GENE WOLFE

by Darrell Schweitzer

WT: You're been writing full time for several years now. How has this changed your perspective?

Wolfe: I'm not sure that it's really changed my perspective at all, and I think that perhaps it should have. You're supposed to be more professional, more bottom-line oriented, and I don't think I am, because I spent too long writing as an avocation rather than a profession. I still tend to write that way. I think I tend to write as I like rather than what might be commercial.

WT: To do that and to do it for a living — isn't that the definition of success?

Wolfe: Well, it is if you live off it. I just hope I can do well enough at it. Writing is a long-lead-time profession. You write something, and if you're lucky you see it in print in three or four years. So it's going to be a while longer before I know that I'm really making a go of this. I *hope* I am.

WT: If you found you weren't making enough, would you branch out into other areas of writing? Would you novelize *Dune*?

Wolfe: [laughs] That's a dirty crack.

WT: Well, Joan Vinge did precisely that. She wrote the story book of the movie.

Wolfe: I would always do that sort of thing if somebody really wanted it and wanted to pay me a lot of money to do it. I doubt if anyone is ever going to be willing to pay me to write movie novelizations. I don't think I'm that kind of writer, and people sense that I'm not that kind of writer. I would probably do it for the money if I could. I doubt if the matter is ever going to come up. I suspect that if things don't go well, eventually I'll have to take a job at the carwash or whatever. I'll have to go out into some non-writing field — I've been there before — and do that to make a living if I can. I hope it's not going to come to that. I like being a full-time writer. I hope I can continue to turn out enough successful work that I can continue to do what I'm doing now.

WT: You don't seem to be the sort of writer who can be rushed. Your books don't read like that. Are you indeed a very slow writer?

Wolfe: I don't know what very slow is. A page of first draft, typically, takes me a half an hour. I can be rushed in the sense that I can be made to work longer hours in the day than I normally do. I normally start somewhere around eight and stop somewhere around noon. As far as the actual writing is concerned, I try to reserve the afternoons for research and correspondence and that sort of thing. If deadlines get tight, if things get hard, then obviously I'm going to start cutting into afternoon and evening time. I could write ten hours a day if I had to, and I think I could write as well as I do writing four hours a day. But it's exhausting; and it means that the correspondence and the research don't get done, because you've taken up the time that normally should be devoted to them and actually spent it putting words on paper.

WT: *THE BOOK OF THE NEW SUN* seems to be something that was slowly and painstakingly done. I can imagine you going over the first four volumes again and again, as well as the upcoming *The Urth of the New Sun*, and adding details. Was it like that?

Wolfe: It was much more a matter of going over it and chopping out details, actually, because I had written in a number of things when I did my original draft of it that either did not work or would have made a long book even longer — *The Urth of the New Sun* is 110,000 words now, which even for me is a long book; as for *THE BOOK OF THE NEW SUN* itself, the first four volumes, that is close to a half a million words — and if I had left certain things in that would have made it longer still. So I cut some things out and condensed scenes to try

23

to bring it down to a reasonable limit.

WT: When you started, did you envision a work of such magnitude?

Wolfe: No, not in the least. I always hate to admit this [laughs] — I started it as a novella for *Orbit*. It definitely got out of control. I wrote on it and I realized I was approaching novella length and it was hardly started. So I thought, well, it's a book. So I did it as a book, which was essentially *The Shadow of the Torturer*; and I realized that I was *still* hardly started, so I said, "Aha! It's a trilogy. I should have known." So I went and did it as a trilogy, and I ended up with three volumes of which the third volume was about half again as long as the first two. I knew I couldn't do a trilogy with a 150,000-word third volume, so I split the third volume into two. That was originally going to be called *The Sword of the Autarch*. It became *The Sword of the Lictor* and *The Citadel of the Autarch*. I had a climactic scene with Baldanders in the middle of the original book, and it became the end of *The Sword of the Lictor*. Then I had room to do some additional things that I hadn't had room to do before, like the story contest in the lazarette when Foila and Melito and Hallvard and Loyal To The Group Of Seventeen all tell their stories. That's the sort of thing that went in, and the story that Severian reads to Little Severian at the foot of Mount Typhon.

WT: How much is there in the way of outtakes?

Wolfe: You mean existing? Well, I don't think any of it exists anymore. I've pretty much scratched it out and thrown it away. Of course in the case of splitting that volume, it wasn't a matter of out-takes. It was a matter of building up. In the case of something like *The Urth of the New Sun* there were out-takes, but usually it was a matter of scrubbing sentences and paragraphs here and there which I had intended to develop into something until I saw that there wasn't *room* — unless I was going to do a whole new series, which I didn't want to do. I wanted to settle the matter of bringing the New Sun and the creation of the new Earth.

WT: Could you tell us something about *The Urth of the New Sun*?

Wolfe: It begins ten years after Severian's story in *THE BOOK OF THE NEW SUN*. If you've read *THE BOOK OF THE NEW SUN* carefully, you know that it's being written just before he leaves to go and bring the New Sun. This is his last act on Earth before he boards the ship and takes off to leave our universe, which is Briah, and enter the universe of the Hierogrimates, which is Yesod. So *The Urth of the New Sun* is the story of what happens to him immediately after he has finished writing *THE BOOK OF THE NEW SUN*, in the time-frame of the novel, if you see what I mean. Now what we're skipping is about ten years in which Severian was the Autarch of the Commonwealth — and also Autarch of Earth in the sense that his title gives him a titular rulership over the planet, which he cannot actually exercise.

WT: It seems to me that the document Severian has produced will be remembered in his world not as an autobiography or historical memoir but as a great myth. It will become like Homer's works and might even be the basis for a religion. Is there any sense of this in the sequel?

Wolfe: Oh, yes. First of all, what you say is absolutely true, and that's why Dr. Talos's play, "Eschatology and Genesis," deals with this sort of thing. For example, if you'll look at the beginning of the play [in Chapter XXIV of *The Claw of the Conciliator*], you'll see that the New Sun is listed as one of the characters in the cast. And of course you never get the complete play because Baldanders goes wild and terrifies the audience and gets shot a little bit and breaks up the show. But what you say has happened, and there's a great deal more in *The Urth of the New Sun* of how it happens and why it happens. You see Severian not only as the New Sun but also as the Conciliator.

WT: I am fascinated by the vaguely historical models in the series. The Commonwealth, for all that it's set in the Southern Hemisphere, reminds me somewhat of Byzantium during one of its four-hundred-year declines, maybe toward the end of the Comnenus period. That is, it is clearly declining and will continue to do so, but it will just as clearly go on well beyond anyone's lifetime. Did you have any of this specifically in mind?

Wolfe: Yes, absolutely. I was very happy to hear you say that, because people look at

The Shadow of the Torturer and they say, "The Torturers' Guild — Ah, this is Medieval Europe." And it isn't. It's Byzantium, and that's where the model for it comes from. I've gotten a lot of criticism about bad Latin in the books, because to a modern Latinist, Latin is the language of Cicero, and I was using the Latin of, say, about A.D. 1000, late Byzantine Latin, which, from the standpoint of a classicist who is interested in Vergil and that sort of writer, is a corrupt Latin because, although Latin is a dead language now, it was a *living* language for two thousand years or so at least; and it developed. It changed. There is an early Latin, an archaic Latin if you want to call it that. There is the classical Latin which you get when you read the classical Latin poets and dramatists, and there is a Byzantine Latin which is really contemporaneous with the early Middle Ages. We tend to think of the classical world as ending with the sack of Rome, and it simply didn't. It continued in the eastern Mediterranean for hundreds and hundreds of years after that. As you've just said yourself, Darrell, it went on lifetime after lifetime. People lived their entire lives in the Byzantine Empire, and their great-grandchildren lived their entire lives in the Byzantine Empire and *their* great-grandchildren lived their entire lives in the Byzantine Empire, until finally Constantinople fell to the Turks. It was only really when Constantinople fell to the Turks that the ancient world came to an end.

WT: One historical footnote: I hadn't realized that the Byzantines used much Latin after about the reign of Heraclius in the early 7th century, when most of the remaining Latin-speaking provinces were overrun by the Avars. Didn't the Empire shift mostly to medieval Greek at that point?

Wolfe: It did. The empire that was supposed to be the Eastern Roman Empire was much more of a Greek empire than it was a Roman one, but Latin continued to be used in various esoteric disciplines. It was not the tongue of the ordinary man, nor was it the common tongue of the court, but it did continue, and it was written by scholars, and it progressed — if you want to call it progress — and changed, or it was corrupted — if you want to call it corruption — under the pens of those scholars.

WT: Would you ever follow the Byzantine model further and have an event like the battle of Mantzikert? After that Byzantium collapsed relatively fast — it only took another four hundred years.

Wolfe: I wouldn't have an event like that. The possibility of that sort of event has been preempted by the things that take place within *The Urth of the New Sun*.

WT: By way of your interest in the classical world, could you give us some of the background for *Soldier of the Mist*? I've just started reading that. My first thought is that I vaguely remember an amnesiac character in *The Iliad* —

Wolfe: Oh. Boy. I've forgotten him, whoever it was. That's something I should be able to answer, but I can't. As for *Soldier of the Mist*, it is laid at the tail-end of the Persian Wars, and in the years just before what we consider the real classical period of Greece. Let's see, we're in 479 B.C. in the book, and I think that Socrates will be born about 475 B.C. or some such date. Of course Pericles is not around and people like Plato and Aristotle are not around. But this is the society that laid the groundwork for the classical age. The book starts with the battle of Platea, which was the last, decisive land battle of the Persian Wars. It came a year after Salamis, which was the decisive sea battle, in which Persia lost control of the sea lanes. Losing control of the sea lanes meant that the Persians could no longer maintain the enormous army with which they had invaded Greece. Herodotus says it was three million men. Most historians think that was an error. The actual number was something like three to four hundred thousand. Whoever is right — for that period, a force of even three hundred thousand men was an *immense* army. The Greeks were accustomed to dealing with hundreds or even thousands of soldiers, and when we're talking three *hundred* thousand we're talking something that was almost *unimaginable* to the Greeks of that period.

WT: The unimaginable part would be how they would feed them.

Wolfe: That was the problem with the loss of the sea lanes. As long as the Persians had control of the eastern Mediterranean, which they did up until the battle of Salamis, they fed them by shipping grain from Egypt and other parts of the Persian Empire; it was possible to supply an army of that size. After the battle of Salamis, most of the soldiers had to be pulled back into the Persian Empire, because you couldn't maintain an army like that. Such an army could not live off the land in a country like Thrace or northern Greece or Bœotia or any of those places. They didn't have that kind of a food supply. So, the Persian army was cut down to a size that was reasonable by Greek standards — let's say, thirty or forty thousand men — and that could live off the land. Of course the Persians still had hopes of defeating the Greeks, the Greeks in this case being the combined armies of Athens and Sparta, with their various satellite states. The battle of Platea was their big chance to do it, and they lost the battle. That, for practical purposes, ended the Persian Wars. But you have to understand that neither the Greeks nor the Persians knew that the war was over. It was only with hindsight that we can look back and say, "Well that was the end of the Persian Wars for all practical purposes." The Persians expected to invade Greece again with another army when they got things built up again. The Greeks expected to be invaded again.

WT: But you've made the whole setting magical, not only because the hero can see the gods, but because you don't ever call Athens and Sparta by the names Athens and Sparta. So it has a very remote feel, almost of an imaginary world. Could you explain the derivation of the names and how they're used?

Wolfe: As for how they're used, that's no great puzzle. Latro calls Athens *Thought* because that's what he thinks it means. As it turns out, he's right. That *is* what it means, although his derivation of it is incorrect. He's connecting Athens with *athanatos*, which anybody with a superficial knowledge of Greek would do — immortal. What's immortal is thought. *Concept* is immortal. Earth may be destroyed, but five times three is always going to be fifteen. That is truly immortal. That's what continues, that thought and many others. Latro also thinks that Sparta means *rope*, because there is a very common Greek word, *spartos*, which is rope, cord, string. Now Sparta did

not mean *rope*. What it actually meant was *scattered*. But it took its name from a Greek word that was obsolete by the time Latro was in Greece. Sparta was one of those places that grew up from more than one center. Sparta was originally four villages, and these four villages became the four quarters of the city. And for a long, long time, each village maintained a separate market. Each village had its own agora. Now to a Greek who had been to Megara and Argos and Olympia and various other Greek cities, this was unheard of. Every Greek city had a central market where people bought and sold and argued politics, and he got to Sparta and discovered that it wasn't that way there at all. There were these four shopping centers around the city. That was what impressed vistors, and that was apparently how the city got its name originally.

As far as the magical end of the novel, that is the way the people of that time saw it. If you read their writings, if you look at their world with their worldview, you will find all this magical stuff right there. You should read Herodotus on the battle of Marathon and all the supernatural occurrences that took place during the battle — the vision of the giant, and so on. Now we *know* that none of that stuff took place, but the Greece of the 5th century B.C. did not know that that stuff did not take place. They knew just the opposite. They knew that it *did*. They knew that when Apollo was really mad, it rained blood, because there was a time when Apollo was really mad and they found blood on all the rooftops in Athens. How it got there, I don't know. Some people think that someone was going around cutting the throats of chickens to panic the populace. But there was blood on the rooftops. And this was what the average man in the street saw. This was the world that he lived in.

These people gave enormous respect to the oracle at Delphi, because they honestly believed that the oracle at Delphi was a pipeline to the god Apollo. If you read their writings, there were just *miraculous* predictions coming out of Delphi. It was marvellous stuff. Maybe it was faked. Maybe it was written after the fact, but that was their thought, that was the mental world they lived in; and I'm not sure that that mental world is necessarily inferior to our rationalist world. Yes, they were certainly duped in some instances. I don't have any question of it. I think that we in our rationalist world are duped in different ways, but we're still duped occasionally. I dislike the tendency to look down on these people because they were making a different set of mistakes than we make. They made their mistakes with much more justification, because they had much less data to work on than we do, and they generally made those mistakes with a better intellect and a better heart than we seem to have.

WT: They didn't reject data as many people do today. We have science now, but *this* is the golden age of sorcery and fortune-telling. There are probably more sorcerers and fortune-tellers alive today than ever before.

Wolfe: There are probably are, not in a per-capita sense, but in a broad sense. Of course in *Soldier of the Mist*, I show one of these itinerant charlatans. He's one of the characters, Eurykles the Necromancer. As frequently happens, quite frankly, to people who get involved in charlatanism, he finds himself mixed up in supernatural activities that are outside his control and are the sort of things that he has been faking and hinting at most of his life. Now he finds himself really caught up in them and destroyed by them.

WT: By way of charlatans of classical Antiquity, have you read Lucian of Samosata's "Alexander the Quack Prophet"?

Wolfe: I have read excerpts of it. I have not read the entire work. I've read it quoted in other books.

WT: Did you have it in mind?

Wolfe: Yes, I did, and there was an actual Eurykles the Necromancer, who shows up in the court records of Athens, and I had him even more in mind.

WT: What sort of background do you have in these matters? Do you read Classical Greek?

Wolfe: "Read" is not the word. I sort of thrash my way through it. When I started this book, I didn't get very far into it before I realized that I was going to have to have some actual, solid Greek and I had none. I thought I knew a lot about the ancient world, and I found that I really had very

superficial ideas and knowledge of it. So I started studying Greek. At this time — this sounds silly, I suppose, or supernatural, if you believe that Somebody looks after writers — a teacher of Classical Greek moved into the house across the street. And I went over to her and said, "I understand you're a teacher of Classical Greek. I'd like to take private lessons." I took private lessons from her at $15.00 an hour for, oh, eight months. Her name was Anne McCausland.

WT: This is a lot more effort than most people go through to write a novel.

Wolfe: Well, you've got to do that if you're going to do the ancient world and do it *right*. Otherwise you find yourself sticking in things that you think ought to be there. I was very tempted to put in sundials, because I thought that the ancient Greeks of that period would have invented the sundial. And, by God, they hadn't. *They didn't have it.* That's all. It wasn't there then. It was probably over in Babylon. I would be amazed to learn that it wasn't in Babylon, but it wasn't in places like Athens and Sparta and Thebes. They had, as strange as it sounds to us, no regular mechanical way of dividing the day. They divided it by the activities that normally went on at a certain hour.

WT: Therefore, precisely *because* there are supernatural elements in *Soldier of the Mist*, it is a strictly realistic novel written from the viewpoint of the 5th century B.C.

Wolfe: Absolutely. When the Persians were going to land at Marathon, the Athenians sent a runner to Sparta to ask Spartan military help. The runner was a professional — these were people you hired to run messages, because that was the fastest way to get a message from Athens to Sparta — and he ran into the Peleponese and across Arcadia and delivered the message. And he got the Spartan reply, which was that they couldn't march until the festival celebrating the full of the moon, and he ran back to Athens with that message. When he reported to the Assembly, he told them that he had encountered the god Pan on the road, and he recounted his conversation with the god Pan.

WT: Presumably everyone did not regard that as particularly extraordinary.

Wolfe: They did not. These were people

who, when the Persian navy was in a bad position, were sacrificing to Boreas to get him to destroy that part of the Persian navy. And he did. The north wind came down and the Persian ships were driven onto the rocks. There was a whole lot of that. There is a period, interestingly, before the battle of Platea really started, where the two armies were facing off. If you understand the strategic situation, you'll see that it was going to be pretty bad for either army to advance. The ideal thing from the Greek standpoint was for the Persians to attack *them* in their present position. The ideal thing from the Persian standpoint was for the Greeks to attack *them* in *their* present position, because the Persians are down on the plain, and the Persians have cavalry, and the Greeks are up in the hills, and they *don't*. They have very little cavalry comparatively. So each of them wants to fight where they are. So each commander has his own mantis, his own wizard, who is sacrifcing and reading the portents and telling what the gods say. In all cases, the gods say, "Stay where you are. Don't attack." Then the Greeks started getting more reinforcements, and the Persian mantis said, "Now's the time to attack," and the Persian army attacked.

WT: I have a theory about this, not about the battle but about the ancient world, which is that if a time-traveller went back and tried to explain to those people scientific rationalism and a completely mechanistic universe which preludes the supernatural, he would not be understood. It would be incomprehensible nonsense.

Wolfe: It would depend on who he is talking to. If he is talking to the average man on the street in Athens, I agree with you completely. It would have been. If you were talking to the sophists, the better educated class, you would be understood. You probably, at that time, simply would not be believed. For example, at this time, the Greeks were being exposed to Persian monotheism, and they had heard it and they understood it; they just didn't believe it. They said, obviously there was the river. You could *see* the damn river, and clearly the river had a god because it acted all the time as if it had a mind of its own. It got mad and it flooded the city. It liked people and it

watered their crops. It did all these things as if it were controlled by its own genius. That was good enough for them. They believed in the genius. Besides, every once in a while somebody saw him.

WT: What I was getting at was that it wouldn't be possible to be an atheist at that time.

Wolfe: I think it would be. I don't think you have to go much later than that to find some people who were getting awfully close to it. But certainly not in popular belief. Never in popular belief, not to this day in Greece. The individual, yes. We're getting very close to the sort of thing that Socrates was killed for. Athens was in big, big trouble in the Peleponesian War and Socrates was going around saying things that a lot of people considered blasphemous. They thought that they'd better put this man to death. He could quite easily have saved himself. Of course he didn't choose to do so.

WT: Could you say something about the sequel to *Soldier of the Mist*? I gather it's a two-volume work.

Wolfe: Well, no. I am hoping to do an open-ended series here. It's a two-volume work only in the sense that I have signed a contract for a second volume. But if people like the books, I'm hoping there will be a third volume and a fourth, because I've fallen in love with the ancient world, and I would like to move Latro around in it. In the next book, I'm hoping to take him to Delphi, which you haven't seen in *Soldier of the Mist*, and I'm hoping to show him the Pythic Games, which will take place in 478 B.C. The ancient Greeks not only had the Olympics every four years; they had other games that fell in the years between. There was always a major set of games dedicated to some important god falling in the dry season of each year, when people could sleep out in the fields without getting rained on and catching cold. In 478 B.C., this would be the Pythic Games, which were held at Delphi and dedicated to Apollo, as opposed to the Olympics which were dedicated to Zeus and held at Olympia. They had the same type of events: boxing, wrestling, javelin-throwing, horse-racing, chariot-racing, lots of foot races of various lengths, and so on.

WT: What else are you working on these days?

Wolfe: I've turned in a book called *There Are Doors*, which is about a department store clerk in our world who falls in love with a visiting goddess from another universe. The visiting goddess is working as his psychiatrist's receptionist for reasons of her own, and she meets this man and lives with him briefly, and then departs, and leaves him with the warning that there are doors between his world and hers and he may find himself accidentally slipping through one of these doors. She tells him how to reverse the situation and get back to his own world.

As you've already guessed, he does indeed slip into her world and he decides he doesn't want to stop and reverse the situation. What he wants to do is find the woman that he loves, whom he knows as Lara Morgan. So he goes hunting for her, gets into various difficulties, has various adventures, acquires a cybernetic doll that was modelled on her a few years back, and by accident finds himself back in his own world after seeing something of hers, which is in many ways the same as ours, and in many ways quite different. The key thing about it that causes the difference is that in her world human males die after intercourse, just as male salmon do, and males of many species of lower animals, which means that the only forty-year-old men, for example, are men who have never had intercourse with women, and women who have children are all widows before the first child is born. The women hold the semen and may have anywhere from three or four to twenty-five children in a lifetime, all from the single experience of intercourse with her mate. For example, queen bees mate once with the drone and produce bees and bees and bees. That's what's going on in her world. Of course this is why she has gone to his world, because she doesn't like the idea of killing the man because he has been her lover.

It gave me a chance to explore a little bit what such a world would be like. For example, a number of wars that have taken place in our world, the American Civil War and the First World War, for examples, have not taken place in her world, because there is a shortage of young men and there is a much greater sense of the value of young men since they will die very shortly if they do reproduce the human race. And of course there are people who are trying to dodge around the biological facts in various ways. Eventually, he does reconnect with the goddess.

WT: How are the feminist critics going to take this?

Wolfe: I think that's going to be interesting, but if I get anything but straight hostility I'll be delighted. What I've gotten from feminist critics has been, by and large, straight hostility to whatever I've written. But I think that feminist critics, like other critics whose orientation is primarily political one way or another, Marxist or whatever, are looking for someone who will write their party line. And I'm not going to do that. I'm not a party-line writer, not for them, not for the Marxists, not for a lot of other people. I am writing the story line, not the party line. I write it the way I think it should be written. In the goddess's universe, obviously the president is a woman. Many, though not all, high officials are women, because very few men live past their twenties.

WT: Well, I'm looking forward to the book in any case. Thank you, Gene. ∎

DEAD MAN

by Gene Wolfe

© G Barr – 1987

Reis surveyed the hull without hope and without despair, having worn out both. They had been hit hard. Some portside plates of Section Three lay peeled back like the black skin of a graphite-fiber banana; Three, Four, and Five were holed in a dozen places. Reis marked the first on the comp slate so that Centcomp would know, rotated the ship's image and ran the rat around the port side of Section Three to show that.

"Report all damage," Centcomp instructed him.

He wrote quickly with the rattail: *"Rog."*

"Report all damage," flashed again and vanished. Reis shrugged philosophically, rotated the image back, and charted another hole.

The third hole was larger than either of the first two. He jetted around to look at it more closely.

Back in the airlock, he took off his helmet and skinned out of his suit. By the time Jan opened the inner hatch, he had the suit folded around his arm.

"Bad, huh?" Jan said.

Reis shook his head. "Not so bad. How's Hap?"

Jan turned away.

"How's Dawson doing with the med pod?"

"I don't know," Jan said, "He hasn't told us anything."

He followed her along the spiracle. Paula was bent over Hap, and Dawson was bent over Paula, a hand on her shoulder. Both looked up when he and Jan came in. Dawson asked, "Anybody left downship?"

Reis shook his head.

"I didn't think so, but you never know."

"They'd have had to be in suits," Reis said. "Nobody was."

"It wouldn't be a bad idea for us stay suited up."

Reis said nothing, studying Hap. Hap's face was a pale, greenish yellow, beaded with sweat; it reminded Reis of an unripe banana, just washed under the tap. So this is banana day, he thought.

"Not all of the time," Dawson said. "But most of the time."

"Sure," Reis told him. "Go ahead."

"All of us."

Hap's breathing was so shallow that he seemed not to breathe at all.

"You won't order it?"

"No," Reis told Dawson, "I won't order it." After a moment he added, "And I won't do it myself, unless I feel like it. You can do what you want."

Paula wiped Hap's face with a damp washcloth. It occurred to Reis that the droplets he had taken for pirspiration might be no more than water from the cloth, that Hap might not really be breathing. Awkwardly, he felt for Hap's pulse.

Paula said, "You're the senior officer now, Reis."

He shook his head. "As long as Hap's alive, he's senior officer. How'd you do with the med pod, Mr. Dawson?"

"You want a detailed report? Oxygen's —"

"No, if I wanted details, I could get them from Centcomp. Overall."

Dawson rolled his eyes. "Most of the physical stuff he'll need is there; I had to fix a couple things, and they're fixed. The med subroutines look okay, but I don't know. Centcomp lost a lot of core."

Paula asked, "Can't you run tests, Sid?"

"I've run them. As I said, they look all right. But it's simple stuff." Dawson turned back to Reis. "Do we put him in the pod? You *are* the senior officer fit for duty."

"And don't you forget it," Reis said. "Yes, we put him in, Mr. Dawson; it's his only chance."

Jan was looking at him with something indefinable in her eyes. "If we're going to die anyway —"

"We're not, Mr. van Joure. We should be able to patch up at least two engines, maybe three, borrowing parts from the rest. The hit took a lot of momentum off us, and in a week or so we should be able to shake most of what's left. As soon as Ecomp sees that we're still alive and kicking, it'll authorize rescue." Reis hoped he had made that part sound a great deal more certain than he felt. "So our best chance is to head back in toward the sun and meet it part way — that should be obvious. Now let's get Hap into that pod before he dies. Snap to it, everybody!"

Dawson found an opportunity to take Reis aside. "You were right — if we're going to get her going again, we can't spare anybody for nursing, no matter what happens. Want me to work on the long-wave?"

Reis shook his head. Engines first, long-wave afterward, if at all. There would be plenty of time to send messages when the ship lived again. And until it did, he doubted whether any message would do much good.

Lying in his sleep pod, Reis listened to the slow wheeze of air through the vent. The ship breathed again, they'd done that much. Could it have been ... admiration, that look of Jan's? He pushed the thought aside, telling himself he had been imagining things. But still?

His mind teetered on the lip of sleep, unable to tumble over.

The ship breathed; it was only one feeble engine running at half force with a doubtful tube, and yet it was something; they could use power tools again — the welder — and the ship breathed.

His foot slipped on an oil spill, and he woke with a start. That had happened years back while they were refitting at Ocean West. He had fallen and cracked his head. He had believed it forgotten. . . .

The ship breathed. She's our mother, Reis thought. She's our mother; we live inside her, in her womb; and if she dies, we die. But she died, and we're bringing her to life again.

Someone knocked on the pod lid. Reis pushed the Retract lever and sat up.

Paula said, "Sir, I'm sorry, but —"

"What is it? Is Jan — "

"She's fine, sir. I relieved her an hour ago. It's my watch."

"Oh," Reis said. "I didn't realize I'd been asleep." He sounded stupid even to himself.

"My orders were to call you, sir, if —"

He nodded. "What's happened?"

"Hap's dead." Paula's voice was flat, its only emotion this very lack of emotion betrayed.

Reis looked at her eyes. There were no tears there, and he decided it was probably a bad sign. "I'm truly sorry," he said. And then, "Perhaps Centcomp —"

Wordlessly, Paula pointed to the screen. The glowing green letters read: *"Resuscitation underway."*

Reis went over to look at it. "How long has this been up?"

"Five minutes, Captain. Perhaps ten. I hoped —"

"That you wouldn't have to wake me."

Paula nodded gratefully. "Yes, sir."

He wrote: *"Resp?"*

"Respiration 0.00. Resuscitation underway."

The ship breathed, but Hap did not. That, of course, was why Paula had called him "Captain" a moment ago. She must have tried pulse, tried everything, before knocking on his pod. He wrote: *"Cortex?"*

"Alpha 0.00. Beta 0.00. Gamma 0.00," Centcomp replied. *"Resuscitation underway."*

Reis wrote: *"Discon."*

There was a noticeable pause before

the alpha, beta, and gamma-wave reports vanished. *"Resuscitation under-way,"* remained stubbornly on screen.

Paula said, "Centcomp won't give up. Centcomp has faith. Funny, isn't it?"

Reis shook his head. "It means we can't rely on Centcomp the way we've been used to. Paula, I'm not very good at telling people how I feel. Hap was my best friend."

"You were his, Captain."

Desperately Reis continued, "Then we're both sorry, and we both know that."

"Sir, may I tell you something?"

He nodded. "Something private? Of course."

"We were married. You know how they still do it in some churches? We went to one. He told them we didn't belong, but we wanted to have the ceremony and we'd pay for it. I thought sure they'd say no, but they did it, and he cried — Hap cried."

Reis nodded again. "You meant a lot to him."

"That's all, sir. I just wanted somebody else to know. Thanks for listening."

Reis went to his locker and got out his suit. It shone a dull silver under the cabin lights, and he recalled a time when he had envied people who had suits like that.

"Aren't you going back to sleep, sir?"

"No. I'll be relieving you in less than an hour, so I'm going hullside to have another look around. When I come back, you can turn in."

Paula gnawed her lower lip. He was giving her something to think about besides Hap, Reis decided; that was all to the good. "Sir, the captain doesn't stand watch."

"He does when there are only four of us, dog tired. Check me through the airlock, please, Mr. Phillips."

"Of course, sir." As the inner hatch swung shut Paula said softly, "Oh, God,

I'd give anything to have him back."

Neptune was overhead now; they were spinning, even if the spin was too slow to be visible. With only a single engine in service it was probably impossible to stop the spin, and there was no real reason to. The gravitational effect was so slight he had not noticed it.

He found Jupiter and then the Sun, slightly less brilliant than Jupiter or Neptune but brighter than any other star. The sun! How many thousands — no, how many millions of his ancestors must have knelt and sung and sacrificed to it. It had been Ra, Apollo, Helios, Heimdall, and a hundred more, this medium-sized yellow star in a remote arm of the Galaxy, this old gas-burner, this space heater laboring to warm infinite space.

If you're a god, Reis thought, why aren't you helping us?

Quite suddenly he realized that the Sun *was* helping, was drawing them toward the circling inner planets as powerfully as it could. He shook his head and turned his attention back to the ship.

A faint violet spark shone, died, and rekindled somewhere on Section Six, indicating that Centcomp had at least one of its mobile units back in working order. Centcomp was self-repairing, supposedly, though Reis had never put much faith in that; human beings were supposed to be self-repairing too, but all too often were not.

And deep space was supposed to make you feel alone, but he had never really felt that way; sometimes, when he was not quite so tired, he was more alive here, more vibrant, then he ever was in the polluted atmosphere of Earth. Now Hap was dead, and Reis knew himself to be alone utterly. As he jetted over to check on the mobile unit, he wished that he could weep for Hap as he had wept for his father, though he had known his father so much less well than

Hap, known him only as a large, sweet-smelling grownup who appeared at rare intervals bringing presents.

Or if he could not cry, that Paula could.

The mobile unit looked like a tiny spider. It clung to the side of Section Three with six legs while two more welded up one of the smaller holes. Centcomp, obviously, had decided to close the smallest holes first, and for a moment Reis wondered whether that made sense. It did, he decided, if Centcomp was in actual fact fixing itself; there would be more units as well as more power available later. He swerved down toward the mobile unit until he could see it for what it was, a great jointed machine forty metres across. Three clicks of his teeth brought ghostly numerals — hours, minutes, and seconds — to his faceplate, which had darkened automatically against the raw ultraviolet from the mobile unit's welding arc. Still twenty-four minutes before he had to relieve Paula.

For a minute or two he watched the fusing of the filament patch. The patch fibers had been engineered to form a quick, strong bond; but a bit of dwell was needed just the same. The mobile unit seemed to be allowing enough, working slowly and methodically. In the hard vacuum of space there was no danger of fire, and its helium valves were on *off* just as they should have been.

Reis glanced at the time again. Twenty minutes and eleven seconds, time enough yet for a quick look inside Section Three. He circled the hull and jetted through the great, gaping tear, landing easily in a familiar cabin that was now as airless as the skin of the ship. The hermetic hatch that sealed Section Two from this one was tightly dogged still. He had inspected it earlier, just after the hit, and inspected it again when he had come with Dawson, Jan,

and Paula to work on the least damaged engine. He threw his weight against each of the latches once again; you could not be too careful.

Nell Upson's drifting corpse watched him with indifferent eyes until he pushed her away, sending her deeper into the dark recesses of Section Three to join her fellows. In time, space would dry Nell utterly, mummifying her; radiation would blacken her livid skin. None of that had yet taken place, and without air, Nell's blood could not even coagulate — she had left a thin, crimson tail of it floating in the void behind her.

Twelve minutes. That was still plenty of time, but it was time to go. When he left the side of Section Three, the mobile unit was at work on a second hole.

"Resuscitation underway," was still on the screen half an hour into Reis's watch. He read it for the hundredth time with some irritation. Was it supposed to refer to Centcomp's self-repair functions? Reis picked up the rat and wrote, *"Who's in resusc?"*

"Capt. Hilman W. Happle. Resuscitation underway."

So that was that. *"Discon."*

"Resuscitation underway."

"Clear screen," Reis scribbled.

"Resuscitation underway."

Reis cursed and wrote, *"What authority?"*

"Capt. Hilman W. Happle."

That was interesting, Reis decided—not sensible or useful, but interesting. Centcomp did not know that Hap was dead. Reis wrote, *"Capt. Happle K. Lt. Wm. R. Reis commanding."*

The screen went blank, and Reis decided to try a general instrument display. *"GID"*

The three letters faded slowly, replaced by nothing.

"Enter — GID"

That, too, faded to an empty screen.

Reis scratched his nose and looked speculatively at the transducer headband. He had ordered the others not to use it — the hard instrumentation was amply sufficient as long as nothing too delicate was being attempted; but it had been sixteen hours since the hit, and Centcomp was still limping at best.

Multiplication became coitus, division reproduction; to add was to eat, to subtract to excrete. Glowing, Centcomp's central processor loomed before him, a dazzling coral palace with twice ten thousand spires where subroutines worked or slept. Tiny and blue alongside it, the lone mobile unit sang a Bach fugue as it labored. Smoldering leaves perfumed the breeze, washed away by a fountain of exponential functions that appeared to Reis to be calculating natural logarithms for purposes both infinite and obscure, pungently returning with each fresh gust of algorithmic air. Interactive matrices sprouted around his feet — the lilies, buttercups, and pale or burning roses that allowed his conscious mind to move here as it did, their blossoms petaled with shining elementary rows and columns.

Hap was sitting astride a tree that sprouted from the coral wall. The smile that divided his dark face when he saw Reis seemed automatic and distracted. Reis saluted, called, "Good evening, Skipper," and leaped across the laughing rill that had overflowed the fountain's rim.

Hap touched his forehead in return. "Hi ya, Bill."

Reis said, "It's damned good to see you here. We thought you were dead."

"Not me, Bill." Hap stared off into the twilight. "You can't die on duty, know that? Got to finish your tick, know what I mean, Bill boy? You want up here on the bridge?" He patted the tree trunk.

"That's okay — I'm fine where I am. Hap . . . ?"

His eyes still upon something Reis could not see, Hap said, "Speak your piece."

"Hap, I checked your cortical activity. There wasn't any. You were braindead."

"Go on."

"That's why it was quite a surprise to run into you here, and I'm not sure it's really you. Are you Hap, or are you just a kind of surrogate, Centcomp's concept of Hap?"

"I'm Hap. Next question?"

"Why won't Centcomp terminate resuscitation?"

"Because I told it not to, as soon as we left Earth." Hap sounded as though he were talking to himself. "Not just on me, on all of us. We're all too necessary, all of us vital. Resusc is to continue as long as — in Centcomp's judgement — there's the slightest possibility of returning a crewman to his or her duty. No overrides at all, no mutinies. Know what a mutiny is, Bill? Grasp the concept?"

Reis nodded.

"Some snotty kid's trying to take over my ship, Billy boy, trying to push me out through a hatch. That's mutiny. It's a certain Lieutenant William R. Reis. He's not going to get away with it."

"Hap . . ."

Hap was gone. Briefly, the tree where he had sat remained where it was, vacant; then it too vanished, wiped from working memory.

Something was wrong: the brilliant garden seemed haunted by sinister shadows, flitting and swift; the chaotic twilight from which Reis had emerged pressed closer to the coral palace. His head ached, there was a chill in his side, and his fingers felt oddly warm. He tried to remove the headband, willing himself to use his real arms, not the proxies that here appeared to be his arms. A hurrying subroutine shouldered him out of the way; by accident he stepped into the laughing rill, which bit his foot like acid. . . .

A smudged white cabin wall stood in place of the wall of the coral palace. Dawson was bending over him, his face taut with concern. "Reis! What happened?"

His mouth was full of blood; he spat it out. "I'm hurt, Sid."

"I know. *Christ!*" Dawson released him; but he did not fall, floating derelict in the cabin air. Dawson banged on Jan's pod.

Reis moved his right arm to look at the fingers; the warmth there was his own blood, and there was more blood hanging in the cabin, floating spheres of bright scarlet blood — arterial blood. "I'm bleeding, Sid. I think he nicked a lung. Better patch me up."

Twilight closed upon the cabin. Reis remembered how they had celebrated Christmas when he was three — somthing he had not known he knew, with colored paper and a thousand other wonderful things. Surely he was peeping through one of the plastic tubes the paper had come on; the few things he could see seemed small, toylike and very bright. Everything in all the universe was a Christmas present, a fact he had forgotten long, long ago. He wondered who had brought them all, and why.

"You have been asleep in the medical pod. There is little cause for concern."

Reis searched the pod for a rat, but there was none. No backtalk to Centcomp from in here.

"Are you anxious? Fearful? Confide your fears to me. I assure you that any information that I provide concerning your condition will be both complete and correct. No matter how bad, reality is never quite so bad as our fears concern-ing reality."

Reis said, "Spare me the philosophy," though he knew that Cencomp could not hear him.

"And your condition is not even crit-ical. You suffered a dangerous lesion between the fifth and sixth ribs of your right side, but you are nearly well."

Reis was already exploring the place with his fingers.

"Please reply."

"Would if I could." Reis muttered.

"You will find a rapid access trace beside your right hand. Please reply."

"There's no God-damned rapid access trace."

A latch clicked. Servos hummed. The pod in which Reis lay rolled forward with stately grandeur, and the pod opened. This time it was Jan who was looking down at him. "Reis, can you sit up?"

"Sure." He proved it.

Low and quick: "I want you to get into your sleeping pod with me, please. Don't ask questions — just do it, fast."

His pod was closed, but not latched from inside. He threw it open and he and Jan climbed in; she lay facing him, on her side, her back to the pod wall. He got in beside her, closed the pod, and threw the latching lever. Jan's breasts flattened against his chest; Jan's pelvis pressed his. "I'm sorry," she whispered. "I hadn't realized it would be this crowded."

"It's all right."

"Even if I had, I'd have had to ask you anyway. This is the only place I could think of where we could talk privately."

"I like it," Reis said, "so you can forget about that part. Talk about what?"

"Hap."

He nodded, though she could not have seen him in the dark. "I thought so."

"Hap was the one who stabbed you."

"Sure," Reis said. "I know that. With the rat from the med pod."

"That's right." Jan hesitated; Reis could feel her sweet breath wash across his face. At last she said. "Perhaps you'd better tell me how you knew. It might be important."

"I doubt it, but there's no reason not to. Hap thinks I'm a mutineer because I took charge when he was hurt — I was talking to him in Centcomp's conscious space. Hap had been in the med pod, and when I woke up in there the rat that should have been there was gone. A rat's stylus is long and sharp, and the whole rat's made of some sort of metal — titanium, I suppose. So a rat ought to make a pretty decent weapon."

Hair brushed his cheek as Jan nodded. "Sid found you. He woke up and realized he should have been on watch."

"Sure."

"He yelled for me, and we put you in the med pod when we saw that it was empty. There's another pod in Section Three, remember?"

"Of course," Reis said.

He waited for her to pursue that line of thought, but she seemed to veer off from it instead. "Hap's resumed command." She swallowed. "It was all right at first — he's the captain, after all. None of us even thought about resisting him, then."

Reis said slowly, "I wouldn't have resisted him either; I would have obeyed his orders, if I'd known he was alive to give them."

Jan said, "He's very suspicious now." There was a queer flatness in her voice."

"I see."

"And Reis, he's going to continue the mission."

For a moment he could not speak. He shook his head.

"It's crazy, isn't it? With the ship ripped up like it was."

"Not crazy," he told her. "Impossible."

Jan took a deep breath — he could feel and hear it, her long gasp in the dark. "And Reis, Hap's dead."

Reluctantly Reis said, "If he really wanted to proceed with the mission,

maybe it's for the best. You didn't kill him, did you? You and Sid?"

"No. You don't understand. I didn't mean . . . Oh, it's so hard to say what I do mean."

Reis told her, "I think you'd better try." His right hand had been creeping, almost absently, toward her left breast. He forced it to stop where it was.

"Hap's still running the ship. He tells us what to do, and we do it because we know we'd better. But our real captain, our friend, is dead. Try to understand. The real Hap died in the med pod, and Centcomp's substituted something else — something of its own — for his soul or spirit or whatever you want to call it. When you've seen him, after you've been around him for a while, you'll understand."

"Then I ought to be outside, where I can see him," Reis said practically, "not in here. But first —"

Jan screamed, a high-pitched wail of sheer terror that was deafening in the enclosed space of the sleep pod. Reis clapped his hand over her mouth and said, "Jesus! All right, if you don't want to, we won't. Promise you won't do that again if I let you talk?"

Jan nodded, and he returned his hand to his side.

"I'm sorry," she said. "It isn't that I don't like you, or that I'd never want to. I've been under such a terrible strain. You missed it. You were in the med pod, and you can't know what it's been like for us."

"I understand," Reis told her. "Oh, Hell, you know what I mean."

"If Hap isn't looking for us already, he will be soon. Or looking for me, anyway. He thinks you're still in the med pod, unless Centcomp's told him I took you out. Reis, you've got to believe me. He's going to courtmartial and execute you; that's what he said when Sid and I told him we'd put you in the pod."

"You're serious?"

"Reis, you don't know what he's like now. It doesn't make any difference, we're all going to die anyway, Sid and Paula and me. And Hap's already dead." Her voice threatened to slip from tears to hysteria.

"No, we're not," he told her. "Hap's been having you fix the ship? He must have, if he's talking about carrying out the mission."

"Yes! We've got three engines running now, and the hull's air-tight. We don't know — Sid and I don't know — whether we can count on Paula. If she sided with Hap it would be two against two, a man and a woman on each side, and . . ."

"Go on," Reis said.

"But if you were with us, that would be two men and a woman on our side. We'd save the ship and we'd save our lives. Nobody would have to know — we'd tell them the truth, that Hap died in the hit."

"You're not telling *me* the truth," Reis said. "If we're going to handle this together, you've got to open up."

"I am, Reis, I swear. Don't you think I know this isn't the time to lie?"

"Okay," he said. "Then tell me who's in the medical pod in Section Three. Is it Sid? Somebody's in there, or you wouldn't have brought it up."

He waited, but Jan said nothing.

"Maybe Hap sleeps in there," Reis hazarded. "Maybe he's getting himself some additional treatment. You want me to pull the plug on him, but why can't you do that yourself?"

"No. I don't think he sleeps at all. Or . . ."

"Or what?"

"He's got Nell with him — Sergeant Upson. Nell was in the pod, but she's out now, and she stays with him all the time. I didn't want to tell you, but there it is. Something else is in Three's med pod. I don't know who it was, but when it gets out we won't have a chance."

"Nell's dead." He recalled her floating body, its hideous stare.

"That's right."

"I see," Reis said, and jerked back the lever that opened the sleep pod.

"Reis, you have to tell me. Are you with us or against us?"

He said, "You're wrong, Jan. I don't have to tell you one God-damned thing. Where's Hap?"

"In Section Five, probably. He wants to get another engine on line."

Reis launched himself toward the airlock, braked on the dog handles, and released them.

Section Three seemed normal but oddly vacant. He crossed to Centcomp's screen and wrote, *"Present occ this med pod for vis check."*

"ID" flashed on the screen.

"Lt. Wm. R. Reis."

"Refused. Resuscitation underway."

Behind him Jan said, "I tried that. Centcomp won't identify it either."

Reis shrugged and pushed off toward the emergency locker. Opening it, he tossed out breathing apparatus, the aid kit, a body bag, and a folding stretcher with tie-downs. Behind them was a steel emergency toolbox. He selected a crowbar and the largest screwdriver and jetted to the med pod.

"Tampering with medical equipment is strictly forbidden. Resuscitation underway."

Reis jammed the blade of the screwdriver into the scarcely visible joint between the bulkhead and the pod, and struck the screwdriver's handle sharply enough with the crowbar to make his own weightless bodymass jump. He let the crowbar float free, grasped the pod latch, and jerked the screwdriver down. That widened the crack enough for him to work one end of the crowbar into it.

Centcomp's screen caught his eye. It read, *"Tampering is strictly Bill stop."*

Reis said, "Jan, tell it to open the God-damned pod if it doesn't want me to mess with it."

Jan found the rat; but before she could write, the screen read, *"Bill, I cannot."*

Jan gasped, "Oh, holy God," and it struck Reis that he had never heard her swear before. He said, "I thought you couldn't hear us, Centcomp. Wasn't that the story?"

"I truly cannot, Bill, and that is no story. But I monitor conditions everywhere in the ship. That is my job, and at times I can read your lips. Particularly yours, Bill. You have very good, clear lip motion."

Reis heaved at the crowbar; tortured metal shrieked.

Jan said, "Centcomp will have told Hap. He and Nell are probably on their way up here right now."

"I have not, Lieutenant van Jure."

Reis turned to face the screen. "Is that the truth?"

"You know I am incapable of any deception, Bill. Captain Hapgood is engaged in a delicate repair. I prefer to take care of this matter myself in order that he can proceed without any interruption."

"Watch the dogs — the moment they start going around, tell me."

"All right," Jan said. She had already pulled a wrench from the toolbox.

"Bill, I did not want to tell you this, yet I see I must."

Reis moved the crowbar to the left and pried again. "What is it?"

You said . . . ?"

"I said what is it, God damn it! Stop screwing around and stalling. It's not going to do you any good."

"Bill, it really would be better if you did not open that."

Reis made no reply. Pale blue light was leaking from the med pod through the crack; it looked as though there might be a lot of ultraviolet in it, and he turned his eyes away.

"Bill, for your own good, do not do that."

Reis heaved again on the crowbar, and the latch broke. The pod rolled out, and as it did a nearly faceless thing inside sat up and caught his neck in skeletal hands. Section Three filled with the sickening sweetish smells of death and gangrene. Reis flailed at the half-dead thing with the crowbar; and its crooked end laid open a cheek, scattering stinking blood that was nearly black and exposing two rows of yellow teeth.

Evening was closing on Section Three. Night's darkness pressed upon Reis; his hands were numb, the crowbar gone.

Jan's wrench struck the dead thing's skull hard enough to throw her beyond the range of Reis's narrowing vision. The bony fingers relaxed a trifle. Reis forced his own arms between the dead arms and tore the hands away.

Then Jan was back, her wrench rising and falling again and again. His crowbar was gone; but the toolbox itself was within reach, with a D-shaped handle at one end. Reis grabbed it and hurled the box at the dead thing. It was heavy enough to send him spinning diagonally across the section, and it struck the head and chest of the dead thing and the end of the pod as well. For a split second Reis seemed to hear a wailing cry; the pod shot back until its bent and battered end was almost flush with the bulkhead.

Jan screamed as the airlock swung open; there was a rush of air and scorching blue flash. Something brushed Reis's cheek. He could scarcely see, but he snatched at it and his still-numb fingers told him he held an emergency mask. He pushed it against his face, shut his eyes, and sucked in oxygen, feeling he drank it like wine. There was another searing burst of heat.

Long training and good luck put the manual control into his hands; he tore away the safety strap and spun the wheel. Driven by a fifty thousand p.s.i. hydraulic accumulator, the airlock door slammed shut, its crash echoing even in the depleted atmosphere of Section Three. Emergency air that Centcomp could not control hissed through the vents, and Reis opened his eyes.

Jan writhed near the airlock door, her uniform smoldering, one hand and cheek seared. The arm and welding gun of a mobile unit, sheered off at the second joint, floated not far from Jan. Reis sprayed her uniform with a CO_2 extinguisher and smeared her face and hand with blue antibacterial cream.

"My eyes . . ." she gasped.

"You've been flashed," Reis told her. He tried to keep his voice low and soothing. "Zapped by an electric arc. Open them, just for a minute, and tell me if you can see anything."

"A little."

"Good," he told her. "Now shut them and keep them closed. After a while your vision should come back a bit more, and when we get home they can give you a retinal —"

His own dimmed sight had failed to note the spinning dogs. The hatch to Section Four swung back, and Hap floated in. His sunken cheeks and dull eyes carried the hideous stamp of death, and his movements were the swift, jerky gestures of a puppet; but he grinned at Reis and touched his forehead with the steel rod he carried. "Hi there, Bill boy."

Nell Upson followed Hap. Her lips seemed too short now to conceal her teeth; it was not until she raised her pistol that Reis felt certain she was not wholly dead. Sid Dawson and Paula lingered at the hatch until Nell waved them forward. Both were terrified and exhausted, Reis decided. There could not be much fight left in either — perhaps none.

"You're supposed to salute your captain, Bill. You didn't even return mine.

If I were running a tight ship, I'd have my marine arrest you."

Reis saluted.

"That's better. A lot of things have changed while you've been out of circulation, Bill. We've got three engines going. We'll have a fourth up in another fourty-eight hours, and we only needed six to break away from the inner planets. Out where we are now, four should be plenty. And that's not all — we've got more air and food per crewman now than we had when we left Earth."

Reis said, "Then there's no reason we can't continue the mission."

"Way to go, Bill! Know what's happened to this old ship of ours?"

Reis shrugged. "I think so, a little. But tell me."

"We've been seized, Bill boy. Taken over, possessed. It isn't Centcomp — did you think it was Centcomp? And it sure as Hell ain't me. It's something else, a demon or what they call an elemental; and it's in me; and in Centcomp; and in you, too. Whatever you want to call it, it's the thing that created the *Flying Dutchman* and so on, centuries ago. We're the first ghost ship of space. You're not buying this, are you, Bill boy?"

"No," Reis told him.

"But it's the truth. There's a ship headed for us, it's coming from Earth right now — I bet you didn't know that. I wonder just how long they'll be able to see us."

Reis spat. The little gray-brown globe of phlegm drifted toward Hap, who appeared not to notice it. "Bullshit," Reis said.

Nell leveled her pistol. The synthetic ruby lens at the end of the barrel caught the light for a moment, winking like a baleful eye.

"Can I tell you what's really happened?" Reis asked.

"Sure. Be my guest."

"Centcomp's brought back you and

Nell at any and all cost, because that's what you programmed it to do. You were both too far gone, but Centcomp did it anyway. You've suffered a lot of brain damage, I think — you move like it — and I don't think you can keep going much longer. If you hit a dead man's arm with a couple of electrodes, his muscles will jump; but not forever."

Hap grinned again, mirthlessly. "Go on, Bill boy."

"Every time you look at yourself, you see what you are — what you've become — and you can't face it. So you've made up this crazy story about the ghost ship. A ghost ship explains a dead captain and a dead crew, and a ghost ship never really dies; it goes on sailing forever."

Reis paused. As he had hoped, the minute reaction created by the act of spitting was causing him to float, ever so slowly, away from Hap and Nell. Soon he would be caught in the draft from the main vent. It would move him to the left, toward the Section Two hatch; and if neither changed position, Nell would be almost in back of Hap.

"Now are you still going to court-martial me?" he asked. As he spoke, fresh cool air from the vent touched his cheek.

Hap said, "Hell, no. Not if —"

Nell's boot was reaching for the edge of the Section Four hatch; in a moment more she would kick off from it. It was now or never.

Reis's hand closed hard on the tube of antibacterial cream. A thick thread of bright blue cream shot into the space before Hap and Nell and writhed there like a living thing — a spectral monster or a tangle of blue maggots.

Nell fired.

The cream popped and spattered like grease in an overheated skillet, wrapping itself in dense black smoke. Alarms sounded. Through billowing smoke, Reis saw Dawson dart toward the airlock control.

Reis's feet touched the bulkhead; he kicked backward, going for Hap in a long, fast leap. Hap's steel bar caught his right forearm. He heard the snap of breaking bone as he went spinning through the rapidly closing Section Four hatch. A rush of air nearly carried him back into Three.

Then silence, except for the whisper from the vents. The alarms had stopped ringing. The hatch was closed; it had closed automatically, of course, when Centcomp's detectors had picked up the smoke from the burning cream, closed just slowly enough to permit a crewman to get clear.

His right arm was broken, although the pain seemed remote and dull. He went to Section Four's emergency locker and found a sling for it. It would not be safe to get in a med pod, he decided, even if Hap was gone; not until somebody reprogrammed Centcomp.

The hatchdogs spun. Reis looked around for something that could be used as a weapon, though he knew that his position was probably hopeless if either Hap or Nell had survived. There was a toolbox in this locker too, but his arm slowed him down. He was still wrestling with the stretcher when the hatch opened and Dawson came through.

Reis smiled. "You made it."

Dawson nodded slowly without speaking. Jan entered; her eyes were closed, and Paula guided her with one hand.

Reis sighed. "You were able to catch hold of something. That's good, I was worried about you. Paula too."

Jan said, "Sid saved me. He reached out and snagged me as I flew past, otherwise I'd be out there in space. Paula saved herself, but Hap and Nell couldn't. It was just like you said: they didn't have enough coordination left. You were counting on that, weren't you? That Nell couldn't hit you, couldn't shoot very well any more."

"Yes," Reis admitted. "Yes, I was, and I didn't think Hap could swat me with that steel bar; but I was wrong."

Jan said, "It doesn't matter now." She was keeping her eyes shut, but tears leaked from beneath their lids.

"No, it doesn't. Hap and Nell are finally dead — truly dead and at rest. Sid, I never thought a hell of a lot of you, and I guess I let it show sometimes; but you saved Jan and you saved the ship. Hell, you saved us all. All of us owe you our lives."

Dawson shook his head and looked away. "Show him, Paula."

She had taken something shining, something about the size of a small notepad, from one of her pockets. Wordlessly, she held it up.

And Reis, looking at it, staring into it for a second or more before he turned away, looked into horror and despair.

It was a mirror. ∎

THE UNLAWFUL HUNTER

by Keith Taylor

As to the pitfall of the unlawful hunter; the deer which he rouses and the deer which he does not rouse come equally to him.

— *Brehon Law.*

The idea was Fal's. He met his father's foster brother, the outlaw Miach, in secret to suggest it. Like all Fal's ideas, it was bold, outrageous — and would work. With winter drawing near, Miach was tempted. He delayed his decision for a while, knowing how angry his foster brother would be if Miach encouraged Fal in more potentially fatal mischief. But Miach owed it to his band to find it food for the winter. Besides, Fal had never stayed out of trouble simply because no man encouraged him.

"Can you and your friends get out of Suibni's dun on the night?"

"No difficulty there, Uncle." Fal did not award the title in irony. No blood tie existed between him and Miach, but fosterage often created closer ties than blood. "I know the paths through the bog, by night or day. By the gods, I ought to. It's a year I have lived in Suibni's house."

He, and others. Many high-born youngsters were sent to Suibni the bard for instruction in poetry and law, as befitted their rank. Fal was different. His ancestors had been bards since time out of mind, and he was expected to become one himself.

He did not wish to.

Miach, who knew him well, sensed his aversion. "Too long for your liking, eh?"

Fal shrugged. "He's a merry man, Suibni, and open of hand. The company's merry, too. Training in poetry is no hardship. The harp I love, but I don't wish to be a bard. It is not my calling. A year is time enough for me to be sure of that."

Miach guessed that he was the first to hear of Fal's decision. It was appropriate, in a way. Refusing to follow the bard's profession would be almost like becoming an outlaw from his clan. Who better to tell than Miach?

"What will you do, then?"

Fal's black brows met, even as his mouth smiled. "Quarrel with Father, I suppose." His forehead grew smooth once more. "The other thing, now . . . Are you ready?"

"I? I asked you whether your friends would do it."

"Six I am sure of. Six are enough, are they not?" And all so bold that they will ride on Samhain Eve. None would think of it, but once I suggest it, they will ride just for the sport."

Miach's mouth formed a somewhat wry shape. He too would not have thought of riding abroad on Samhain Eve until Fal suggested it. Samhain was the night between summer and winter, between life and death, when extremes were united and strange creatures travelled freely. Sometimes the dead came home — and if they did, they found food and drink and a fresh bed prepared. The lords of the Tuatha Dé Danann, that fair and awesome race which had been defeated by the first iron-users to invade Erin, often returned at Samhain to the land they loved and had never forgotten. No matter how men might revel and jest indoors, they seldom went out. Not on that night; not once the Sun had set.

Fal had less awe than most of Samhain Eve. It was his birth-night, and of course there had been talk on that account. Many had watched him grow, remarking his beauty, recklessness, and unpredictability, and spoken the word *changeling* with solemn nods. Knowing this was nonsense, Fal tended to disbelieve the other things he heard about Samhain. At least to doubt them.

"Bring your friends, then," Miach said. "I'll have my band in place."

The seven youths rode to their appointment not long after sunset upon the night. Leaving Suibni's crowded dun unnoticed was easy, with the riotous feasting and drinking under way, half the folk either masked or painted. The seven went disguised in bizarre tatters, fur, and animal masks; any man who saw them riding would shiver and look away.

By winding paths they crossed the ice-crusted bog, and next a plain of white grass beneath glittering stars. Their breath and their horses' smoked in the bitter night. The cold grew sharper each hour. Rime whitened young moustaches and frosted spearheads.

Three hours before midnight, they came to the rendezvous, a tumble of weathered boulders patched with lichen. Beside it, a pine tree creaked as the cold applied a slowly tightening wrestler's grip. Something hooted softly from the darkness under the branches — something, Fal knew, which lacked feathers. He hooted twice in reply.

"Fal?"

"It is I."

Miach trod forward to embrace his foster-brother's son. Fal's companions saw a man of middle height, dark-haired and fork-bearded. The night and his heavy cloth hid details of build.

"You come in good time," Miach said. "Midnight's hours away yet." His gaze travelled to the six mounted figures in their several masks: otter, bear, wildcat, owl, fanged demon, and dog. Fal's mask, an eagle, hung by his saddle; and he wore a cloak of crimson feathers as magnificent as it was warm.

Youth, Miach thought, and smiled.

"I am Miach mac Ringabra," he said to the six. "Some call me Redfist and Kinslayer, and all I will say about that is that I killed a man who betrayed me when I trusted him enough to stand hostage for him. It was an ill business for all concerned, and it made me an outlaw. If you'd be courteous, forget you saw me tonight.

"But first I'll ride with you. I know something of the work."

The mounted figures chuckled. One laughed aloud.

"We have done it a time or two ourselves," the youth in the bear-mask said.

"You know the plan," Fal declared, "or if you do not, go home. Two hours' ride from here is the steading of Srem the cattle-lord. He has two hundred beasts of his own and his neighbours', penned for slaughter, and we lift them tonight. The steading has two ramparts faced with stone, a log palisade, and a gate which will be unguarded. None will expect a raid at this time. Even when his dogs raise a racket, Srem will likely think the restless dead are abroad."

There were more chuckles, and exaggerated eerie moans. Fal detected hidden tension behind his friends' mirth; they mocked their own terrors.

"Cahal and I will open the gate, Miach will lead you in. If we act quickly, we can be away before Srem knows what is happening."

"Once in the bogs, we will lose them!" Lurgan cried. A scion of the conquering uí Néill was this one. "They don't know their way, and we do, to the inch!"

"Aye!" laughed Ebenár of Cétcha. "And then — and then!"

"We'll drive the beasts through the lake!" Art enthused. "Half a hundred beasts, wet and bawling, in the dun in the blue frosty dawn! That's the way to wake them!"

"Out stamps the Lord Suibni, roaring—"

"— a blanket kilted about him —"

"— and sets his foot in a fresh steaming cowpat!"

"Right," Miach said, in a voice which ended the nonsense. "If we succeed, it will be merry. There is never certainty. We'll be pursued hard. You may have to abandon the cattle and your joke with the Lord Suibni. Expect the men who follow to be enraged. It's a dark night. We're all coarsely clad. The pursuit won't know or care that you are well born, highly connected. Be ready for that — or go home, as Fal says."

An outlaw spoke, a man whose life and freedom were carried in his swordsheath, or on the legs of a fast horse. But he spoke to hothead aristocrats too young to really believe they could die. They howled him down. They reached eagerly for the weapons he had brought. In a rush of hoofbeats, they left the meeting-place deserted.

Fal, the youngest rider there, was filled with hard, gleeful exaltation. Come what might, this was man's work. It pleased him mightily to know he had devised the plan.

They came to the steading of Srem. Its stone-faced ramparts enclosed what amounted to a village. By the nearby stream stood a water-mill, its wheel removed and stored for the winter, dead leaves silted against the walls. Miach's lieutenant waited there. He confirmed that Miach's outlaws were in position, ready to act, and that nothing had happened to make any change of plan needful.

Fal and Cahal the Burly dismounted. Silently, they climbed across the deserted ramparts and opened the gate. Dogs barked. The barking became frenzied clamor as Miach led five youths galloping through the gates. Two led Fal and Cahal's horses. A run, a leap and they were mounted again, racing among the barns and byres, sweeping around the kiln. Finding the cattlepens was easy, with the bawling that issued from within. The raiders opened and emptied them in moments. Nightriding and cattle-lifting were second nature to Fal's cronies.

Two hundred beasts and four streamed out the gates, Miach's dogs bounding at their tails. They rushed down the slope. Behind them, in the dun, startled men ran for the stables, to saddle and mount.

"We should ha' scattered their horses!" Ebenár yelled.

"Too late it is now!" Fal yelled back.

Nor had it been a part of the plan. He and Miach *wished* to be followed closely by Srem's angry men. Now they wrought confusion in the pursuit by sending three parts of the herd in all directions, riding hard through the frigid darkness, whooping and goading until only fifty-odd beasts remained together. Then they wheeled after their companions, who had stayed with the remnant, herding it urgently across the plain.

Srem and his kindred were practised trackers, by day or night. The ruse would not confuse them for long, nor was it meant to. They would discover that while most of the herd had been scattered and left, fifty cattle were yet in the raiders' hands. Belike they would follow those, holding their recovery the more urgent matter. The abandoned beasts would not stampede far. They could always be gathered later.

So Srem would assume, but he would be mistaken. Miach's men were waiting, three dozen strong, to round up those hundred and fifty beasts and drive them south, while the owners chased a far smaller number westward. Fal and Miach had every hope of keeping the pursuit occupied until dawn.

Fal led. Miach seconded him. This was no nominal thing, agreed for appearances' sake. Fal had always taken command and led among his friends, first to think of a thing, most forceful in performing it. The youths all knew the region better than Miach. They might not be outlaws, but they had spent their lives in the open, riding and hunting. None lacked training in weapon-use or some acquaintance at least with raid, ambush, feud, and affray. Cattle-lifting was an accepted pastime to them; sport, a way of making war, a way for neighbours to quarrel. Such things went naturally with the proud, jealous ties of kinship that were as real to them all as the breath between their ribs. They covered the miles at a devouring pace.

Fal began to have a sense of something being wrong. The pursuit seemed to have failed, and Srem's night tracking was known to be better than that. They might have been alone in a frozen, brittle world.

Further, he grew more aware each moment that Samhain was indeed a night like no other in the year, for all his disbelief. The knowledge seeped into him through his skin. Fallen leaves lay in drifts, some pallid, some hectic, already spotted with decay. The naked trees rubbed creaking branches together, groaning in the cold. Samhain, night of the world's death and promise of its rebirth. Fal's birth night. He realised that at some time in the past few hours he must have turned thirteen.

"Are you wandering, Fal? We must keep these beasts to their pace!"

"So we must," Fal answered, recovering swiftly, "but keep your weapons ready. I hear something yonder. Srem may have found us."

As he spoke, a huge, misshapen thing rose out of the ground, almost under his horse's hoofs. The horse shied violently. So did Fal's heart, as he drew his sword. What — ?

The thing was long, with too many legs. It staggered like a drunkard. As Fal controlled his panicking horse, the monster made a great despairing sound from the humped centre of its form. Fal suddenly knew what it was; two stags with locked antlers. They had fought in the rutting time, and their contest had been drawn in this worst of ways. The riders had disturbed them where they lay weakened and dying.

The hapless pair blundered away, losing themselves among bushes and bracken. Centipedes crawled in Fal's belly. Although no Druid, he could recognise an evil omen of that strength and plainness.

"Bunch the cattle closer," Miach said urgently. "They are spreading among the trees."

Fal thought, *There should not be so many trees here.*

Yet there were. They grew thicker as he rode, leaning towards each other and reaching down to bar his way with their branches. One great limb swatted at his horse like a malformed, many-fingered hand, making it leap to the right. Somewhere the cattle bawled in fear, though he could no longer find them in the forest — this forest which should not exist.

Fal gripped his frightened horse hard with his knees and drew rein, holding it still. Using a steely self-control beyond his years, he curbed his imagination also. Rather than shouting to his friends for the comfort of hearing a voice, even his own, he listened.

Other horses trampled and crashed

nearby. The echoes had a strangely constricted sound. Fal sensed that however he had come there, he sat in some great forest. It did not *feel* like any little coppice or stand of timber. It was too completely dark, the trees near him too mighty.

"Fal!" Miach cried. "Are you with us, lad?"

"I am. Do you wish your hand held?"

Miach made a wry noise which blended exasperation with relief. "That'll be you and no other, indeed. Come here. Join us, if you are not too proud."

Fal walked his horse between the massive trees. "Suppose we name ourselves. Fal and Miach are here."

"Art is before you."

"And Amergin."

"Cahal over here."

"Ebenár of Cétcha beside him."

"Lurgan is here."

"Tadg, this leaves you," Fal said.

"I'm here, Fal."

"Ha. Shy, were you?"

"It was in my mind that fetches or demons had maybe borrowed your voices. But the Redfist is right. No fetch could imitate the edge that's upon your tongue. Now, where are we?"

"In difficulties, I would say."

Miach's dry comment was the aptest response he could make to such an unanswerable question. As he spoke, the darkness lightened in an odd way, like dye diluted with clear water. Sourceless and shadowless, pale illumination seemed to distil from the air — or else the band's surroundings became visible to them without light.

"Magic," whispered Cahal the Burly.

Trees of no earthly kind surrounded them. Spiral flutings characterised the trunks, and the branches wove together above their heads, making an impenetrable dome. Smaller trees, or perhaps one multiple growth, filled the gaps, while thorn and creeper wove through the chinks remaining, to bind it all in one tough, resistant mass. A wall of great stones could not have imprisoned them better.

"Hahahaha! Welcome, reckless ones!"

The monstrous bellow had a club's force. Horses reared, screaming. A couple tried to bolt. After one glimpse of the thing that had lumbered into view, Fal was glad to distract himself by curbing his mount. That done, sorrowfully, he had to look again.

She was the hugest and most disgusting hag he'd ever seen.

The tattered, stinking cowhide she wore covered only some of her noisomeness. Through all the dirt she carried, Fal could just discern that her hide was scabbed, scaled, fissured, horny, and wattled. Despite her bulk, it hung loosely upon her, swinging in folds when she moved. Her legs were mismatched. Teeth like tether stakes pushed a flabby upper lip far back from her gums. She had one live, yellow, and flaming eye; and another like a dead oyster in its shell. She smelled worse than she looked.

"Welcome!" she thundered again.

The dogs crept whining to the far end of the glade.

"Now you are here, and I have you," she went on, softening her voice to a mere bawl. "Be sure you will not go from this place until one of you has done as I wish. If none obliges me, I will slay you all."

Cahal and Ebenár rode at her, shouting in anger. Cahal drove his spear at her neck. Ebenár dealt an expert swordcut from horseback, no easy matter for one who had never heard of stirrups. His blade cut a wedge of meat from her back. Not quite severed, it hung flapping, and she ignored it. One-handed, she caught Cahal's plunging spear, to rend it from his grip and him from the saddle.

Her other hand clenched. She swung her fist at Cahal's breast-bone. His chest caved in. His heart spasmed like a flapping bird, and grew still.

The she-monster turned, that slab of muscle dangling from her back. She lifted Cahal's body — and he was appropriately called "the burly" — and threw him at Ebenár. The latter was knocked from his horse. In a lurching rush she reached him, seized him and broke him across her knee.

"Stand!" she howled. "Stand, the rest of you, or be killed like the weak things you are! See what I think of your weapons, by what I do!"

Contemptuously, she turned her back. Her wound gaped like a mouth. The wedge of meat hanging loose moved, flexing and hunching itself back into place with sounds like those of some huge, mannerless tongue.

It healed as they stared. There was not even much gore. What she had bled covered her back in thick glossy layers like pitch.

She turned without haste to confront them. "Will another of you attempt it?"

"No," Fal said. "What will you?"

He felt none of the self-possession or heartless pragmatism those words conveyed to his comrades. Four short words were all he could force past the horror clogging his throat. Yet someone had to speak.

"I will have a lover," she told him. "I will have one of you to swive me here in the glade. Well and completely must it be done. Do not hang back, as you are men!" She guffawed and spread her arms. "To be bashful is to die."

Fal's skin moved in cold ripples above his flesh. Behind him, Miach and the other youths looked at each other.

"Let us suppose that one tries and fails," Fal said.

"I shall rend him! I shall scatter his limbs from tree to tree and call upon the next worthless worm of you!"

"Then I'll be first."

"Fal! No!"

"Yes!" the boy answered violently. "Yes! Yes! Yes! I devised this raid. I led you here. Now Cahal and Ebenár lie dead." He snapped his jaw shut, for it had begun to vibrate. Miach, who had uttered the protest and sat closest to Fal, distinctly heard him grind his teeth as he sought control. "I will be first," he said again, after a time. "But you must make us private, hag. I'll not lie with you on the ground in view of all."

"Ah, the handsome, shy boy," she chuckled. "I'll do that much, if you shame so easily. Come!"

"It's impatient you are," he said, dismounting, "but I will not make you wait long. Only as long as it takes me to vomit."

He did precisely that, bending and spewing for nasty moments. Then he walked past the broken corpses of Cahal and Ebenár, to the grinning she-creature at the glade's end. The tangled brush opened before him, a gap with moss thick as a bed beyond it.

The brush wove together as the pair vanished from sight.

Lurgan blew a shaken outward breath. "Macha! If, if Fal can achieve a stand, confronted by *that*, he's the bravest youth in Erin!"

"We had better draw lots, in case he cannot," Miach said.

Voiding his stomach had done Fal a certain amount of good. His frozen disgust was melting. Although he loathed the creature no less, a heat of anger and hatred began to seethe in him now, boiling away the paralysis. From violent feeling he drew strength.

The nameless being threw off her cowhide and lay upon it. Reaching under her hams, she drew her nether lips wide apart in the posture of a bawdy *sheela-na-gig* carving. Her open womb smelled more like an open grave.

Fal's lips skinned back from his clamped teeth. Swiftly he threw off his clothes, while his courage remained. He'd ceased thinking some time before.

She was as hideous to touch as to see. Fal gripped handfuls of flesh in a wild blind darkness, making rage do the work of lust, turning revulsion inside out, making fear a goad to his body instead of a shackle, stopping thought and knowledge. Clawing his toes into the moss, he brought each shuddering thrust from the soles of his feet. It was more like mortal combat in the bitterest extreme of hatred than any kind of desire. It went on forever; he dared not stop, dared not pause, wanted to rend, to savage; and the longer it lasted the less it could be endured.

It ended at last, with a sensation like being racked apart. He arched backward and fell away from the creature. Landing on his back with wild spasms running through the deep muscles by his spine, he shuddered from neck to hips, and his legs flew about like jerking flails. Too quickly he grew still, locking those tremors unreleased into his muscles. He would have done better to tremble and thrash until his body found its own peace — but in the presence of his enemy, he would not.

Once his breathing grew steady, he opened his eyes.

The sourceless light was different, somehow. Perhaps it had grown brighter, but the quality of the change was that it seemed more healthy, more right. Fal turned his head.

The verminous cowhide had become a soft, luxurious fur pelt. Seated upon it was a girl, chin resting on her knees, arms clasped about her legs, watching him.

No. She could not be a girl. Too slender and long-limbed for humanity, she had blankly glowing eyes, blue-white from lid to lid with no pupil or iris that he could discern; blind-seeming eyes.

But she saw him more clearly than he did her.

Her skin had the whiteness of royal salt, and it too was over-smooth and fine for the earthy crudities of human existence.

"Look as much as you will," she said in a voice like wind-chimes. "What you see is your own work. I was a prisoner in the shape of the hag until a mortal man should join with me. Now I am free, Fal mac Umai."

Ordinarily quick-witted, Fal felt sluggish then. "You were the hag?"

"I was the hag. You have done me the best of turns."

"Pleasant!" Fal said with sudden, aware viciousness. "You have done me the worst!"

He reached for her delicate throat. She made no attempt to stop him. As his hands found a grip, numb helplessness flowed up his arms to the shoulders, robbing him of strength so that his hands fell slackly by his sides. He could neither lift them nor do more than twitch his fingers.

"I have my full powers, natural to myself, now that I have my own shape. I need not attack you with trees or strike you with my arm. You cannot harm me, Fal. Curb your resentment. What harm have I done you?"

"What harm? You murdered two friends of mine! You take that lightly!"

"You were prepared to do murder tonight for lighter reasons than mine. What if the owners of your lifted cattle had found you before I did? Your friends might well have suffered no less. I do not see that you have cause to hate me.

"Nor am I other than well-disposed to you. Fal, if you consider I have done you wrong, name an honour-price or compensation and I will pay it if I can."

"I'll accept nothing less than your life."

The being shook her head. "You are vengeful and arrogant, and that will bring you more grief than I have done. Put on your clothes and go home with nothing, then. Except your cattle. They have not strayed far."

"Wait," Fal said. Slowly, he stretched his recovering limbs and touched her shoulders.

The skin was cooler than mortal flesh, too smooth, too fine, and far too flawless. And she did not see that she had wronged him. Beautiful she might be now, but if anything she was less human than the hag had been.

"Since I've asked what you will not give, I'll demand another thing," he said. "Never let me look upon you again."

"As you wish."

The legends were wrong, Fal thought. Many were the tales of enchanted folk who regained their true shapes through the love of a mortal, but always in the tales the love had to be willingly given, or it effected nothing. Outside legend, it seemed the act was all that mattered, and not its meaning; that anything one wanted could be coerced.

Fal's slow smile would have looked unpleasant on the face of a man a hundred years old.

Yes, faerie woman. Maybe I should have been more gracious after all. Maybe you did teach me a thing worth knowing.

There was nothing around him now but a few thin bushes on a frosty plain. The woman had vanished. Shivering, Fal clad himself. Then he strode to his horse.

"The cattle will not have roved far," he said. "They were penned within thickets, as we were. Let's ride. We have still to get them safely through the bogs."

"By the Cross and the Wounds!" Amergin cried. "You mean to carry through your plan?"

"What has happened that we should not? As someone said to me, had Srem's riders come up with us, Cahal and Ebenár might well have suffered no less. We were all prepared to kill or die tonight — or meet what was not canny. Else we should have stayed in the dun." Fal gathered his strength and sprang to the saddle. "Come. We have cattle to find."

"What of Cahal and Ebenár?" Art demanded in anger. "Will you leave them where they lie?"

"I was supposing you'd placed them on their horses," Fal answered, unmoved. "And why didn't you? Had you something better to do while I was giving joy to that tender lady?"

"Easy, Fal," Miach cautioned. "It's in my mind that you are ripe for a quarrel, and that is a thing we can forgo. I too say we should gather the beasts. It may be better than brooding on what has passed. I take oath *I* would rather do some hard work."

One by one, the youths murmured agreement.

None drove himself harder than Fal in finishing what they had begun. In the sunrise, when he could see the face of his foster-brother's son, Miach grew more concerned than ever. The boy had a dark look upon him.

"Fal, visit your mother," Miach advised him.

His mother was Umai, the poetess and seeress of her people, famed for her ability to see the future, and her prophetic sayings. But it was her power to see into the human heart and share pain that Miach was thinking of. That, and her particular kinship of soul with her son.

He would need it.

After looking into Fal's eyes, Miach feared this mischief would outlast the night that had seen it committed. ■

Ménage à Trois

by F. Paul Wilson

Burke noticed how Grimes, the youngest patrolman there, was turning a sickly shade of yellow-green. He motioned him closer. "You all right?"

Grimes nodded. "Sure. Fine." His pitiful attempt at a smile was hardly reassuring. "Awful hot in here, but I'm fine."

Burke could see that he was anything but. The kid's lips were as pale as the rest of his face and he was dripping with sweat. He was either going to puke or pass out or both in the next two minutes.

"Yeah. Hot," Burke said. It was no more than seventy in the hospital room. "Get some fresh air out in the hall."

"Okay. Sure." Now the smile was real — and grateful. Grimes gestured toward the three sheet-covered bodies. "I just never seen anything like this before, y'know?"

Burke nodded. He knew. This was a nasty one. Real nasty. He swallowed the sour-milk taste that puckered his cheeks. In his twenty-three years with homicide he had seen his share of crime scenes like this, but he never got used to them. The splattered blood and flesh, the smell from the ruptured intestines, the glazed eyes in the slack-jawed faces — who could get used to that? And three lives, over and gone for good.

© G. Barr - 1987

"Look," he told Grimes, "why don't you check at the nurses' desk and find out where they lived. Get over there and dig up some background."

Grimes nodded enthusiastically. "Yes, sir."

Burke turned back to the room. Three lives had ended in there this morning. He was going to have to find out what those lives had been until now if he was ever going to understand this horror. And when he did get all the facts, could he ever really understand? Did he really want to?

Hot, sweaty, and gritty, Jerry Pritchard hauled himself up the cellar stairs and into the kitchen. Grabbing a beer from the fridge, he popped the top and drained half the can in one long, gullet-cooling swallow. Lord, that was *good!* He stepped over to the back door and pressed his face against the screen in search of a vagrant puff of air, anything to cool him off.

"Spring cleaning," he muttered, looking out at the greening rear acreage. "Right." It felt like August. Who ever heard of eighty degrees in April?

He could almost see the grass growing. The weeds, too. That meant he'd probably be out riding the mower around next week. Old Lady Gati had kept him busy all fall getting the grounds perfectly manicured; the winter had been spent painting and patching the first and second floors; April had been designated basement clean-up time, and now the grounds needed to be whipped into shape again.

An endless cycle. Jerry smiled. But that cycle meant job security. And job security meant he could work and eat here during the day and sleep in the gatehouse at night, and never go home again.

He drained the can and gave it a behind-the-back flip into the brown paper bag sitting in the corner by the fridge.

Home . . . the thought pursued him. There had been times when he thought he'd never get out. Twenty-two years in that little house, the last six of them pure hell after Dad got killed in the cave-in of No. 8 mine. Mom went off the deep end then. She had always been super religious, herding everyone along to fire-and-brimstone Sunday prayer meetings and making them listen to Bible readings every night. Dad had kept her in check somewhat, but once he was gone, all the stops were out. She began hounding him about how her only son should join the ministry and spread the Word of God. She submerged him in a Bible-besotted life for those years, and he'd almost bought the package. She had him consulting the Book upon awakening, upon retiring, before eating, before going off to school, before buying a pair of socks, before taking a leak, until common sense got a hold of him and he realized he was going slowly mad. But he couldn't leave because he was the man of the house and there was his younger sister to think of.

But Suzie, bless her, ran off last summer at sixteen and got married. Jerry walked out a week later. Mom had the house, Dad's pension, her Bible, and an endless round of prayer meetings. Jerry stopped by once in a while and sent her a little money when he could. She seemed to be content.

Whatever makes you happy, he thought. He had taken his own personal Bible with him when he left. It was still in his suitcase in the gatehouse. Some things you just didn't throw away, even if you stopped using them.

The latest in a string of live-in maids swung through the kitchen door with old lady Gati's lunch dishes on a tray. None of the others had been bad looking, but this girl was a knockout. "Hey, Steph," he said, deciding to put off his return to the cellar just a little bit longer. "How's the Dragon Lady treating you?"

She flashed him a bright smile. "I don't know why you call her that, Jerry. She's really very sweet."

That's what they all say, he thought, and then *wham!* they're out. Stephanie Watson had been here almost six weeks — a record in Jerry's experience. Old lady Gati went through maids like someone with hayfever went through Kleenex. Maybe Steph had whatever it was old lady Gati was looking for.

Jerry hoped so. He liked her. Liked her a *lot*. Liked her short tawny hair and the slightly crooked teeth that made her easy smile seem so genuine, liked her long legs and the way she moved through this big old house with such natural grace, like she belonged here. He especially liked the way her blue flowered print shift clung to her breasts and stretched across her buttocks as she loaded the dishes into the dishwasher. She excited him, no doubt about that.

"You know," she said, turning toward him and leaning back against the kitchen counter, "I still can't get over the size of this place. Seems every other day I find a new room."

Jerry nodded, remembering his first few weeks here last September. The sheer height of this old three-storey gothic mansion had awed him as he had come through the gate to apply for the caretaker job. He had known it was big — everybody in the valley grew up within sight of the old Gati House on the hill — but had never been close enough to appreciate *how* big. The house didn't really fit with the rest of the valley. It wasn't all that difficult to imagine that a giant hand had plucked it from a far-away, more populated place and dropped it here by mistake. But the older folks in town still talked about all the trouble and expense mine-owner Karl Gati went through to have

it built.

"Yeah," he said, looking at his calloused hands. "It's big all right."

He watched her for a moment as she turned and rinsed out the sink, watched the way her blond hair moved back and forth across the nape of her neck. He fought the urge to slip his arms around her and kiss that neck. That might be a mistake. They had been dating since she arrived here — just movies and something to eat afterwards — and she had been successful so far in holding him off. Not that that was so hard to do. Growing up under Mom's watchful Pentacostal eye had prevented him from developing a smooth approach to the opposite sex. So far, his limited repertoire of moves hadn't been successful with Steph.

He was sure she wasn't a dumb innocent — she was a farm girl and certainly knew what went where and why. No, he sensed that she was as attracted to him as he to her but didn't want to be a pushover. Well, okay. Jerry wasn't sure why that didn't bother him too much. Maybe it was because there was something open and vulnerable about Steph that appealed to a protective instinct in him. He'd give her time. Plenty of it. Something inside him told him she was worth the wait. And something else told him that she was weakening, that maybe it wouldn't be too long now before . . .

"Well, it's Friday," he said, moving closer. "Want to go down to town tonight and see what's playing at the Strand?" He hated to sound like a broken record — movie-movie-movie — but what else was there to do in this county on weekends if you didn't get drunk, play pool, race cars, or watch tv?

Her face brightened with another smile. "Love it!"

Now why, he asked himself, should a little smile and a simple *yes* make me feel so damn good?

57

No doubt about it. She did something to him.

"Great! I'll —"

A deep, gutteral woman's voice interrupted him. "Young Pritchard! I wish to see you a moment!"

Jerry shuddered. He hated what her accent did to the *r*'s in his name. Setting his teeth, he followed the sound of her voice through the ornate, cluttered dining room with its huge needlepoint carpet and bronze chandeliers and heavy furniture. Whoever had decorated this house must have been awfully depressed. Everything was dark and gloomy. All the furniture and decorations seemed to end in points.

He came to the semi-circular solarium where she awaited him. Her wheelchair was in its usual position by the big bay windows where she could look out on the rolling expanse of the south lawn.

"Ah, there you are, young Pritchard," she said, looking up and smiling coyly. She closed the book in her hands and laid it on the blanket that covered what might have passed for legs in a nightmare. The blanket had slipped once and he had seen what was under there. He didn't want another look. Ever. He remembered what his mother had always said about deformed people: That they were marked by God and should be avoided.

Old lady Gati was in her mid-sixties maybe, flabby without being fat, with pinched features and graying hair stretched back into a severe little bun at the back of her head. Her eyes were a watery blue as she looked at him over the tops of her reading glasses.

Jerry halted about a dozen feet away but she motioned him closer. He pretended not to notice. She was going to want to touch him again. God, he couldn't stand this!

"You called, ma'am?"

"Don't stand so far away, young Prit-chard." He advanced two steps in her direction and stopped again. "Closer," she said. "You don't expect me to shout, do you?"

She didn't let up until he was standing right next to her. Except for these daily chats with Miss Gati, Jerry loved his job.

"There," she said. "That's better. Now we can talk more easily."

She placed a gnarled, wrinkled hand on his arm and Jerry's flesh began to crawl. Why did she always have to touch him?

"The basement — it is coming along well?"

"Fine," he said, looking at the floor, out the window, anywhere but at her hungry, smiling face. "Just fine."

"Good." She began stroking his arm, gently, possessively. "I hope this heat wave isn't too much for you." As she spoke she used her free hand to adjust the blanket over what there was of her lower body. "I really should have Stephanie get me a lighter blanket."

Jerry fought the urge to jump away from her. He had become adept at masking the revulsion that rippled through his body everytime she touched him. And it seemed she *had* to touch him whenever he was in reach. When he first got the caretaker job, he took a lot of ribbing from the guys in town down at the Dewkum Inn. (Lord, what Mom would say if she ever saw him standing at a bar!) Everybody knew that a lot of older, more experienced men had been passed over for him. His buddies had said that the old lady really wanted him for stud service. The thought nauseated him. Who knew if she even had —

No, that would never happen. He needed this job, but there was nothing he needed *that* badly. And so far, all she had ever done was stroke his arm when she spoke to him. Even that was hard to take.

As casually as he could, he moved out of reach and gazed out the window as if something on the lawn had attracted his attention. "What did you want me to —"

Stephanie walked into the room and interrupted him.

"Yes, Miss Gati?"

"Get me a summer blanket, will you, dear?"

"Yes, ma'am." She flashed a little smile at Jerry as she turned, and he watched her until she was out of sight. Now if only it were Steph who couldn't keep her hands off him, he wouldn't —

"She appeals to you, young Pritchard?" Miss Gati said, her eyes dancing.

He didn't like her tone, so he kept his neutral. "She's a good kid."

"But does she *appeal* to you?"

He felt his anger rising, felt like telling her it was none of her damn business, but he hauled it back and said, "Why is that so important to you?"

"Now, now, young Pritchard, I'm only concerned that the two of you get along well. But not *too* well. I don't want you taking little Stephie away from me. I have special needs, and as you know, it took me a long time to find a live-in maid with Stephie's special qualities."

Jerry couldn't quite buy that explanation. There had been something in her eyes when she spoke of Steph "appealing" to him, a hint that her interest went beyond mere household harmony.

"But the reason I called you here," she said, shifting the subject, "is to tell you that I want you to tend to the roof in the next few days."

"The new shingles came in?"

"Yes. Delivered this morning while you were in the basement. I want you to replace the worn ones over my room tomorrow. I fear this heat wave might bring us a storm out of season. I don't want my good furniture ruined by leak-ing water."

He guessed he could handle that. "Okay. I'll finish up today and be up on the roof tomorrow. How's that?"

She wheeled over and cut him off as he tried to make his getaway. "Whatever you think best, young Pritchard."

Jerry pulled free and hurried off, shuddering.

Marta Gati watched young Pritchard's swift exit.

I repulse him.

There was no sorrow, no self-pity attached to the thought. When you were born with twig-like vestigial appendages for legs and only half a pelvis, you quickly became used to rejection — you learned to read it in the posture, to sense it behind the eyes. Your feelings soon became as callused as a miner's hands.

He's sensitive about my little Stephie, she thought. Almost protective. He likes her. He's attracted to her. *Very* attracted.

That was good. She wanted young Pritchard to have genuine feelings for Stephie. That would make it so much better.

Yes, her little household was just the way she wanted it now. It had taken her almost a year to set it up this way. Month after month of trial and error until she found the right combination. And now she had it.

Such an arrangement would have been impossible while Karl was alive. Her brother would never have hired someone with as little experience as young Pritchard as caretaker, and he would have thought Stephie too young and too frail to be a good live-in maid. But Karl was dead now. The heart attack had taken him quickly and without warning last June. He had gone to bed early one night complaining of what he thought was indigestion, and never awoke. Marta Gati missed her brother and mourned his loss, yet she was revelling in the freedom his passing had left her.

Karl had been a good brother. Tyrannically good. He had looked after her as a devoted husband would an ailing wife. He had never married, for he knew that congenital defects ran high in their family. Out of their parents' four children, two — Marta and Gabor — had been horribly deformed. When they had come to America from Hungary, Karl invested the smuggled family fortune in the mines here and, against all odds, had done well. He saw to it that Lazlo, the younger brother, received the finest education. Lazlo now lived in New York where he tended to Gabor.

And Marta? Marta he had kept hidden away in this remote mansion in rural West Virginia where she had often thought she would go insane with boredom. At least he had been able to persuade him to decorate the place. If she had to stay here, she had a right to be caged in surroundings to her taste. And her taste was Gothic Revival.

Marta loved this house, loved the heavy wood of the tables, the carved deer legs of the chairs, the elaborate finials atop the cabinets, the ornate valances and radiator covers, the trefoil arches on her canopy bed.

But the decor could only carry one so far. And there were only so many books one could read, television shows and rented movies one could watch. Karl's conversational capacity had been limited in the extreme, and when he had spoken, it was on business and finance and little else. Marta had wanted to be out in the world, but Karl said the world would turn away from her, so he'd kept her here to protect her from hurt.

But Marta had found a way to sneak out from under his overprotective thumb. And now with Karl gone, she

no longer had to sneak out to the world. She could bring some of the world into the house.

Yes, it was going to be so nice here.

"Tell me something," Steph said as she rested her head on Jerry's shoulder. She was warm against him in the front seat of his old Fairlane 500 convertible and his desire for her was a throbbing ache. After the movie — a Burt-Reynolds-type car-chase flick, but without Burt Reynolds — he had driven them back here and parked outside the gatehouse. The top was down and they were snuggled together in the front seat watching the little stars that city people never see, even on the clearest of nights.

"Anything," he whispered into her hair.

"How did Miss Gati get along here before she had me?"

"A lady from town used to come in to clean and cook, but she never stayed over. You're the first live-in who's lasted more than a week since I've been working here. The old lady's been real choosy about finding someone after the last live-in . . . left."

Jerry decided that now was not the time to bring up the last maid's suicide. Steph was from the farmlands on the other side of the ridge and wouldn't know about her. Constance Granger had been her name, a quiet girl who went crazy wild. She had come from a decent, church-going family, but all of a sudden she became a regular at the roadside taverns, taking up with a different man every night. Then one night she became hysterical in a motel room — with two men, if the whispers could be believed — and began screaming at the top of her lungs. She ran out of the room jaybird naked and got hit by a truck.

Jerry didn't want to frighten Steph with that kind of story, not now while they were snug and close like this. He steered the talk elsewhere.

"Now you tell me something. What do you think of working for old lady Gati?"

"She's sweet. She's not a slave driver and the pay is good. This is my first job since leaving home and I guess I'm kinda lucky it's working out so well."

"You miss home?"

He felt her tense beside him. She never talked about her home. "No. I . . . didn't get along with my father. But I get along just fine with Miss Gati. The only bad thing about the job is the house. I gives me the creeps. I get nightmares every night."

"What about?"

She snuggled closer, as if chilled despite the warmth of the night. "I don't remember much by morning, all I know is that they're no fun. I don't know how Miss Gati lived here alone after the last maid left. Especially without any legs. I'd be frightened to death!"

"She's not. She tried out girl after girl. No one satisfied her till you came along. She's a tough one."

"But she's not. She's nice. A real lady. You know, I make her hot chocolate every night and she insists I sit down and have a cup with her while she tells me about her family and how they lived in 'the Old Country.' Isn't that nice?"

"Just super," Jerry said.

He lifted her chin and kissed her. He felt her respond, felt her catch some of the fervor running through him like fire. He let his hand slip off her shoulder and come to rest over her right breast. She made no move to push him away as his fingers began caressing her.

"Want to come inside?" he said, glancing toward the door at the gatehouse.

Steph sighed. "Yes." She kissed him again, then pulled away. "But no. I don't think that would be such a good idea, Jerry. Not just yet. I mean, I just met you six weeks ago."

"You know all there is to know. I'm not hiding anything. Come on."

"I want to . . . you know I do, but not tonight. It's time for Miss Gati's hot chocolate. And if I want to keep this job, I'd better get up to the house and fix it for her." Her eyes searched his face in the light of the rising moon. "You're not mad at me, are you?"

"Nah!" he said with what he hoped was a reassuring grin. How could he look into those eyes and be mad? But he sure as Hell *ached*. "Crushed and heartbroken, maybe. But not mad."

She laughed. "Good!"

There's plenty of time, he told the ache deep down inside. And we'll be seeing each a lot of other.

"C'mon. I'll walk you up to the house."

On the front porch, he kissed her again and didn't want to let go. Finally, she pushed him away, gently. "She's calling me. Gotta go. See you tomorrow."

Reluctantly, Jerry released her. He hadn't heard anything but knew she had to go. He wondered if her insides were as churned up as his own.

"Hurry and drink your chocolate before it gets cold," Marta Gati said as Stephie returned from down the hall.

Stephie smiled and picked up her cup from the bedside table. *A lovely child*, Marta thought. *Simply lovely.*

Her own cup was cradled in her hands. It was a little too sweet for her taste, but she made no comment. She was propped up on her bed pillows. Stephie sat in a chair pulled up to the side of the bed.

"And what did you and young Pritchard do tonight?" Marta said. "Anything special?" She watched Stephie blush as she sipped her chocolate.

Marta took a sip of her own to hide the excitement that swept through her.

They're in love! This was perfect. "How was the movie?" she managed to say in a calm voice.

Stephie shrugged. "It was okay, I guess. Jerry likes all those cars racing around and crashing."

"Don't you?"

She shrugged. "Not really."

"But you go because young Pritchard likes them. And you like him, don't you?"

She shrugged shyly. "Yes."

"Of course you do. And he likes you. I can tell. I just hope he hasn't taken any liberties with you."

Stephie's color deepened. Marta guessed she wanted to tell her it was none of her damn business but didn't have the nerve. "No," Stephie said. "No liberties."

"Good!" Marta said. "I don't want you two running off and getting married. I need the both of you here. Now, finish your chocolate and get yourself to bed. Never let it be said I kept you up too late."

Stephie smiled and drained her cup.

Yes, Marta thought. *A lovely girl.*

The gatehouse was one room and a bathroom, furnished with a small desk, a chair, a bureau, and a hide-a-bed that folded up into a couch during the day. A sort of unattached motel room. But since he took his meals up at the house, it was all that Jerry needed.

The lights had been off for nearly an hour but he was still awake, rerunning his favorite fantasy, starring the voracious Steph and the inexhaustible Jerry. Then the door opened without warning and Steph stood there with the moonlight faintly outlining her body through the light cotton nightgown she wore. She said nothing as she came forward and crawled under the single sheet that covered him.

After that, no words were necesssary.

Dawnlight sneaking through the spaces between the venetian blinds on the gatehouse window woke Jerry. He was alone. After she had worn him out, Steph had left him. He sat on the edge of the hide-a-bed and cradled his head in his hands. In the thousand times he had mentally bedded Steph since her arrival, he had always been the initiator, the aggressor. Last night had been nothing at all like the fantasies. Steph had been in complete control — demanding, voracious, insatiable, a wild woman who had left him drained and exhausted. And hardly a word had passed between them. Throughout their lovemaking she had cooed, she had whimpered, she had moaned, but she had barely spoken to him. It left him feeling sort of . . . used.

Still trying to figure out this new, unexpected side to Steph, he walked up to the house for breakfast. The sun was barely up and already the air was starting to cook. It was going to be another hot one.

He saw Steph heading out of the kitchen toward the dining room with old lady Gati's tray as he came in the back door.

"Be with you in a minute," she called over her shoulder.

He waited by the swinging door and caught her as she came through. He slipped his arms around her waist and kissed her.

"Jerry, no!" she snapped. "Not here — not while I'm working!"

He released her. "Not your cheerful old self this morning, are you?"

"Just tired, I guess." She turned toward the stove.

"I guess you should be."

"And what's that supposed to mean?"

"Well, you had an unusually active night. At least I hope it was unusual."

Steph had been about to crack an egg on the edge of the frying pan. She stopped in mid motion and turned to face him.

"Jerry . . . what on earth are you talking about?"

She looked genuinely puzzled, and that threw him. "Last night . . . at the gatehouse . . . it was after three when you left."

Her cranky scowl dissolved into an easy smile. "You must really be in a bad way!" She laughed. "Now you're believing your own dreams!"

Jerry was struck by the clear innocence of her laughter. For a moment, he actually doubted his memory — but only for a moment. Last night had been real. Hadn't it?

"Steph . . ." he began, but dropped it. What could he say to those guileless blue eyes? She was either playing some sort of game, and playing it very well, or she really didn't remember. Or it really never happened. None of those choices was the least bit reassuring.

He wolfed his food as Steph moved in and out of the kitchen, attending to old lady Gati's breakfast wants. She kept glancing at him out of the corner of her eye, as if checking up on him. Was this a game? Or had he really dreamed it all last night?

Jerry skipped his usual second cup of coffee and was almost relieved to find himself back in the confines of the cellar. He threw himself into the job, partly because he wanted to finish it, and partly because he didn't want too much time to think about last night. By lunchtime he was sweeping up the last of the debris when he heard the sound.

It came from above. The floorboards were squeaking. And something else as well — the light sound of feet moving back and forth, rhythmically. It continued as he filled a carboard box with the last of the dirt, dust, and scraps of rotten wood from the cellar. He decided to walk around the south side of the house on his way to the trash bins. The sound seemed to be coming from there.

As he passed the solarium, he glanced in and almost dropped the box. Steph was waltzing around the room with an invisible partner in her arms. Swirling and dipping and curtsying, she was not the most graceful dancer he had ever seen, but the look of pure joy on her face made up for whatever she lacked in skill.

Her expression changed abruptly to a mixture of surprise and something like anger when she caught sight of him gaping through the window. She ran toward the stairs, leaving Miss Gati alone. The old lady neither turned to watch her go, nor looked out the window to see what had spooked her. She just sat slumped in her wheelchair, her head hanging forward. For a second, Jerry was jolted by the sight: She looked dead! He pressed his face against the solarium glass for a closer look, and was relieved to see the gentle rise and fall of her chest. Only asleep. But what had Steph been doing waltzing around like that while the old lady napped?

Shaking his head at the weirdness of it all, he dumped the box in the trash area and returned to the house through the back door. The kitchen was empty, so he made his way as quietly as possible to the solarium to see if Steph had returned. He found all quiet — the music off and old lady Gati bright and alert, reading a book. He immediately turned back toward the kitchen, hoping she wouldn't spot him. But it was too late.

"Yes, young Pritchard?" she said, rolling that "r" and looking up from her book. "You are looking for something?"

Jerry fumbled for words. "I was looking for Steph to see if she could fix me a sandwich. Thought I saw her in here when I passed by before."

"No, dear boy," she said with a smile. "I sent her up to her room for a nap almost an hour ago. Seems you tired her out last night."

"Last night?" He tensed. What did she know about last night?

Her smile broadened. "Come now! You two didn't think you could fool me, did you? I know she sneaked out to see you." Something about the way she looked at him sent a sick chill through Jerry. "Surely you can fix something yourself and let the poor girl rest."

Then it hadn't been a dream! But then why had Steph pretended —?

He couldn't figure it. "Yeah. Sure," he said dully, his thoughts jumbled. "I can make a sandwich." He turned to go.

"You should be about through with the basement by now," she said. "But even if you're not, get up to the roof this afternoon. The weatherman says there's a sixty percent chance of a thunderstorm tonight."

"Basement's done. Roof is next."

"Excellent! But don't work *too* hard, young Pritchard. Save something for Stephie."

She returned to her book.

Jerry felt numb as he walked back to the kitchen. The old lady hadn't touched him once! She seemed more relaxed and at ease with herself than he could ever remember — a-cat-that-had-swallowed-the-canary sort of self-satisfaction. And she hadn't tried to lay a single finger on him!

The day was getting weirder and weirder.

Replacing the shingles on the sloping dormer surface outside old lady Gati's bedroom had looked like an easy job from the ground. But the shingles were odd, scalloped affairs that she had ordered special from San Francisco to match the originals on the house, and Jerry had trouble keeping them aligned on the curved surface. He could have used a third hand, too. What would have been an hour's work for two men had already taken Jerry three in the broiling sun, and he wasn't quite finished yet.

While he was working, he noted that the wood trim on the upper levels was going to need painting soon. That was going to be a hellish job, what with the oculus windows, the ornate friezes, cornices, brackets, and keystones. Some crazed woodcarver had had a field day with this stuff — probably thought it was "art." But Jerry was going to be the one to paint it. He'd put that off as long as he could, and definitely wouldn't do it in summer.

He pulled an insulated wire free of the outside wall to fit in the final shingles by the old lady's window. It ran from somewhere on the roof down to the ground — directly *into* the ground. Jerry pulled himself up onto the parapet above the dormer to see where the wire originated. He followed it up until it linked into the lightning rod on the peak of the attic garret. *Everything* connected with this house was ornate — even the lightning rods had designs on them!

He climbed back down, pulled the ground wire free of the dormer, and tacked the final shingles into place. When he reached the ground, he slumped on the bottom rung of the ladder and rested a moment. The heat from the roof was getting to him. His tee-shirt was drenched with perspiration and he was reeling with fatigue.

Enough for today. He'd done the bulk of the work. A hurricane could hit the area and that dormer would not leak. He could put the finishing touches on tomorrow. He lowered the ladder to the ground, then checked the kitchen for Steph. She wasn't there. Just as well. He didn't have the energy to pry an explanation out of her. Something was cooking in the oven, but he was too bushed to eat. He grabbed half a six pack of beer from the fridge and stumbled down to the gatehouse. Hell with dinner. A shower, a few beers, a good night's sleep, and he'd be just fine in the morning.

It was a long ways into dark, but Jerry was still awake. Tired as he was, he couldn't get to sleep. As thunder rumbled in the distance, charging in from the west, and slivers of ever-brightening light flashed between the blinds, thoughts of last night tumbled through his mind, arousing him anew. Something strange going on up at that house. Old lady Gati was acting weird, and so was Steph.

Steph . . . he couldn't stop thinking about her. He didn't care what kind of game she was playing, she still meant something to him. He'd never felt this way before. He —

There was a noise at the door. It opened and Steph stepped inside. She said nothing as she came forward, but in the glow of the lightning flashes from outside, Jerry could see her removing her nightgown as she crossed the room. He saw it flutter to the floor and then she was beside him, bringing the dreamlike memories of last night into the sharp focus of the real and now. He tried to talk to her but she would only answer in a soft, breathless "uh-huh" or "uh-uh" and then her wandering lips and tongue wiped all questions from his mind.

When it was finally over and the two of them lay in a gasping tangle of limbs and sheets, Jerry decided that now was the time to find out what was going on between her and old lady Gati, and what kind of game she was playing with him. He would ask her in a few seconds . . . or maybe in a minute . . . soon . . . thunder was louder than ever outside but that wasn't going to bother him . . . all he wanted to do right now was close his eyes and enjoy the delicious exhaustion of this after-glow a little longer . . . only a little . . . just close his eyes for a few

seconds . . . no more . . .

"Sleep well, my love."

Jerry forced his eyes open. Steph's face hovered over him in the flashing dimness as he teetered on the brink of unconsciousness. She kissed him lightly on the forehead and whispered, "Good-night, young Pritchard. And thank you."

It was as if someone had tossed a bucket of icy water on him. Suddenly Jerry was wide awake. *Young Pritchard?* Why had she said that? Why had she imitated old lady Gati's voice that way? The accent, with its roll of the "r," had been chillingly perfect.

Steph had slipped her nightgown over her head and was on her way out. Jerry jumped out of bed and caught her at the door.

"I don't think that was funny, Steph!" She ignored him and pushed the screen door open. He grabbed her arm. "Hey, look! What kind of game are you playing? What's it gonna be tomorrow morning? Same as today? Pretend that nothing happened tonight?" she tried to pull away but he held on. "Talk to me Steph! What's going on?"

A picture suddenly formed in his mind of Steph going back to the house and having hot chocolate with old lady Gati and telling her every intimate detail of their lovemaking, and the old lady getting excited, *feeding* off it.

"What's going *on!*" Involuntarily, his grip tightened on her arm.

"You're hurting me!" The words cut like an icy knife. The voice was Steph's, but the tone, the accent, the roll of the "r"s, the inflection — all were perfect mimicry of old lady Gati, down to the last nuance. But she had been in pain. It couldn't have been rehearsed!

Jerry flipped the light switch and spun her around. It was Steph, all right, as achingly beautiful as ever, but something was wrong. The Steph he knew should have been frightened. The Steph

65

before him was changed. She held herself differently. Her stance was haughty, almost imperious. And there was something in her eyes — a strange light.

"Oh, sweet Jesus! What's happened to you?"

He could see indecision flickering through her eyes as she regarded him with a level stare. Outside, it began to rain. A few scattered forerunner drops escalated to a full-scale torrent in a matter of seconds as their eyes remained locked, their bodies frozen amid day-bright flashes of lightning and the roar of thunder and wind-driven rain. Then she smiled. It was like Steph's smile, but it wasn't.

"Nothing," she said in that crazy mixed voice.

And then he thought he knew. For a blazing instant, it was clear to him: "You're not Steph!" In the very instant he said it he disbelieved it, but then her smile broadened and her words turned his blood to ice:

"Yes, I am . . . for the moment." The voice was thick with old lady Gati's accent, and it carried a triumphant note. "What Stephie sees, *I* see! What Stephie feels, *I* feel!" She lifted the hem of her nightgown. "Look at my legs! Beautiful, aren't they?"

Jerry released her arm as if he had been burned. She moved closer but Jerry found himself backing away. Steph was crazy! Her mind had snapped. She thought she was old lady Gati! He had never been faced with such blatant madness before, and it terrified him. He felt exposed, vulnerable before it. With a trembling hand, he grabbed his jeans from the back of the chair.

Marta Gati looked out of Stephie's eyes at young Pritchard as he struggled into his trousers, and she wondered what to do next. She had thought him asleep when she had kissed him good night and made the slip of calling him

"Young Pritchard." She had known she couldn't keep her nightly possession of Stephie from him for too long, but she had not been prepared for a confrontation tonight. She would try for sympathy first.

"Do you have any idea, young Pritchard," she said, trying to make Stephie's voice sound as American as she could, "what it is like to be trapped all your life in a body as deformed as mine? To be repulsive to other children as a child, to grow up watching other girls find young men and go dancing and get married and know that at night they are holding their man in their arms and feeling all the things a woman should feel? You have no idea what my life has been like, young Pritchard. But through the years I found a way to remedy the situation. Tonight I am a complete woman — *your* woman!

"Stephanie!" young Pritchard shouted, fear and disbelief mingling in the strained pallor of his face. "Listen to yourself! You sound crazy! What you're saying is impossible!"

"No! Not impossible!" she said, although she could understand his reaction. A few years ago, she too would have called it impossible. Her brother Karl had devoted himself to her and his business. He never married, but he would bring women back to the house now and then when he thought she was asleep. It would have been wonderful if he could have brought a man home for her, but that was impossible. Yet it hadn't stopped her yearnings. And it was on those nights when he and a woman were in the next bedroom that Marta realized that she could sense things in Karl's women. At first she thought it was imagination, but this was more than mere fantasy. She could feel their passion, feel their skin tingling, feel them exploding within. And one night, after they both had spent themselves and fallen asleep, she found herself in the other woman's body — actually lying in Karl's bed and seeing the room through her eyes!

As time went on, she found she could enter their bodies while they slept and actually take them over. She could get up and walk! A sob built in her throat at the memory. To *walk!* That had been joy enough at first. Then she would dance by herself. She had wanted so much all her life to dance, to waltz, and now she could! She never dared more than that until Karl died and left her free. She had perfected her ability since then.

"It will be a good life for you, young Pritchard," she said. "You won't even have to work. Stephie will be my maid and housekeeper during the day and your lover at night." He shook his head, as if to stop her, but she pressed on. "And when you get tired of Stephie, I'll bring in another. And another. You'll have an endless stream of young, willing bodies in your bed. You'll have such a *good* life, young Pritchard!"

A new look was growing in his eyes: belief.

"It's really you!" he said in a hoarse whisper. "Oh, my dear sweet Lord, it's really you in Steph's body! I . . . I'm getting out of here!"

She moved to block his way and he stayed back. He could have easily overpowered her, but he seemed afraid to let her get too near. She couldn't let him go, not after all her work to set up a perfect household.

"No! You mustn't do that! You must stay here!"

"This is sick!" he cried, his voice rising in pitch as a wild light sprang into his eyes. "This is the Devil's work!"

"No-no," she said, soothingly. "Not the Devil. Just me. Just something —"

"Get away from me!" he said, backing toward his dresser. He spun and pulled open the top drawer, rummaged through

it and came up with a thick book with a cross on its cover. "Get away, Satan!" he cried, thrusting the book toward her face.

Marta almost laughed. "Don't be silly, young Pritchard! I'm not evil! I'm just doing what I have to do. I'm not hurting Stephie. I'm just borrowing her body for a while!"

"Out, demon!" He said, shoving the Bible almost into her face. "*Out!*"

This was getting annoying now. She snatched the book from his grasp and hurled it across the room. "Stop acting like a fool!"

He looked from her to the book and back to her with an awed expression. At that moment there was a particularly loud crash of thunder and the lights went out. Young Pritchard cried out in horror and brushed past her. He slammed out the door and ran into the storm.

Marta ran as far as the doorway and stopped. She peered through the deluge. Even with the rapid succession of lightning strokes and sheets, she could see barely a dozen feet. He was nowhere in sight. She could see no use in running out into the storm and following him. She glanced at his keys on the bureau and smiled. How far could a half-naked man go in a storm like this?

Marta crossed the room and sat on the bed. She ran Stephie's hand over the rumbled sheets where less than half an hour ago the two of them had been locked in passion. Warmth rose within her. *So good.* So good to have a man's arms around you, wanting you, needing you, *demanding* you. She couldn't give this up. Not now, not when it was finally at her disposal after all these years.

But young Pritchard wasn't working out. She had thought any virile young man would leap at what she offered, but apparently she had misjudged him. Or was a stable relationship within her household just a fool's dream? She had so much to learn about the outside world. Karl had kept her so sheltered from it.

Perhaps her best course was the one she had taken with the last housekeeper. Take over her body when she was asleep and drive to the bars and roadhouses outside of town. Find a man — two men, if she were in the mood — and spend most of the night in a motel room. Then come back to the house, clean her up, and leave her asleep in her bed. It was anonymous, it was exciting, but it was somehow . . . empty.

She would be more careful with Stephie than with the last housekeeper. Marta had been ill one night but had moved into the other body anyway. She had lost control when a stomach spasm had gripped her own body. The pain had drawn her back to the house, leaving the woman to awaken between two strangers. She had panicked and run out into the road.

Yes, she had to be very careful with this one. Stephie was so sensitive to her power, whatever it was. She only had to become drowsy and Marta could slip in and take complete control, keeping Stephie's mind unconscious while she controlled her body. A few milligrams of a sedative in her cocoa before bedtime and Stephie's body was Marta's for the night.

But young Pritchard wasn't working out. At least not so far. There was perhaps a slim chance she could reason with him when he came back. She had to try. She found him terribly attractive. But where could he be?

Sparks of alarm flashed through her as she realized that her own body was upstairs in the house, lying in bed, helpless, defenseless. What if that crazy boy — ?

Quickly, she slid onto the bed and closed her eyes. She shut out her senses one by one, blocking off the sound of the rain and thunder, the taste of the saliva in her mouth, the feel of the beclothes against her back . . .

. . . and opened her eyes in her own bedroom in the house. She looked around, alert for any sign that her room had been entered. Her bedroom door was still closed, and there was no moisture anywhere on the floor.

Good! He hasn't been in here!

Marta pushed herself up in bed and transferred to the wheelchair. She wheeled herself out to the hall and down to the elevator, cursing its slow descent as it took her to the first floor. When it finally stopped, she propelled herself at top speed to the foyer where she immediately turned the dead bolt on the front door. She noted with satisfaction that the slate floor under her chair was as dry as when she had walked out earlier as Stephie. She was satisfied that she was alone in the house.

Safe!

She rolled herself into the solarium at a more leisurely pace. She knew the rest of the doors and windows were secure — Stephie always locked up before she made the bedtime chocolate. She stopped before the big bay windows and watched the storm for a minute. It was a fierce one. She gazed out at the blue-white, water-blurred lightning flashes and wondered what she was going to do about young Pritchard. If she couldn't convince him to stay, then surely he would be in town tomorrow, telling a wild tale. No one would believe him, of course, but it would start talk, fuel rumors, and that would make it almost impossible to get help in the future. It might even make Stephie quit, and Marta didn't know how far her power could reach. She'd be left totally alone out here.

Her fingers tightened on the arm rests of her wheelchair. She couldn't let that happen.

She closed her eyes and blocked out the storm, blocked out her senses . . .

. . . and awoke in Stephie's body again.

She leapt to the kitchenette and pulled out the drawers until she found the one she wanted. It held three forks, a couple of spoons, a spatula, and a knife — a six-inch carving knife.

It would have to do.

She hurried out into the rain and up the hill toward the house.

Jerry rammed his shoulder against the big oak front door again but only added to bruises the door had already put there. He screamed at it.

"In God's name — open!"

The door ignored him. What was he going to do? He had to get inside! Had to get to that old lady! Had to wring the Devil out of her! Had to find a way in! Make her give Steph back!

His mother had warned him about this sort of thing. He could almost hear her voice between the claps of thunder: *Satan walks the earth, Jerome, searching for those who forsake the Word. Beware — he's waiting for you!*

Jerry knew the Devil had found him — in the guise of old lady Gati! What was happening to Steph was all his fault!

He ran back into the downpour and headed around toward the rear. Maybe the kitchen door was unlocked. He glanced through the solarium windows as he passed. His bare feet slid to a halt on the wet grass as he stopped and took a better look.

There she was: old lady Gati, the Devil herself, zonked out in her wheelchair.

The sight of her sitting there as if asleep while her spirit was down the hill controlling Steph's body was more than Jerry could stand. He looked around for something to hurl through the window, and in the next lightning

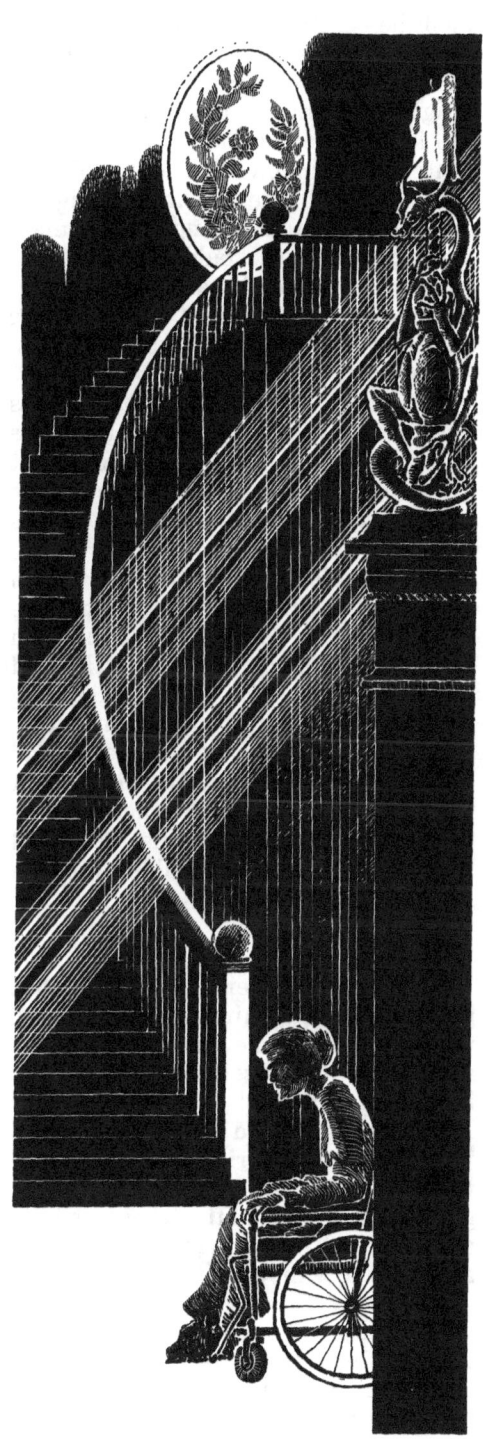

flash he spotted the ladder next to the house on the lawn. He picked it up and charged the solarium like a jousting knight. Putting all his weight behind the ladder, he rammed it through the center bay window. The sound of shattering glass broke the last vestige of Jerry's control. Howling like a madman, he drove the ladder against the window glass again and again until every pane and every muntin was smashed and battered out of the way.

Then he climbed in.

The shards of glass cut his bare hands and feet but Jerry barely noticed. His eyes were on old lady Gati. Throughout all the racket, she hadn't budged.

Merciful Lord, it's true! Her spirit's left her body!

He stumbled over to her inert form and stood behind her, hesitating. He didn't want to touch her — his skin crawled at the thought — but he had to put an end to this. Now. Swallowing the bile that sloshed up from his stomach, Jerry wrapped his fingers around old lady Gati's throat. He flinched at the feel of her wrinkles against his palms, but he clenched his teeth and began to squeeze. He put all his strength into it —

— and then let go.

He couldn't do it.

"God, give me strength!" he cried, but he couldn't bring himself to do it. Not while she was like this. It was like strangling a corpse! She was barely breathing as it was!

Something tapped against the intact bay window to the right. Jerry spun to look — a flash from outside outlined the grounding wire from the lightning rods as it swayed in the wind and slapped against the window. It reminded him of a snake —

A snake! And suddenly he knew: *It's a sign! A sign from God!*

He ran to the window and threw it open. He reached out, wrapped the wire

around his hands, and pulled. It wouldn't budge from the ground. He braced a foot against the window sill, putting his back and all his weight into the effort. Suddenly the metal grounding stake pulled free and he staggered back, the insulated wire thrashing about in his hands . . . just like a snake.

He remembered that snake handlers' church back in the hills his mother had dragged him to one Sunday a few years ago. He had watched in awe as the men and women would grab water moccasins and cotton-mouths and hold them up, trusting in the Lord to protect them. Some were bitten, some were not. Ma had told him it was all God's will.

God's will!

He pulled the old lady's wheelchair closer to the window and wrapped the wire tightly around her, tying it snugly behind the backrest of the chair, and jamming the grounding post into the metal spokes of one of the wheels.

"This is your snake, Miss Gati," he told her unconscious form. "It's God's will if it bites you!"

He backed away from her until he was at the entrance to the solarium. Lightning flashed as violently as ever, but none came down the wire. He couldn't wait any longer. He had to find Steph. As he turned to head for the front door, he saw someone standing on the south lawn, staring into the solarium. It was Old Lady Gati, wearing Steph's body. When she looked through the broken bay window and saw him there, she screamed and slumped to the ground.

"Steph!" What was happening to her?

Jerry sprinted across the room and dove through the shattered window onto the south lawn.

Marta awoke in her own body, panicked.

What has he done to me?

She felt all right. There was no pain,

MENGE Á TROIS

no —
My arms! Her hands were free but she couldn't move her upper arms! She looked down and saw the black insulated wire coiled tightly around her upper body, binding her to the chair. She tried to twist, to slide down on the chair and slip free, but the wire wouldn't give an inch. She tried to see where it was tied. If she could get her hands on the knot . . .

She saw the wire trailing away from her chair, across the floor and out the window and up into the darkness.

Up! To the roof! The lightning rods!
She screamed, "*Nooooo!*"

Jerry cradled Steph's head in his arm and slapped her wet face as hard as he dared. He'd hoped the cold pounding rain and the noise of the storm would have brought her around, but she was still out. He didn't want to hurt her, but she had to wake up.

"Steph! C'mon, Steph! You've got to wake up! Got to fight her!"

As she stirred, he heard old lady Gati howl from the solarium. Steph's eyes fluttered, then closed again. He shook her. "Steph! Please!"

She opened her eyes and stared at him. His spirits leaped.

"That's it, Steph! Wake up! It's me — Jerry! You've got to stay awake!"

She moaned and closed her eyes, so he shook her again.

"Steph! Don't let her take you over again!"

As she opened her eyes again, Jerry dragged her to her feet.

"Come on! Walk it off! Let's go! You've *got* to stay awake!"

Suddenly her face contorted and she swung on him. Something gleamed in her right hand as she plunged it toward his throat. Jerry got his forearm up just in time to block it. Pain seared through his arm and he cried out.

"Oh, God! It's you!"

"*Yes!*" She slashed at him again and he backpedaled to avoid the knife. His bare feet slipped on the grass and he went down on his back. He rolled frantically, fearing she would be upon him, but when he looked up, she was running toward the house, toward the smashed bay window.

"No!"

He couldn't let her get inside and untie the old lady's body. Steph's only hope was a lightning strike.

Please, God, he prayed. *Now! Let it be now!*

But though bolts crackled through the sky almost continuously, none of them hit the house. Groaning with fear and frustration, Jerry scrambled to his feet and sprinted after her. He had to stop her!

He caught her from behind and brought her down about two dozen feet from the house. She screamed and thrashed like an enraged animal, twisting and slashing at him again and again with the knife. She cut him along the ribs as he tried to pin her arms and was rearing back for a better angle on his chest when the night turned blue white. He saw the rage on Steph's face turn to wide-eyed horror. Her body arched convulsively as she opened her mouth and and let out a high-pitched shriek of agony that rose and cut off like a circuit being broken —

— only to be taken up by another voice from within the solarium. Jerry glanced up and saw old lady Gati's body juttering in her chair like a hooked fish while blue fire played all about her. Her hoarse cry was swallowed and drowned as her body exploded in a roiling ball of flame. Fire was everywhere in the solarium. The very air seemed to burn.

He removed the knife from Steph's now limp hand and dragged her to a safer distance from the house. He shook her. "Steph?"

He could see her eyes rolling back

and forth under the lids. Finally they opened and stared at him uncomprehendingly.

"Jerry?" She bolted up to a sitting position. "Jerry! What's going on?"

His grip on the knife tightened as he listened to her voice, searching carefully for the slightest hint of an accent, the slightest roll of an "r." There wasn't any he could detect, but there was only one test that could completely convince him.

"My name," he said. "What's my last name, Steph?"

"It's Pritchard, of course. But —" She must have seen the flames flickering in his eyes because she twisted around and cried out. "The house! It's on fire! Miss Gati — !"

She had said it perfectly! The real Steph was back! Jerry threw away the knife and lifted her to her feet. "She's gone," he told her. "Burnt up. I saw her."

"But how?"

He had to think fast — couldn't tell her the truth. Not yet. "Lightning. It's my fault. I must have messed up the rods when I was up on the roof today!"

"Oh, God, Jerry!" She clung to him and suddenly the storm seemed far away. "What'll we do?"

Over her shoulder, he watched the flames spreading throughout the first floor and lapping up at the second through the broken bay window. "Got to get out of here, Steph. They're gonna blame me for it, and God knows what'll happen."

"It was an accident! They can't blame you for that!"

"Oh, yes they will!" Jerry was thinking about the ground wire wrapped around the old lady's corpse. No way anyone would think that was an accident. "I hear she's got family in New York. They'll see me hang if they can, I just know it! I've got to get out of here." He pushed her to arm's length

and stared at her. "Come with me?"

She shook her head. "I can't! How — ?"

"We'll make a new life far from here. We'll head west and won't stop till we reach the ocean." He could see her wavering. "Please, Steph! I don't think I can make it without you!"

Finally, she nodded.

He took her hand and pulled her along behind him as he raced down the slope for the gate house. He glanced back at the old house and saw flames dancing in the second floor windows. Somebody down in town would see the light from the fire soon and then half the town would be up here to either fight it or watch it being fought. They had to be out of here before that.

It's gonna be okay, he told himself. They'd start a new life out in California. And someday, when he had the nerve and he thought she was ready for it, he'd tell her the truth. But for now, as long as Steph was at his side, he could handle anything. Everything was going to be all right.

Patrolman Grimes looked better now. He was back from the couple's apartment and stood in the hospital corridor with an open notebook, ready to recite.

All right," Burke said. "What've we got?

"We've got a twenty-three year old named Jerome Pritchard. Came out here from West Virginia nine months ago."

"I mean drugs — crack, Angel Dust, needles, fixings."

"No, sir. The apartment was clean. The neighbors are in absolute shock. Everybody loved the Pritchards and they all seem to think he was a pretty straight guy. A real churchgoer — carried his own Bible and never missed a Sunday, they said. Had an assembly line job and talked about starting night courses at UCLA as soon as he made the

residency requirement. He and his wife appeared to be real excited about the baby, going to Lamaze classes and all that sort of stuff."

"Crack, I tell you!" Burke said. "Got to be!"

"As far as we can trace his movements, sir, it seems that after the baby was delivered at 10:06 this morning, he ran out of here like a bat out of hell, came back about an hour later carrying his Bible and a big oblong package, waited until the baby was brought to the mother for feeding, then . . . well, you know."

"Yeah. I know." The new father had pulled a 10 gauge shotgun from that package and blown the mother and kid away, then put the barrel against his own throat and completed the job. "But why, dammit!"

"Well . . . the baby did have a birth defect."

"I know. I saw. But there are a helluva lot of birth defects a damn sight worse. Hell, I mean, her legs were only withered a little!"

■

COMING IN OUR SUMMER, 1988 ISSUE!

The Wonderful Wallstretcher

by Felix C. Gotschalk

It was the hot summer of 1939, and ten-year-old Jody walked, silent as a cat, through the equally silent alley, on his way to Mike Braur's tiny grocery store to get a watermelon. His new, high-quarter tennis shoes enabled him to sprint like a cheetah, to leap across the algae-green creek in one arcing bound, and to twist and dodge and forage and escape the adventures always available on the hot asphalt flats of the neighborhood playground. In his new shoes, Jody was in new and sensitive contact with the gritty hard dirt, the leaf-stained sidewalks, the resilient grass, the hot streets, and even the cool marble halls of the school.

Skeeter, the skinny Irish Setter, galloped, mongrel-like, to Jody, his tail fanning the August air, a poignantly lower-class wag, for Skeeter was gun-shy and cringing, and his pedigree meaningless in light of his overt manner. A Best of Show Irish Setter could prance like a graceful, dancing stallion, but Skeeter's body language was sadly introversive. Jody found a fat gray tick in Skeeter's heavy silky ear, and pried it loose. The tick was swollen with blood and was shaped rather like a kernel of corn, but soft and rubbery to the touch. The slowly waving legs and the forked-needle snout were so small in comparison with the bloated body that they looked like hairs instead of true appendages. Jody put the tick down on a large flat rock and then crushed the resilient body with a smaller rock. Dark blood shot out, the tick now looked like a grape-skin, and Jody felt he had performed a significant act.

He walked on. Insects sawed in the tall grasses behind the Jeters' high white-washed fence, and Jody could already hear the buzzing of the big green flies that swarmed around the dented metal cans behind Braur's store. Coming onto the street from the alley, he saw Mister Akers's Packard at the curb, all regal and heavy and sombre. There was no doubt that cars wore different facial expressions, and that of the Packard was sombre. Jody had ridden in the car once, and he remembered the scratch of the mohair seats against his bare legs, and how he had listened for the marvelous singing transmission sounds Mister Akers had told him about. He opened the beveled glass door to the store and went inside. It was dim and cool, and the smell was a mixture of the mystical aromatic and the grossly domestic. Mike was in the back, behind the refrigerated meat cases, and there was some sort of a commotion going on there. Jody spotted Mike's familiar blood-stained apron, and then he saw that Mike was holding a puppy down on the huge meat-cutting block. As Jody watched, fascinated, Mike cut off the pup's tail with a long, curved, razor-sharp knife. The pup yelped, and Mike brushed the tiny severed tail onto the sawdust covered floor. The man standing next to Mike wrapped the rear end of the dog in brown paper, thanked Mike, and left by the back door where the green flies lived. Jody stood and looked at the meats in their cold display case, the various cuts all red and thick and wet. There were smooth squab, goose-bumped chickens, shiny fish with dilated pupils, leathery pigs' feet, and mounds of hamburger.

"Maw wants a watermelon," Jody said to Mike, as the muscular butcher hefted a leg of lamb up onto the cutting block and reached for his saw.

"Joe'll get it for you," Mike said, beginning to saw away at the lamb, "You gonna pay for it?"

"Maw said put it on her bill." Mike gave Jody a look that seemed to say that the bill was already too big, and Jody could feel his reaction. He turned to go to where Joe Willard was arranging the produce.

"Hey, Jody," Mike's voice took on a new and interesting tone, and he put the saw down. He leaned his heavy, hairy forearms on the top of the counter where the potato salad lay in cellophane-topped containers. "I want you to do me a favor." Jody felt flooded with excitement. "I want you to go to the drugstore and ask Frank Johnson for the wallstretcher."

A *wallstretcher,* Jody exulted, silently. That sounded important. He wondered how such a device would work. He looked up earnestly into Mike's twinkling pig-eyes, and felt a cone of true masculine camaraderie beaming down on him.

"Take the watermelon on home, and then straight on up to the drugstore, okay?" Jody's look was almost worshipful. Mike was an important man. He had a big house in the country, a fat wife and sassy kids that never came near the store, and he always had a big roll of money in his pocket. Jody felt under the umbrella of all this importance.

The watermelon was heavy and cold, and Jody almost fell on the rutted, sloping part of the alley behind his house.

He left the huge green blimp on the worn linoleum of the kitchen floor and ran for the drugstore, the wind in his ears; past the Jeters' ungainly large house, past the dry cleaners on the corner, then the stucco church, and the big square house where the five old-maid sisters lived. He was breathless as his new shoes smoked to a halt at the drugstore; and he stood for a minute at the magazine rack, looking at the airplane books. Jody loved airplanes and built models as a hobby.

"Mike wants the wallstretcher," he said to Frank Johnson, the clerk at the back counter. Frank was a man of wholly bent frame and beaten facial cast. He combed his thinning, greasy black hair straight back; strands of it were forever falling loose; and he was forever brushing them back with his hand. He looked down at Jody, and the faintest smile formed on his lips. There was a pause, and Jody knew that the wonderful wallstretcher must be in the back, where the medicines were all ranked up in soldierly bottles and boxes, standing at permanent attention on merthiolate and iodine-smelling shelves.

"Go ask Tate for it," Frank said, finally, "I think he's got it." There was some kind of sly look on Frank's face, some little glint that Jody couldn't puzzle out; an elusive, knowing look in his sad eyes, and a look that was not at all appropriate to the serious nature of the job at hand. But, to work, Jody thought, and left immediately for Tate's barbershop, just half a block away. The wallstretcher was in demand, he thought to himself, only the important people have access to it. Perhaps it was used and shared several critical times this very day. It was vital that he locate it.

Tate was shaving Dick Glover, the local drunk, who, when not stumbling in and out of Nader's Bar, was said to be the most skillful brick mason in the entire city. The barber chairs were enormous thrones, somehow human or robot-looking, and the smell of bay rum mixed with the smell of the hot towel that Tate was lowering down on to Dick's craggy face.

"Frank sent me to get the wallstretcher. He said you had it."

"The what?" Tate said, patting the soggy steaming towel, adjusting it, like pieces of soft, wide taffy.

"The wallstretcher!" Jody said, importantly, "Mike's got to use it today, and Frank said you had it."

"Oh — Oh yeah," Tate's voice broadened, and he laughed. "'Let's see, what did I do with that thing?" Jody looked all around the shop but did not see the marvelous device. "I do believe Miz Childress came and got it. Yeah, you go ask her. I recollect she's the one's got it."

Miz Childress, Jody thought. She was the wide-faced little lady who ran the candy store three blocks away, the lady who had a pretty daughter and two scrappy Pomeranians, and the lady who had given Jody his first and only taste of whiskey. It had been last Christmas, when the snow was deep and the cold was bone-chilling; and Jody remembered the fumes up his nose, and the warmth of the liquor in his throat and chest and stomach. It had been a very masculine feeling and he had never told anyone about it. Perhaps Miz Childress was going to enlarge her little store. The wallstretcher would be vital for her. Wouldn't it be wonderful to have the grocery store, the drugstore, the barber shop *and* the candy store all larger? There were important ramifications here: the expansion of three-dimensional space, the burgeoning of cubic yardage — why, it was an actual growth process! Surely the wallstretcher must be a landmark invention.

Jody didn't want Mike or Joe to see him walk past the grocery again (par-ticularly without the wallstretcher), and he hesitated before finally striding by, his new tennis shoes firmly in command of the smooth hot sidewalk. He could feel some sweat in the small of his back now, and he was glad that his pants were old and smooth and cottony in the summer heat. The Chinaberry trees were getting full of green marbles that would soon be picked and cached away for the autumn times when they would be thrown in battle, boys pitching them at each other from across their streets. The Fairmount bus hissed its noisy airbrakes and pulled to a stop across the street. Young Stagg was driving and he curled his lip at Jody. Stagg liked to have the young women sit close to him on the bus as he turned the huge flat steering wheel and double-clutched through the grinding gears. But Jody could feel important also, knowing that all he had to do was stand at the bus stop, and Stagg would have to stop the huge metal monster for him. The big door would open, Jody would stomp up the cross-hatched metal steps, slam his six cents in the glass fare-box, and then sit anywhere he wanted. And Stagg would have to take him anywhere he wanted to go, and stop the bus when Jody pulled the cord.

He walked more slowly now, the urgency of his mission somehow lessened, the criticality of his assignment temporarily suspended in his mind, the logistics of the plan in flux, uncertain and reconnoitering. A locust built up its seesaw message from high in an elm tree, and a biplane chattered overhead, low, wobbling, free, and dominant. Jody had flown once in an open-cockpit Stearman, and he counted this as one of his greatest thrills. Now, as he walked toward the candy store, his feelings of territoriality weakened, for he was no longer on the familiar ground of his own block. Here the houses looked more substantial, with fresh paint and brightly contrasting trim. The grass in the small elevated plots was thicker and more carefully tended than the grass on Jody's block, and all the stone steps looked well swept. Jody had heard that some of the people here had woolen rugs on their floors instead of linoleum, and that their ice-boxes had big coils on top, with a black wire that plugged into the lamp socket, and, because of this, the ice-man didn't have to leave ice there at all. Some of the people even had water that would turn hot right out of the faucet, and they had stoves called oil circulators that sat in the dining room and had a flue-pipe that sent heat into the fireplace in the living room, and even up through the ceiling to where the bedrooms were. Jody saw the black wreath on Miz Hite's door, and knew this was for 19-year-old Roy, who had been killed in an auto accident. He did not know that Roy's handsome face and strong young body had been all but destroyed in the crash, and he had wondered why the casket was closed at the funeral.

Now Jody passed Nader's Bar and could see the big brown Lebanese man inside, drying glasses behind the counter. Another block of row houses, all alike and yet slightly different, and Jody saw Miz Childress's store. Now he would complete his mission, for here reposed the magic space-enlarger, the alterer of angles, the displacer of bulkheads; the pressing, straining, powerful Open-Sesame prize. The bell jangled as Jody entered, and the wooden floor was resonant beneath his new shoes, smelling lumberish and old, like a secret attic. Twisted licorice snakes lay in flaccid parallel strips beneath the glass counter top, and there were peppermint barberpoles, gumdrops like translucent jewels, orange slices, lemon drops, and thick jellied mint leaves crusted with tiny perfect cubes of sugar. A pendulum clock hung on the wall, like a walking

stick-man, and it ticked and tocked slowly and somberly in the stillness of the store.

"Hi Jody," Miz Childress said, her wide face puffy, like a tomato, "How's your mother?"

"Fine. Mike wants to borrow the wallstretcher. I went to the drug store and the barber shop, and they told me you had it. Mike wants it back real bad. I think he has to have it today." Miz Childress looked a little bit surprised, then she smiled, and then she looked kind or sympathetic; and again, Jody couldn't quite puzzle out her look. She pushed a jelly mint leaf over the counter to him, and it left a little trail of cubed sugar.

"I don't have any money," Jody said, and there was a hint of defiance in his voice that he hadn't intended.

"Pay me the next time you come." Miz Childress's face took on a look of resolve, and there was just the faintest edge of indignation in her voice: "Mike and Frank and Tate never could get the hang of using that wallstretcher," she began, and Jody marveled that a woman would talk that way about masculine things. "The rig is new, hasn't been used very much; and, well, maybe it's too advanced for them to know how to make it work right. You go on home. I'll phone Mike and tell him."

"But where is it? I want to see it."

"It's packed away in the basement. Now you get on home, and tell your mother to be sure to come to PTA this week."

Jody lay on his bed and looked up at the model airplanes hanging from the long string that ran from one corner of the ceiling diagonally across to the other. The planes turned slowly in the slight breeze: fragile, airy birds of balsa sticks glued in bodysides, cross members, angled longerons, notched formers, 3/32″ stringers, all covered with tissue paper, wetted, dried taut, and brushed with banana oil and dope. There was the gull-winged Stinson Reliant, the Ryan, the Waco, and the Taylorcraft, the small high-ruddered Stinson Sport, and his prize: a big Spad from the World War, with struts and N-bracings and thread for the X-rigging between the wings. Jody lowered his head, face up, far down over the edge of the bed and looked, upside down, out the window. From this position, he could imagine he was fixed to the bed, that the bed was pinned to the ceiling, that up was really down, and that the vast blue sky he was looking at was really beneath him. He imagined that if he fell, he would fall forever downward, never stopping, and never striking anything. He enjoyed this little visual game, and could do it so intently he occasionally scared himself. When it worked well, it was apparent that his squarish wooden house was hanging on the absolute flat underside of the Earth, and that beneath there was endless deep space.

He thought about the wallstretcher. How well and simple it must look, and yet how revolutionary! It would have to be made of light-weight angle-irons, or maybe telescoping steel tubes, with sliding lock-collars and thumbscrews and heavy pins to prevent slippage. Perhaps it could retract into a small space, he reasoned, picturing a carrying case about six feet long. There would be strong steel threads cut into the sections, he was convinced of that; and maybe a wormgear somewhere in the maze; and for the final expansive power, perhaps a ring-geared hand-crank or even a torque-bar of some sort. Jody enjoyed working out the mental pictures of the device. Surely the frame would have to be three-dimensional. The angle-irons and tubing would have to form some sort of *box;* that is, unless you wanted to stretch one wall at a time, or one floor (he assumed it would stretch walls and floors and ceilings equally well). The frame would have to fit very precisely against the ceilings and corners and baseboards, and there would be the most basic considerations of horizonality and verticality. Surely this box-frame would have to be connected to a geared power source; so that meant that the tubing would have to be positioned in azimuths that merged somewhere in the exact volumetric center of the room. It would have to be a winch-like device, Jody figured, or like a chain-hoist, or maybe even a capstan. After all, capstans could hold giant ships to their docks, and winches could hold a dirigible down, and a chain-hoist could lift a motor up out of a car. With all this power, wall stretching should be no problem. The gear ratio in the winch could be fixed so as to make the turning easy, and a pawl and ratchet would keep it locked in place as the stretching continued. There would be turning and rotating and inexorable fulcrumic power, there would be force vectors in measurable foot-pounds, the plaster would give and stretch — wait, Jody thought, plaster doesn't stretch — it cracks and crumbles and falls. A piece of plaster ceiling had fallen on him once. And then the idea came to Jody that the wallstretcher could not possibly work. No wonder Mike and Frank and Tate couldn't use it. Why, he thought, it damages the very rooms it purports to stretch! In expanding the cubic yardage, it displaced the fixed vertical risers and the undergirding beams. It distended framing and stressed the gussets and palings. It would, Jody thought, incredulously, *actually crack the ceilings and bow the floors!* It was a crazy invention, the wallstretcher. Far ahead of its time, bizarre in its impractical function, cumbersome and unwieldy, an altogether strange bit of airframe and winch — it must be a bewildering topologic maze of bars and rods and groaning sleeves on tortured metal threads. Jody pictured himself turning the winch, supra-alert to the movement of any surface, every cracking cue monitored precisely, his body tingling with the requisite anticipatory skill, even as the floor lowered and the ceiling rose and all four walls moved slowly outward. I would have to be very careful, Jody reasoned, because the dining room is right below my room, the attic right above, and my sister's room is right through the wall. It would take a skill to do it right. And it would take some re-designing to build a wallstretcher that would expand the lifespace in my room without encroaching on the space in the adjoining rooms. But Jody saw this as a technical problem, an engineering problem amenable to scientific law. He was certain he could work it out.

Jody's mother had plugged the watermelon, extracted and examined the plug, proclaimed the melon good and ripe, and began to cut it, as the circle of children pressed against each other, waiting and watching. She called for Jody to come down and get his slice, but

Jody lay on the bed awhile, thinking. He was developing his plan. He would have to break the news to the other men that, in its present stage of development, the wallstretcher was unworkable. He hoped to make it clear to them that the device was insufficiently refined, and that the best place for it was where it was, at Miz Childress's, packed away. And he thought he would tell them that, in the meantime, he would strive to re-design the device himself, that he would make carefully scaled drawings, and maybe even a 1/8th" scale working model. He was thinking that helical or planetary gears could be tried on the winch. And, in the purity of his mind's eye, he could see the beautifully, infinitely telescoping rods and the ranked and stacked angle-irons of the wonderful wallstretcher, laying under a tarp in the driest corner of the candy store's white-washed basement. Surely that was the best place for it now, and he knew that he would go see Miz Childress sometime in the future and that she would show it to him.

His mother called again, and Jody went down to get his watermelon. ∎

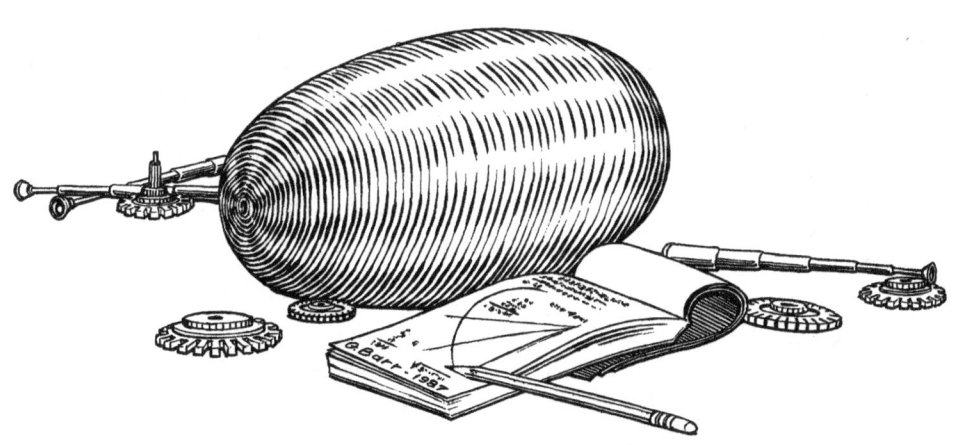

Boiled Alive
by Ramsey Campbell

Each weekday morning Mee was first in the pay office. He would sip coffee from a dwarfish plastic cup and watch the car park rearrange itself as the factory changed shifts, several thousand random blocks of colour gathering about his green car on the concrete field. He would spend the next four hours at the computer, and three hours after lunch. The chirping cursor leapt to do his bidding, danced characters onto the screen. He had charge of half the payroll, half of the three-letter codes that denoted employees so secretively that he didn't even know if he was in his own batch. Now and then Clare trotted in from the outer office with a handful of changes of tax coding; but Mee was mostly unaware of Till, who computed the other half of the payroll, and Macnamara the supervisor, who was always repeating himself, always repeating himself.

Each day after work Mee listened in his car to wartime crooners rhyming the moon and waited until he had a clear path through the car park. The music rode with him along the motorway to the estate that was mounting the sandstone hills. His street was of sandy bungalows, identical except for curtains or cacti or porcelain in the windows. He parked his car in the garage that took the place of one front room and walked down the drive, round the end of his strip of lawn like a hall carpet, and up the path to his front door.

Each night he prepared the next day's dinner and stored it in the refrigerator. He would eat it facing the view back towards the factory, miles away. Roads and looped junctions left no room for trees, but the earliness of headlights signified the onset of winter. He was digging at his dessert with his fork and watching the swarming of lights, the landscape humming constantly like a dynamo, when the telephone rang.

A darts match at the pub, he guessed, or a message from the Homewatch leader, probably about youngsters using the back alleys to take drugs, as if reality weren't enough for them. Munching, he lifted the receiver, and a voice said, "Boiled alive."

"Pardon?" Mee wondered if the man had mistaken him for a restaurant — but the voice was too lugubriously meaningful. "Boiled alive," it repeated in an explanatory tone that sounded almost peevish, and rang off.

No doubt the caller was on drugs and phoning at random, and Mee wanted to believe the phrase was just as meaningless. He switched on the television and watched manic couples win holidays on a quiz show. A dentist's receptionist was leaping and squealing and popping her eyes at her prize when the phone rang again. "Is this the house of Dr Doncaster?" a voice said.

"I'm afraid not. Sorry." Mee waited politely for a response, and was about to break the connection when the voice said, "Is this the house of Dr Doncaster?"

"I've already said not. Can't you hear me?" Perhaps deafness was why the man was calling. "You've got a wrong number," Mee said, so loudly that the mouthpiece vibrated.

This time the silence was shorter. "Is this the house of Dr Doncaster?"

"Don't be ridiculous. What do you want?" The doctor, Mee thought, and felt somewhat ridiculous himself. It wasn't the voice that had called earlier; it had an odd quality — a blandness, a lack of accent. "Is this —" it recommenced, and he cut it off.

Had its silences really been exactly the same length? Certainly it had repeated itself with precisely the same intonation. He might have been talking to a robot, he thought, but that seemed to miss the point somehow. He went out to the pub, a longer bungalow, and tried to interest himself in the quiz league's semi-final, questions about places he'd never heard of.

Next day the lassitude he always suffered after a morning at the computer was worse, but the sight of men from the assembly line swapping pirated videos in the windowless canteen wakened him and a memory he'd been trying to gain access to. He stopped at the video library in the wine shop on his way home after work. Horror films had occupied the shelves nearest the window: *Shriek of the Mutilated, Headless Eyes, Nightmares in a Damaged Brain, Boiled Alive.*

The box showed photographs of people reddening and screaming, presumably the actors who were listed, though they sounded like pseudonyms. He would learn no more unless he hired a videorecorder. At home he ate boiled beef and watched the lights until he felt their swarming was preventing him from thinking. He was late for the committee meeting at the church hall, and had to struggle to interest himself in the question of rents to be charged for jumble sales and Boy Scout gatherings. He voted against letting the peace movement use the hall. Life wasn't as precarious as they made it out to be, he thought as he strode home; it had a pattern you could glimpse if you had faith.

The phone was ringing as he reached his path. He slammed the door, dashed to the phone, snatched the receiver. "Is this the house of Dr Doncaster?" the voice said.

Mee let out a long sigh, which his panting interrupted. "Do I get a prize for the right answer?"

Silence. It really was a total silence, empty even of static. "Is this the house of Dr Doncaster?"

"Where you are, you mean? It may be, for all I know."

Silence. Mee found he was counting the seconds. If the silence was even fractionally longer he would know he'd thrown the caller, as he realized he very much wanted to do. But no: "Is this —"

"Go to the devil where you belong, you lunatic," Mee shouted, and chopped at the cradle with the edge of his palm. He nursed his bruised hand and thought of contacting the police. They would only tell him to keep on receiving the calls so that the caller could be traced, and he wouldn't be able to sleep for waiting tensely. He left the phone off the hook overnight and watched *Boiled Alive*, which varied wildly from dream to dream. Whenever he awoke he felt colder, as if the dreams were draining him.

Next morning he said to Till, "You've a videorecorder, haven't you?"

Till blinked at him under his perpetual grey-browed scowl. "Used to have. Can't afford it with the kids at private school. Besides, most of the films weren't fit for them to watch. Puts ideas in people's heads, that sort of thing."

"Something you wanted to watch, Mr Mee?" Macnamara said across the room, his hollow drone resounding. "Was there something you wanted to see?"

"A tape in my local library."

"Bring it round on Sunday. Come for dinner after church, my mother likes the company. You can't get too much use out of a machine, am I right? You can't get too much use out of a machine."

Should Mee let him know the kind of film it was? But he might seem to be rejecting Macnamara's gesture. He busied himself at the screen, wondering afresh whether any of the three-letter codes coincided with the employee's car registration or whether someone had ensured they did not. Certainly none of his highest earners had the same codes as the limousines outside.

That night he hired *Boiled Alive* for the weekend. He'd finished eating dinner and watched the racing lights for some time before he realized the phone hadn't rung. He had a sudden irrational conviction that it wouldn't while he had the videocassette. Such thoughts were dangerous; things didn't work like that. All the same, the only call that weekend was from Macnamara, to make sure Mee was coming.

Macnamara lived in the town beyond the factory, in a house at the top of a flight of railed steps. "Here he is," he announced as he let Mee into the long narrow hall beneath a lampshade like a flower of stained glass. "He's here."

His mother darted out from the farthest doorway. She couldn't really be that small, Mee thought nervously; but when she squeezed alongside her son her head was barely as high as his chest. Otherwise, apart from having all the hair, she looked much like Macnamara: thin oval face, sharp nose, colourless lips. "Didn't you bring the film?" she said in a stage whisper. "Sidney said you were bringing a film."

They made Mee think of the voice on the phone, but neither of them would be capable of that voice. He dug the cassette out of his pocket. "Some kind of comedy, is it?" Macnamara said, raising his eyebrows at the title, and to his mother, "Some kind of comedy."

She herded them into the dining room then — to Mee's acute embarrassment, she pretended to charge at them like a goat, emitting sounds of shooing. Dinner was Greek, and went on for hours. Whenever he thought the end was near she produced another course. "Is it good?" she demanded anxiously before he'd had a mouthful, and as soon as he had: "It's good, isn't it?" Her whispering was the result of a throat disease, he realized, but nevertheless she talked constantly, interrogating him about himself long after the details ceased to interest him. Worse, she told him in intimate detail about her problems in bringing up her son after his father had deserted them. "How's my Sidney getting on at work?" she asked Mee, and wouldn't let him mumble vaguely. "Fine, I'm sure," he stammered, yearning for it to be time to watch the film.

Macnamara's reluctance was obvious as he picked up the cassette. "Sounds exciting, *Boiled Alive*," his mother whispered enthusiastically, and he slipped it into the player with a despairing shrug. "That's funny. Isn't it?" she suggested as several thin flat scientists squeezed into sight behind the wide-screen credits, then she gasped as they inflated, released from the bonds of the words. Whatever they were doing to measure psychic energy, their experiment was going wrong: laboratory monitors were melting, a man's face was blistering. "How do they do that?" Mrs Macnamara cried in a whisper, and Mee had to restrain himself from hushing her, for one of the scientists had just been called Doncaster.

She talked throughout the film. Mee wondered if she was trying to shut out the sight of people being boiled alive by some vindictive psychic power. "Is that the kind of car you make at the factory?" she whispered as a scientist's hands fused to a steering wheel. Another man's eyes burst one by one, and she struggled to her feet, croaking "I think I'll go to bed now."

Mee stared open-mouthed at the screen, which was filled with a telephone dial. A detective's finger was dialling Mee's phone number. "My mother wants to go to bed," Macnamara growled, but Mee barely noticed he was speaking as the detective, mouthing, said "Is this the house of Dr Doncaster?"

"I'll see you up, mother," Macnamara said furiously, and Mee lurched forward to listen to the detective. "Is Dr Doncaster there?" . . . "What do the words 'boiled alive' mean to you?" . . . "We all have hidden powers that only need to be unlocked" . . . "We can't talk now, this may be being traced" . . . "Right, I'll meet you in an hour." But he was boiled en route, leaving only his girlfriend, a reporter, to gun down the culprit in a refrigerator. Suddenly the gun was too hot to hold, and as she dropped it, a silhouette stepped out from behind a side of beef. "I am Dr Doncaster," it said.

"The End." Had something been missed out? The tape began to rewind, and as Mee picked up the remote control he noticed Macnamara, who was watching him from the hall. "That wasn't funny," Macnamara said, even slower than usual. "Not funny at all."

Mee thought of apologizing, but wasn't sure what for. Had Dr Doncaster really been the culprit, or only in English? The question formed a barrier in his mind as he followed taillights home. Even the inclusion of his number in the film couldn't quite break through.

In the morning he tried to phone the distributor of *Boiled Alive*, but whenever the number wasn't engaged there was no answer. He had to desist when Macnamara kept glaring at him. Otherwise Macnamara behaved as if Mee's visit had never taken place. Mee crouched over the screen and tried to interest himself in the dance of the symbols, telling himself that they were as real as he was.

He had to make himself return the cassette, for his notion that its presence precluded the calls was even stronger. In the library the proprietor held up a box to the bars of his cage. "Lots of naked women being tortured. By the feller who made the one you just had."

"I've no interest in that kind of thing. I only borrowed this because they used my phone number in it."

"I'd sue them. Or send reporters after them, they'll cough up some quick enough."

Mee had meant to consult the factory's lawyers, but the nearest television station was less than half an hour's drive away. His phone call was put through to a bright young woman who wanted him to come in straight away and record an interview for the local news programme. They made up his face, sat him in a puffy leather chair on a metal stalk, shone lights on him while the bright young woman asked him if he thought films like *Boiled Alive* should be banned and how "being haunted by phone" was affecting him. On his way out, his head swimming, he made her promise not to broadcast his number.

Why did the interview persist in troubling him? He spent the evening in trying to think, and flung the phone off the hook when it rang just before midnight. Next day he was so preoccupied that he almost deleted his morning's work on the computer. Working at a screen while waiting to watch himself on another didn't help. He was home well before the six o'clock news. Rising crime and unemployment, nuclear escalation, famines, terrorism. . . . The bright young woman appeared at last, and there was Mee, trying to look as if he belonged in the leather chair. How plump and red and blotchy his face was! His voice sounded bland and timid as he said that he believed films should be banned if they did harm, he didn't think much of the film anyway, his privacy had been invaded, at the very least the number should be changed in every copy of the film. . . . They might just as well have broadcast his number, since he'd named the film. His consciousness lurched at that, and then he wondered if he had actually just said, "It's Dr Doncaster's number, not mine."

The co-presenter turned from the interview with a look that all but winked. "We tried to contact the film's distributor in Wigan but we understand they're bankrupt. Serves them right, our friend at the wrong end of the phone might say. Now, if you've ever wondered where flies go to in the wintertime —"

Mee turned him off and waited for the phone to ring. Eventually he realized he'd been waiting for hours, hadn't even eaten his dinner. Of course, he thought, people couldn't phone until they'd seen the film. By midnight he thought they might have, but the phone was a black lump of silence. Even when he closed his eyes and tried to sleep, it stood out from the dark.

At least now Macnamara ought to know why Mee had been interested in the film — but neither he nor Till gave any sign of having seen the interview. Their silence unnerved Mee, made him feel guilty about letting himself be interviewed, but why should he blame himself? In the canteen he sensed that half the people who weren't looking at him had only just looked away. They'd better not offend him. Maybe they hadn't been impressed by his appearance on the screen, but they ought to see themselves, bunches of letters he could treat however he liked.

The calls began that evening. Mee heard smothered laughter and sounds of a party in the background every time a different voice asked for Dr Doncaster. None of them was the bland voice that had plagued him with the exact information of the line from the film. To his confusion, he found he almost missed that voice. After the fourth call he went to the pub.

Though he didn't recognize many of the drinkers, he thought they all recognized him. Freddy from the darts team bought him a drink, but his small talk sounded stiffer than the dubbing in the film, and so, when Mee listened, did all the conversations around him. When he began to suspect that some of the drinkers were assuming more than one voice, he stalked home through the floodlit identical streets.

He waited for the voice that knew its lines, but there were no more calls. He slept unexpectedly, woke late, drove hastily to work. He had to park at the far side of the concrete field and trudge between the cooling cars in a drizzle. Several people and some kind of machine paced him beyond two ranks of cars.

"How's your mother now?"

"Getting better, getting better," Macnamara told Till, and they fell silent as Mee came in. If they blamed him for that too, let them say so. Maybe he sounded like three letters on a screen, but they mustn't treat him as if he weren't real. Perhaps the voice that knew its lines hadn't been able to reach him last night because of the hoax calls, he was thinking.

Despite Macnamara's disapproval, Mee switched off his computer in time to beat the homeward rush. But by the time his car started, there was a long queue for the exit. Car, he thought, feeling trapped in three letters. He swung into the course of light at last and edged into the middle lane as soon as he could. He was almost unaware that the car was moving when light blazed into the vehicle and flung his silhouette onto the windscreen.

He thought of the floodlights at the television interview. But it was a lorry, blaring at him to force him into the outer lane, where lights were racing faster than he was. When he trod on the accelerator the car jerked toward the taillights beyond the half-blinded windscreen, too fast, too close. He swerved into a momentary gap in the outer race, overtook the car in the middle lane, dodged in ahead of it. He was groaning with relief when the entire lorry slewed toward him.

It had jackknifed, swinging across all three lanes. It struck the car behind Mee's, hurling it into the inside lane, where it smashed into another vehicle. The impact jarred a roof light on, and Mee glimpsed the driver's face, lock-jawed with terror, in the instant before it went out. As he sped onward he heard traffic crashing into the far side of the lorry and into one another, the tardy screech of brakes, crash upon crash, screams of the injured and dying. When he reached home he could see fires from his window, vehicles blazing hundreds of yards apart. Behind the blaze headlights bunched for miles, a comet's tail.

The local newscast was devoted to the crash. "Some of the drivers were driving as if they had no sense of reality," a police spokesman said. He couldn't mean Mee, since Mee hadn't been involved. Later, at the committee meeting in the church hall, Mee mentioned how he'd been ahead of the crash. How could he have known that the chairman's sister and nephews had been killed in the pileup? The committee seemed almost to blame Mee for surviving. As he trudged home he recognized screams in an empty street. Someone must be watching the nude women being tortured in one of the neat bright houses.

In the morning there was no sign of the crash. A sprinkling of snow covered any traces it had left on the motorway. Till asked how close to it Mee had been, but Mee denied all knowledge and stood

at the window, hardly aware of the plastic tumbler of coffee in his reddening hand. Surely the car park hadn't always looked so short of perspective.

He was restless all day. He felt as if the heat of the fires on the motorway, or of the guilt that everyone was trying to make him accept, were building up in his skull. Even the green screen wasn't soothing. He kept straying near Till's desk, but was never in time to see the letters of his name. If they were there, what would it prove? They couldn't reduce him, nor could Macnamara's inability to get his lines right first time, nor the unnatural silence when the computers were switched off.

There had been no calls while he was at home last night, but tonight the phone greeted him with the young shrill voice of an admirer of *Boiled Alive*, accusing Mee of having put the distributor out of business just because he wasn't able to distinguish between fiction and reality. When it wouldn't listen to his objections, Mee cut it off. On television a streetful of identical houses let out their men to advertise a car, and he saw that one of the men who had the wrong car was himself.

Did they think they could do what they liked with him? Now that he'd appeared before the cameras, was he fair game for however they wanted to edit him? They were trying to undermine his sense of reality, he thought; the police spokesman had as good as said Mee's was above average. That would explain why, when he went shopping at the supermarket, everyone not only pretended not to recognize him but acted like extras around him, most of them using the same voice. When he strode home the only sounds in the glaring streets were his footsteps, as if someone had turned off the other sounds or forgotten to record them.

The idea of living in a film wasn't entirely unappealing. If it had been a better film he might even have been flattered. Being able to repeat favourite moments and speed up the boring parts was certainly tempting, not to mention the ability to say of bad times, "it's only a film," or to have a hidden voice explain things when he looked at them. But how much control would he have? About as much as one generally has of one's life, he thought, then felt as if the voice that knew its lines could put him right if he could just work out how to respond.

Next day the snow had melted, but there were no marks of the crash. The view from his car trembled slightly in the frames of the windscreen and windows. It must be the car that was shaking, not the image, for he noticed cameras in several of the vehicles that passed him, filming him. They must have been filming him before the crash — that was how they'd been on the scene so quickly. Why, the camera car might have made the lorry jackknife!

He would have pointed this out to his colleagues, except that they didn't seem real enough to be worth telling, Macnamara and his dogged repetitions, Till and his switched-off silences. The computer screen seemed more real, and took more out of him. But in the canteen at lunchtime, he was unexpectedly upset by the sight of two men smirking at him as they exchanged cassettes, for one of the cassettes was *Boiled Alive*.

They wanted him to see them, did they? Then let them see what he could do. At last he knew why he'd been missing the voice on the phone: he wanted to be told about the hidden powers — but he didn't need it to unlock him. As he stared at the cassette of *Boiled Alive* the fire in his head flared up, yet he didn't feel as if he was focusing it, he felt reality focusing through him, the cassette and the man who held it growing intensely real. "Shit," the man cried, and dropped the cassette deafeningly to clutch the fingers of one hand with the other.

"Hot stuff, eh? Too hot to handle?" Mee suggested, and felt he was cheapening himself. He swung away and hurried through the corridors, past the unstable windowscapes. The shaking of his reality had just been a step in the process of unlocking, then. In an impersonal way, he had never felt nearly so real.

He sat in the pay office and gazed at his blank monitor. What would happen when they realized what he'd done in the canteen? They already disapproved of him, but now they'd try to use him or stop him, not realizing how they would be endangering themselves. It wasn't as if he was sure he could control the power: he felt more like a channel for reality, far harder to close than to open. The inside of his head felt dry and hot and shrunken. He had to think what to do before Till and Macnamara came back.

He prowled the office, staring at the blank walls, at his car in the midst of the random pattern of cars. He even switched on Till's screen and scanned the columns. There were the letters of his name, against a salary several times the size of his. Something about the sight of a version of himself he would have liked to be inspired him. He turned off the computer and slipped down to his car.

Between the factory and home he managed not to pass or be passed by another vehicle. It was a question of balance, He thought. He had to preserve a balance between reality before he'd seen the film and after, between himself and the way the world saw him, between the governments that would want to use him as a weapon. His street was deserted, which was welcome: to be seen at the start of his mission, to have to cope with someone else's perception of him, would only confuse him. It seemed wholly appropriate that he would start by entering so unremarkable a house.

He bolted the front and back doors and secured all the windows. He hadn't prepared tonight's dinner, he saw. That didn't matter; the less he ate, the sooner he would finish. He was surprised how easy it was to take responsibility for the world. He'd expected to feel lonely, but he found he didn't; perhaps there were others like himself. He used the toilet, combed his hair in front of the mirror, straightened his tie, brushed his shoulders, and then he sat down by the phone with his back to the window and dialled his own number. When the phone rang he picked it up, knowing that he wouldn't get the intonation quite right and that he'd have to go for retake after retake, especially if he heard any kind of a response.

"Is this the house of Dr Doncaster?" he said. ∎

John Mason Sidd

He did the right things at all the right times;
he was always proper and he was always nice.
His deportment was impeccable, his manners were sublime;
his talk was fascinating, flawless, and concise.
There was never a drawing room that found him at a loss;
his compliments were lavish, not once did he offend.
He was never brusk nor even mildly cross;
he was your and my and everybody's friend.
The day they found him hanging from a branch,
half the town was shocked and mystified and mute;
they passed the hours in a sort of solemn trance.
A morgue attendant saw the note pinned inside his suit:
"I wanted everyone to like me, and I think they did,
everyone, that is, except John Mason Sidd."

— **Joseph Payne Brennan**

IMPROBABLE BESTIARY: The Bigfoot

While thrashing about in the Oregon woods
(And my haversack filled overflowing
With camping equipment, provisions and goods)
I lost track of which way I was going.
With no rescue in sight, I made camp for the night,
Pitched a tent, and ignited a fire.
And then in the dark I was startled to see
A huge hairy creature as high as a tree.
"Hello there," he rumbled, *"I happen to be
Mister Bigfoot J. Sasquatch, Esquire."*

"Folks would pay through the nose for a look at those toes,"
I remarked, when I saw his huge footsies.
"With your feet on display we'll get rich right away
Showing off your miraculous tootsies.
I know just what to do: come with me to the Zoo!
Have you got any brothers or sisters?"
"I can't go into town!" Bigfoot roared with a frown,
"For the streets give my poor old feet blisters."

"I've twenty-six bunions the size of spring onions,"
The Bigfoot explained, *"And my toes are so sore.
The sidewalks have got holes, the highways have potholes;
The street hurts my feet, as I mentioned before."*
"Don't worry," I said, while the tears filled his eyes.
"I'll treat your poor feet with my camping supplies.
I have here two war-surplus hammocks, for starters;
On legs of *your* size, they'd make excellent garters.
To save your poor feet from the harsh pavement's shocks
These two sleeping-bags will make excellent socks.
And now you'll need shoes; I know just what to use:
Stick your feet in these extra-large birchbark canoes.
Try 'em on," I remarked. "If your feet like the fit
You can walk twenty miles without hurting a bit."

So Bigfoot J. Sasquatch, not skipping a beat,
Quite rapidly garbed his voluminous feet.
"THEY FIT!" he exclaimed. *"Life is nearly complete!
All I need now is LOTS OF NICE HUMANS TO EAT!"*
Then he hightailed it off towards the city.
Where's he *now?* Need you *ask?* Watch
Out, folks; Mister Sasquatch
Is heading *your* way . . . What a pity.

— F. Gwynplaine MacIntyre

The Mysteries

by
Darrell
Schweitzer

When I was eight, my father took me deep into the forest to see the altar of the Faceless King. Voinos, my elder brother, came too; mostly because, as I was smugly certain at the time, Father didn't trust him out of his sight. Voinos was fourteen then; and he hated everyone: me, Father, Mother, the town elders, and even, I think, himself. That year, when he was fourteen, was the last time anyone was ever able to control him.

It was in the autumn, when the leaves had turned brilliant red and gold and yellow, on the morning of the Festival of the Masks, when children make masks out of those leaves and try and go into other people's houses and impersonate other children, only to receive treats when they are discovered. But the Festival of Masks is for younger children, and that year my father de-

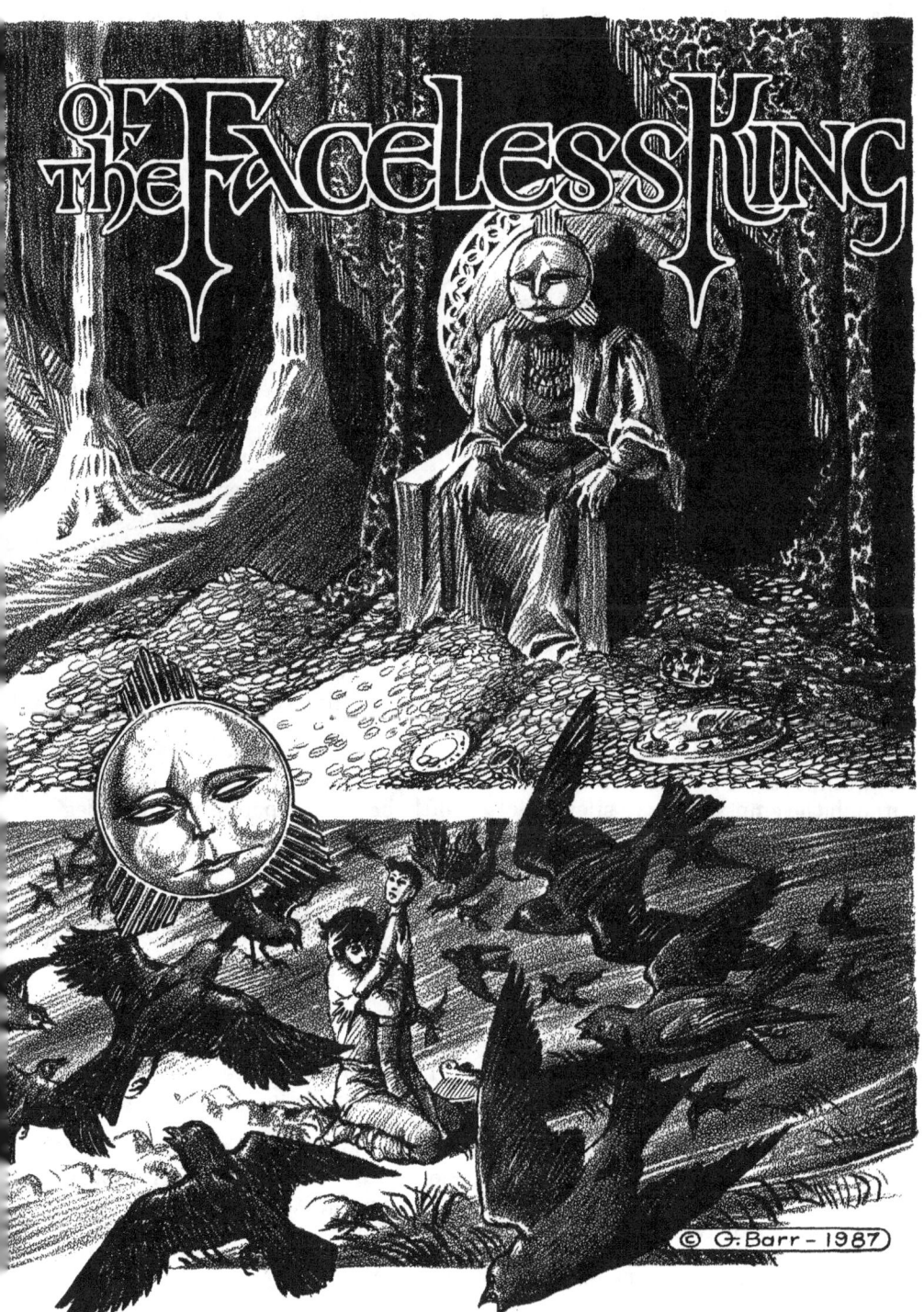

OF THE FACELESS KING

© G. Barr - 1987

cided that I was older. Only fathers can know when this happens, and when they do it is the time of *going*, when fathers and sons go off together, to some private place the gods reveal, to learn together such wisdom as the gods see fit to inspire. In this way, boys become men. So I came a man at the age of eight, and Voinos at fourteen because Father did not trust him.

Going. Old Decronos, the chief priest of our town, was there by the gate, seated at a table sipping broth. He barely looked up when the three of us knelt before him and Father said softly, "Going."

The priest touched Voinos and me on the shoulder with his feather-tipped cane and waved us away. Then the guards opened the heavy log gates, and off we went.

The terraced fields above the Great River were places of mud and dead corn stalks. It was bad to be there at this time of year, I knew, because sometimes ancestors rise up out of the mud, begging to be remembered; and if you don't remember them, it can bring a curse. I wanted to get away quickly, but we walked for most of the morning through the empty fields in silence, following the river. Once we came to a calf's skull and some beads stuck on a post. It was a charm, Father explained, to make the ancestors gather *there* and not bother anyone. We walked a wide half-circle around it.

Going. By noon we were far from any path, in the unbroken twilight beneath heavy pine branches. No birds sang. No animals ran before us. The forest stood silent and expectant all around, the bright leaves of autumn now a memory among the faded blue-greens and browns and the all-pervasive grey.

Voinos complained a lot. He would insist we stop to rest, then sit down; and Father would have to drag him up by the scruff of the neck. Then he'd try

to run off, but Father was too quick and his long arms would always have him. Voinos made a fist once, but Father just swatted it aside. He could have hurt Voinos. He was a big, agile, powerful man. That alone my brother respected in him.

The shadows deepened, and it seemed night already. The soft needles muffled our footsteps. The horizontal rays of the setting sun flickered between the black trunks.

We paused then, built a fire and had our supper, then sat without a word while the flames burned low, Voinos glowering, I almost too excited to be still, a little scared, expecting wonders.

After the sun had been gone for perhaps an hour, the moon rose, gleaming among the branches, like a huge penny.

Father was a bard, one of the very best. He was often called to recite in the halls of the great lords. There, in the forest before his sons, he got out his harp and began to make a story — for a bard is a *maker;* he calls up his matter out of nothing, and when he has finished, it lives.

He sat for a moment with his eyes closed, gazing into himself, strumming softly on the harp; and when he began to speak, it was with all the intensity of a bardic tale, for all that his words were less formal.

"These things came to me in a dream," he said, "and that was why I brought you here. The dream came from the gods."

"Well, what did the gods *say?*" Voinos demanded.

I gasped and looked away, shocked at the interruption; but Father merely answered.

"I dreamed of Verunnos-Kemad, the most secretive of the gods. He is known by the wind in the night, by the pattern of the leaves as they fall, by the voice of the river and the running beasts, by the multitudes of birds. All these are signs of him. I dreamed that the holy one stood here, almost where we sit, in the darkness of a night a few scant centuries after the creation of the world. His whole body shone like the pale moonlight. There was a man here too, prostrate on the ground before him. The name of the man I do not know. Nor did I see his face. It does not matter. He was but one man of many.

"In this time, so long ago, there were dragons in the land, swarming thick as starlings." Father turned to me suddenly, still strumming the harp. "Did you know about the dragons, Evad?"

"There's bones," I said, startled. "Bones in the cliff by the river road."

"Yes, one of the last of the dragons died there, and his bones remain for all to see; but these were *living* dragons, great and terrible. They hovered in black flocks, their wings like thunder. Sometimes people make offerings to them, gold, animals, even their children; and the dragons would go away for a while. But sometimes they would just burn the towns with their breath and swoop down to devour the fleeing people."

Voinos shifted about, rustling.

"You're changing the subject," he said. "What do dragons have to do with Veruna — Vero — whatever his stupid name is?"

Again I was afraid of my father's sudden anger, but as long as he was telling the story, his patience seemed limitless.

"I think the man's children had been taken by the dragons, or perhaps they were about to be. I don't know. But I saw, in my dream, the man lying there and the god bending down over him. The hand of Verunnos-Kemad glowed softly, like a paper lantern. He touched the man on the shoulder and raised him up, and placed on the man's face a mask of brilliant silver, shaped like the full Moon, mottled, with thin rays. And he gave him a silver staff and a silver-bladed sword, and said to him in terrible, relentless whispers, *You are the first. Let it begin.*

"Then he was gone, and the man stood alone in the forest darkness, until the first light of dawn touched the mask and staff, and they shone more brilliantly than the sunrise. But in the full day they were merely silver, for their power and their glory were of the night.

"This man was the Faceless King. Whoever he had been previously had ceased to exist, for he could never remove the mask, never return to being just an ordinary man. He emerged from the forest in the evening with his sword drawn, and the bravest of heroes followed him, and together they slew all the dragons, including the one who died by the river. At last they slew even the mighty Mother of Dragons in her cavern at the center of the world. Then the Faceless King parted from the heroes. He sent with them his farewell to all he had ever known, and he remained in the cavern of the Mother Dragon, among the treasures and the pillars of stone the color of blood. He sits there still, watching over the world. The wisest and the bravest know his sendings, for he is their lord."

"It's just an old story," Voinos said. "You've taken us all the way out here to tell us an old story. We could have stayed home. You could have told it any market day."

Father stiffened. I could hear barely restrained rage in his voice.

"Some of it I could tell again, as a story, for it is good to have the truth in a story. But the dream itself is a secret thing, between me, your father, and Voinos and Evad, my sons. I do not know why the Secret God sent it to me. That is a mighty and even terrible mystery. But I am sure that your lives will be shaped by it. This is the night of *going* and now I have told you all that I have to tell you."

93

"But — but, Father," I asked softly, as respectfully as I could, "what does it *mean?*"

Father pointed to a rise of land, a tree-lined ridge I could barely make out in the darkness. It looked like the back of a huge, sleeping dragon to me.

"There. Just beyond is a little valley. The heroes built an altar there, in secret, for the Faceless King. Sometimes he would manifest himself there and even give them gifts, rare crowns and jewels from the Mother Dragon's hoard, and he would speak to them in prophecies, for he shared the thoughts of Verunnos-Kemad, and at such times his voice was the voice of the god."

Suddenly Voinos was up and running toward the ridge.

"Where are you —?" I managed to say.

Father cursed, grabbed his staff and a burning brand from the fire, and took after him. I followed.

But as we were running the shadows of the night began to move. I thought it was black smoke at first, rushing silently between the trees, but then I saw that it was an enormous flight of birds rising from the earth. Soon the whole forest shook with the whirring of their wings.

I knew this was a sign, a miracle, for there were millions of them. The very air shuddered with their passage, yet not a single bird cried out. Pine needles and twigs rained down on us. Above, the Moon vanished, like a shiny pebble beneath a dark tide.

"Father!" I shouted.

He dropped his staff and brand, then fell to his knees, covering his face. I think he was weeping. I groped toward him, bent against the mighty wind of countless wings, hundreds of birds colliding with me. I reached out. His hand found mine and I embraced him, and so we remained, he kneeling and I standing hunched against him for what

seemed like hours, until at last the night was still. The Moon reappeared. There was no wind. Not a branch rustled. I could hear my father's heart, and my own, racing.

"Father . . . ? Voinos, he —"

"Come!"

Still holding my hand, he leapt to his feet, snatched up his staff, and yanked me along as he ran. We topped the rise and looked down into a hollow, where Voinos stood in the moonlight before a roughly rectangular slab of white marble.

"What have you done?" Father shouted as we approached.

Voinos turned slowly. He spoke with open contempt.

"It's just an old rock."

He spat on the altar stone. I let out a sudden cry of "No!" and cringed at the desecration. It was then that my eyes met my brother's, and I *knew* that the sign had not been for him. He had seen no flight of birds.

Father demanded again, *"What did you do?"*

"Nothing. I was looking for gold. I wanted to see if there was any treasure left." Voinos acted as if it were a commonplace, completely ignoring Father's mounting rage.

"You didn't intend to share it."

"What matter? There's nothing *to* share. The Faceless King is dead, if there ever was any Faceless King. He'd have to be a god himself to live so long. It's just a stupid old story."

"He is but a man," Father said, intoning his words as if speaking a doom. "Some say that the mask extends his life, and he lives for many centuries, but in the end, he dies like any man. When he is dying, he summons his successor from out of the world, and someone else becomes the Faceless King. He dies in secret. No one, not his attendants, not his messengers, ever sees his face."

Voinos laughed, shockingly. "Then how do they know it's *him?*"

Even Father was stunned at that.

I merely said, "Huh?"

Voinos turned to me sharply. "Idiot, if they can't see his face, it could be just anybody." He leaned over and poked my chest viciously. "Even *you.*"

Father still held my hand. I felt him tremble.

"The one who wears the mask *is* the Faceless King. He hears every leaf that falls —"

Voinos mimicked him in sing-song mockery, "He hears every piece of dung plop in every privy in the whole wide world —"

Father let out a terrible cry, almost a scream, shoved me aside, and swung his staff, Voinos rolled out of his way and ran. The unexpended force of the stroke sent Father reeling. He slipped in mud and pine needles, and fell face down before the altar of the Faceless King.

Voinos laughed as he ran, then turned and shouted filthy names, ran again, and was gone.

Strangely, Father made no attempt to pursue him.

He sat up slowly. I crouched down by his side.

"Father . . . I . . . *saw* the Faceless King. So I know you're telling the truth."

He grabbed me with both hands and shook me so hard it frightened me.

"When?"

When the birds . . . I saw the silver mask in the darkness, coming toward me. The eyes were open. The mouth was about to say something."

Father began to weep. I stood there, bewildered. I did not even know if I was telling the truth. I *wanted* it to be true, but my mind was in such a muddle I couldn't be sure.

But Father believed me.

"No matter where you go or how you live, my son, this night will remain with you, and you will spend all your days uncovering its mysteries. *That* is the meaning of your *going.*"

"What about . . . Voinos?"

"It's his night too. Already he is searching for the answers."

Voinos kept on running. I did not see him again for many years, although sinister rumors soon reached us of how he had gathered a band of ruffians around himself and had begun to rob travellers. By the time I was fifteen, there were more than rumors, and Voinos was widely feared. The bodies of his victims were always found mutilated — no one knew why — their faces slashed beyond recognition, or even burned until no trace of the features remained.

Mother died that year, more of grief than anything else, and Father placed *two* wooden skulls above the doorway of our house. He told everyone he had only one son now, and the chief priest — the new one, Hamilcestos, for Decronos had been murdered on a journey — came to exorcise the spirit and memory of Voinos.

But it did little good. The next day, as if to mock us, three faceless corpses were found seated in a neat row against the town's stockade. Thereafter, whenever I walked anywhere, people would turn and stare, then glance away quickly if they thought I'd noticed them. Sometimes I even overheard a whisper. "There! That's him! The brother of Voinos the madman."

People even said that Voinos came to us at night by a secret tunnel, and that we lived better than we should off of our share of his loot.

I followed my father in his profession, and he and the other bards trained me in the ways of the art. I spent long days reciting to myself, chanting all the old stories of our people. And when it came time for me to recite in the market-place, people listened, perhaps out of respect for the stories, not the teller. But I was never summoned to the halls of the lords, either because I lacked skill, or because I was the brother of of a murderer.

At seventeen, I managed to marry, a year and more later than most young men of the town. My wife was called in public merely Evad-ka, the woman of Evad, but I alone called her by the name I had given her, Rael-Hisna, the Flower of the River. She had come from the Great River, with traders on a barge from a strange place far upstream, where villages perch on cliffs above steep gorges, and the people do not worship the gentle gods of the fields and forest, but only the terrible Ragun-Temad, who commands eagles from mountaintops above the clouds.

I truly loved my Flower of the River. She was the one great joy in my life, which was otherwise often bitter. Father was growing old more rapidly than his years, weighed down by his sorrows. One winter, his voice left him, and he was reduced to playing the harp while *I* sang or recited, desperately trying to reconstruct the wonder of *his* half-remembered performances. He never saw the inside of a lord's hall again.

Gossips said the gods had cursed him for having sired Voinos, to which he replied hoarsely that such a son was curse enough, and the gods didn't have to do anything.

Then Rael-Hisna gave birth to a son, my son, and Father was glad again for the first time in a long while.

But that very day Voinos's band, now hundreds strong, seized nine barges on the river. Faceless corpses floated by our town for a week.

It was a sign. I knew that I had to go into the forest as my father had, in secret, and pray before the altar of the Faceless King, that perhaps the King

or even Verunnos-Kemad might look on me and restore some order to my life. I wanted things to be better for my son. When he was grown, I would take him to that altar as I had been taken, and things would work out better at his *going*. Mine had been such a disaster.

The path seemed longer this time. Perhaps I strayed from it. I walked all night through the forest. A fog had come in and the needles were wet, so I made no sound as I went. I listened always, but heard nothing, and still I was afraid. The whole countryside was infested with bandits, with wild beasts, or worse. Toward dawn I slept seated against a tree and dreamed that hundreds of armed men stood before me, all of them wearing the silver mask of the Faceless King, like a mirror image endlessly repeated. I cried out, in my dream, and was answered with familiar laughter. The masks came off. Each face was that of my brother. He made to speak, but the only sounds were the crackling of flames, and all those faces burned away like parchment. The rising sparks cried out fragments of words.

I fell forward, suddenly awake. I knew where I was. The familiar, dragon-backed ridge rose before me in the twilight. I ran, looking for some other sign, another flight of birds perhaps, but there was only the mist and the dank smell of the deep forest.

And there was Voinos, waiting for me. He had changed much since we had last been here together, and was now a black-bearded, barrel-chested giant nearly twice my size, who wore jewels in his hair and rings dangling from his ears, and a wildly colorful costume which seemed all bright sashes and pantaloons.

He stood leaning on a hammer, catching his breath. He had been working hard. He had broken the altar of the Faceless King to bits. Now he watched me coldly, as if I were mere prey.

"Are you . . . still looking for treasure?"

He made no reply.

I spread my hands apart from my body to show that I was not armed, all the while glancing furtively about, certain his men had arrows trained on me every step of the way.

Suddenly a morning bird began to chirp merrily, followed by a chorus of others, announcing the new day.

I stood there, facing my brother, while the sky lightened. A light spray of rain blew in my face.

At last I said, "You've changed a lot."

And with terrifying suddenness he lunged forward and grabbed the front of my jacket with a meaty hand and yanked me off my feet as if I were a rag doll.

"Yes!" he said, holding me inches from his face. His breath stank. "I've changed. I'm no longer a child and you *still are*. You always will be a child, Evad."

"Why —?"

"*Why?* I came here to put an end to an old story. *How?* No magic. I had the town watched. I *know* you, child-brother. I knew you'd come here eventually. When you set out, that was the signal."

I barely managed to gasp, "The signal for . . . what?"

"For a little homecoming." He shook me, again like a doll or a small child. "I haven't been back to my town for such a long time. My men are there even now, delivering my regards. When they are done, I'll go piss in the ashes."

I struggled against him. He only laughed. It was then that I understood that there were no hidden archers in the bushes. Voinos had only contempt for me. He was certainly not afraid.

"You're not going back, child-brother. I've spared you, just you, because you are my *dear* brother."

Suddenly he was pressing the point of a knife under my chin. He pressed harder. I felt it slicing the skin and tried not to breathe. There was a warm trickle of blood.

Then he held the knife up where I could see it. The blade was silver, the handle gold inset with jewels. The sign on it, in relief on the blade, was of the lunar-mask, the emblem of the Faceless King.

"Pretty, isn't it? In found it inside the altar. There was a secret compartment. Think of it was one last gift from the gods to our loving family. And because we love each other so much, child-brother, you are going to perform a task for me."

I thought of our family now, Father and my wife and child probably butchered by Voinos's men, and I said grimly, "Just kill me and get it over with. I'll do nothing for you."

Incredibly, he forced the knife into my hand and closed my fingers around the grip. Then he flung me to the ground, hard, and I lay stunned, while he stood astride me.

"Well? You might kill me with that." He indicated the knife. "But you can't, can you?"

"Yes," I said. "I can."

He slammed his foot down on my chest.

"I don't think so. I am not planning on it. Instead, you will help me carry out my beautiful scheme. Do you remember, dear child-brother, what we talked about when last we, ah, *enjoyed* each other's company here?"

"I . . . remember." I gasped for breath. His foot was crushing me.

"I reasoned then that if nobody has ever seen the face of the Faceless King, he could be, well, *anybody*. Remember?"

He leaned harder. There was a sharp pain as ribs cracked. I could only sob hoarsely.

"That is the point, child-brother. The

knife is a token from the god. With it, you will journey very far. All men will make way for you. And, if such a person as the Faceless King really exists — you know, I have never made up my mind about that — you will return his token, *preferably in the heart.* If there is no such King, then you'll wander forever, which I think will be very funny. But if there is, well, you will use this dagger. Then the face behind the mask will be *yours.* No one will ever now, will they? Just you and me. A secret between brothers."

He let up the pressure a little and I whispered, "Why . . . ?

He shrugged. "I want to pray to you, child-brother. It's good to have family connections in high places."

"I won't," I said.

"You will. What else can you do?"

With that, he took his foot away, hefted the hammer onto his shoulder, and vanished into the forest on long, relentless strides.

It rained all day. Late in the afternoon, I approached the town. The smell of burnt wood carries very far in the rain, so I knew that everything my brother said was true. I believed, too, that he had gone out of his way to piss in the ashes. That would have been just like him.

I was utterly alone, and moreover, incomplete. The pain had not settled yet. I was like a warrior in battle who has just received a terrible wound, but so far has only felt a light blow. He has a little momentum left.

I had a little momentum left as I turned, clutching the sacred dagger Voinos had given me, and walked *away* from the town and everything I had ever known in my life. I refused to see with my own eyes that my wife and child and everyone else in my world — except Voinos! — were dead. That way there would always be the nagging

doubt that I had dreamt it, and eventually the nagging would drive me mad, and in madness there would be some relief.

But the smell of the wood followed after me, and in time I stopped and sat down on a stone and just waited there, shivering, until it was almost evening and the rain ceased. Then I entered the town and saw the blackened logs and the heaps of ashy mud. An occasional corpse lay half-buried. Shadows lengthened as night came on, and I could not tell who any of the dead people were.

The place was very quiet. Here and there smoke rose. Crows cawed in the distance. Above me, the first stars began to appear.

I think I went mad then, for a little while. I screamed and wept and did a strange dance, kicking the heaps of ash and splintered wood, cursing the gods and the Faceless King and even my Father who had, after all, sired Voinos to kill and me to suffer.

And I held up the sacred dagger to the night sky. It gleamed a brilliant silver, like a moonrise. Then I threw it from me, as hard as I could. But I ran after it, and found it glowing where it had fallen. I picked it up, and suddenly the ashes all around me heaved and burst, as if the earth were boiling, and once again there was a miraculous flight of thousands upon thousands of grey and black birds buffetting me, their wings like thunder, rising to fill the sky. I lay huddled there, clutching the knife, and when I closed my eyes I saw the Faceless King clearly this time, sitting on a silver throne in the darkness behind tapestried curtains woven silver on black. His mask seemed to float in the air like a pale moon. He leaned forward, his robes wrinkling, and I was certain he was about to speak, but then the birds were gone and the vision passed.

I hated him. I swore that if I ever did

find him, I *would* kill him, not because Voinos wanted me to, but because *I* wanted to.

But then I walked a little ways in a direction I somehow knew and there on the ground was my father's harp, coated with ash but whole. It seemed to me then the most precious object in the world. I sat down and placed it on my lap, weeping softly, and my rage passed as I spent hours carefully cleaning the harp and tuning its strings.

I wore the sacred dagger of the Faceless King around my neck on a cord, the blade exposed and dangling before me. Wherever I travelled, men recognized it and stood aside to let me pass. Even among the wildest mountain trails, in countryside filled with robbers, I was not molested.

I was summoned to the halls of the great lords as my father had been in the old days, but my song was not what the lords commanded. It was always the same, though the words changed like the passing waters of the Great River. There was anger in it and I sang of bloody vengeance; and then there was sorrow; and longing; and I sang of memories and my soul was purged. At the end I always sang of the Faceless King, whose ways are ever a mystery, who yet guides each one of us on the pathway of this life.

Men came to me from many lands asking to know the secrets of the Faceless King: when this or that lord would die, how a certain god must be placated, the answer to some ancient riddle. When I told them I did not know, they continued to follow me from place to place, saying, "He is testing us," or, "We are not yet worthy to know his mind." When I sang to them, they went away appeased, and yet I myself was not appeased for to me the mysteries remained mysteries, and I could find no reason for all the things that had happened.

I saw the Faceless King often in my dreams, always leaning forward in the darkness behind the curtains, about to speak but never speaking.

I thought this was because I was not worthy to know his mind.

When a youth came to me and said, "Make me your apprentice. Your singing is the most beautiful I have ever heard," I replied sadly, "You are as I once was. Remain so."

But he would not go away. He followed me for days. At last I turned to him and said, "You must chose to follow your own path, your own way, wherever it may lead you. I don't know what you want or need or will ever find. It is a mystery to me."

I just mumbled the first words that came into my mind and tried to make them sound like instruction. When I had finished, the youth touched his forehead to the ground at my feet and remained crouched down like that as I walked away from him. Later, I learned that he had founded a sect of mendicant philosophers called The Wanderers, whose symbols are the shoe and the staff, and the empty bag which remains empty because they have not yet found wisdom. Each of them takes a vow never to sleep in the same place for two nights until that bag is filled.

I came to many places I had never even known existed; and after many years reached the City of the Delta, where the Great River empties into a sea like a blue-metal shield beneath the hot sun. My fame had preceded me. People gathered by the thousands on the beach before the white-walled city. I sang for them of sorrow and longing and of the mysteries of the Faceless King. Many fell to their knees as I approached and begged to become my disciples. But I told them that my mission, or curse, or whatever it was, was for me alone; and I would not wish it on anyone else. Still the great mob of them followed me shouting into the city.

The priests summoned me; and I sang for them in the temple, before the enormous image of the god of the city, Bel-Hemad. Afterwards the mob proclaimed that the image had shifted, grinding its stone guts like an earthquake, so that the god might lean down and hear me better. Up near the ceiling, amid the shadows and the pigeons, Bel-Hemad smiled his inscrutable smile and said nothing.

"This man is possessed of an evil spirit," the chief priest said. "He drives the people to blasphemy!"

I was immediately arrested. Soldiers drove the mob from the temple, while the priests demanded of me the true meaning of my message.

I could only tell them that the Faceless King was an instrument of the secret god Verunnos-Kemad, and I in turn was an instrument of the King, even as my harp was my instrument. I knew that much. I no longer had any doubt.

But the priests were not satisfied. There was money in it, they said. Travellers would come from every land to heap gold on the altars to hear me sing.

"The Faceless King dwells amid the treasure-hoard of the Mother Dragon," I said. "What need has he of your money? I am filled with his music. What need have I?"

The priests brought the King of the city to me, an old, feeble man they had to hold up by either arm. He commanded me to explain the magic of my song, and I told him the story of my life, but that was not enough.

The King stared at me intently. He pursed his lips as if about to spit. Just then he looked like an ancient mummy, not a living man.

"Each man hears something different in your song," the King said at last, "and his soul is touched by it. Even I

cannot touch a man's soul. Your song is a greater treasure than all my riches. I would possess it."

"Majesty," I said with bowed head. "You are not worthy. Nor am I."

Then the King gave me over to his torturers and they tortured me with great cunning, so that my pain would never end even after many years, but they did not let me die. And they would not take away my hands, lest I could no longer play the harp, nor my voice; nor did they dare steal the holy dagger I wore around my neck.

In the end, they put out my eyes with it.

There were many times when I fell into a delerium and dreamed that I was home, that I was still a boy in the walled town by the river, and none of this had ever happened.

Once I sat up suddenly in my bed at home, alarmed by some sudden noise in the night. My father stood there at the foot of my bed holding a lantern which was not a lantern at all, but the glowing mask of the Faceless King. He came forward to put the mask on me, but I struggled and cried out and woke with a start in utter darkness, rattling my chains.

Twenty years passed. My former life fell away like old leaves. I could no longer remember my wife's name, nor summon her face into my memory. I still knew Voinos. He was but a minor agony among many.

I saw the Faceless King every night as I slept. He was always there, leaning forward, about to speak.

At last I screamed to him, whether waking or asleep I do not know, "Let it end! Let me come to you!"

And at last he did speak, saying, "Then come to me right now."

That night ships arrived from across the sea to sack the City of the Delta. They must have taken the city by surprise. In the morning, I could hear the fighting below my window, and I could smell the smoke of burning houses. By evening there was only the smoke and an occasional cry. Then the lock on my door was being smashed, and a wild-voiced, strange-smelling barbarian burst into my cell, panting with exertion. But then I heard only shuffling. I groped about and found his shoulder level with my waist. He was kneeling before me. Gently, he pressed my harp into my hands.

My chains fell off of their own accord. The barbarian did not strike them.

"I must follow my own path," I said aloud. I remembered my conversation with the young man on the road, so many years before. "I am like a man on a swaying rope bridge above a deadly gorge. I cannot remain there. I must go either forward or back, and after so much travelling, I do not wish to go back."

The barbarian cried out something in his own language. I could only make out a few words. He was afraid. I am sure he thought me mad, and to barbarians, madness is a sure sign of the presence of the gods.

I hobbled through the city unopposed. Often someone would take me gently by the arm and guide me a little ways. Once I heard many women weeping. Often I heard masonry crashing, as if the conquerers did not intend to leave any stone atop another.

Finally I was on the beach, the sea breeze blowing in my face, driving away the smoke of the dying city. The lukewarm surf broke around my ankles.

I began to play my father's harp softly, and sing of my home for the first time in a long while. All the good memories came back. That was the greatest mystery of the Faceless King now, that I could remember a time when I had not known him, and had lived in a remote town and been happy.

Then I began to see stars in the dark sky. I thought for a moment that they were an illusion of my brain, like an itch in an amputated limb, but I went on singing, and I called on the Faceless King.

A silver glow spread across the sea and sky; and the huge mask of the Faceless King rose above the midnight waters; and thousands of black ships bobbed on the waves, their masts hung with lanterns; and these lanterns were the stars. Millions upon millions of birds soared up from between the ships, their wings like murmuring thunder, the stars flickering at their passage. Then I walked upon the water amid huge trees of utterly black stone, while the ships with their lanterns drifted among the trunks, and the birds flew in an endless, swirling mass before the Faceless King. I walked until I came to a dark place in the heart of the black stone forest, where silver-masked priests came out of a temple and challenged me. But I showed them the dagger I still wore around my neck; and they let me pass up the high, black steps of the temple, past endless rows of pillars, until, almost imperceptibly at first, the smooth floor gave way to tumbled stone and the pillars were rough fangs dripping from the ceiling and uncountable treasures lay about in heaps, glowing like coals in the darkness. I knew where I was then, that my quest had come to an end, that I had arrived by strange and devious ways at the Earth's heart, in the lair of the Mother Dragon.

I stood at the lip of an alcove, before black curtains embroidered with silver thread.

I began to sing once more, the song of the secret god; and for the only time in my life my song was completely pure, devoid of any longing or hatred or wish, as eternal as the wheel of the sky.

But the Faceless King spoke harshly from behind the curtain.

"Well, what have you come for?"

Astonished beyond all reason, I dropped the harp. It struck the ground with a resonant clang. It was as if *I* had been dropped suddenly from a great height.

"Evad," the King said. "You know for what purpose you have come here."

I could not bring myself to reply, so stricken was I with a terror that goes beyond any mere dread of danger.

"Come to me," the King said, his voice grating.

I opened the curtains. The masked King leaned forward on his throne, regarding me.

"You know the reason," he said.

I lifted the cord from around my neck and held the sacred dagger in my hand. I thought back, then, over many terrors and many years. *No*, I told myself. *It is all too insane. I will not.*

But the Faceless King spoke *with my brother's voice*, saying, "you will always be a child, Evad." And he began to laugh, and it was my brother's laugh.

It all came back to me, my fear, my hatred of Voinos, the deaths of everyone I had ever known, the laughter of Voinos in the forest where he'd smashed the altar.

And the King said in my brother's voice, *"It's good to have family connections in high places."*

Screaming, I lunged forward and grabbed the Faceless King by the front of his robe, yanking him off his throne and onto the blade of my knife. I held him in a terrible embrace while I stabbed him again and again and again.

When he was still and limp, and I felt his hot blood on my hands, I stood there trembling, not so much out of fear, but out of an appreciation of the sheer absurdity of my position. I let the knife and the body of the King drop to the cavern floor.

But the King was not quite dead. He whispered in tho voice of my father.

"It is finished."

I began to sob with crazy remorse. I fell to my knees beside him. I cradled his head in my hands.

"Why?"

"Why?" he said. "Because I am weary. Because I wanted to die. When you have heard every leaf fall and known the flight of every sparrow, when the thoughts of all men living and the cries of their ghosts have merged into an endless babble for *so long*, one can only yearn for an ending. Therefore I caused you to be born, Evad. I made you as you are and Voinos as he had to be, shaping your lives, directing every step of your wanderings, all as part of my plan to bring you here. It was a long labor, but now it is done. Have I not concluded it well?"

"No," I said, feeling rising anger within myself, all the while shocked into terror at the mere fact that I *could* be angry at such a time in such a place. "You have not. What about me? I am merely left here."

"Oh yes, you," he said. His voice was now that of a stranger, very old, very tired. "I had nearly forgotten." He laughed softly, sadly. "It must have been the confusion of the moment. Forgive me."

He was silent for a moment, and I shook him in my terror. "Tell *me*."

"You may turn from your path even now. You may go back to the village by the river and live as you always did. That much I can promise you. I will restore you to your former state."

I shook my head sadly. "It cannot be so. I would remember all these things, if only in dreams; and the memories have changed me. I am no longer that Evad who dwelt by the river. I have travelled too far and too long, and learned too much — and not enough."

And, one last time, he had my father's voice.

"It is finished," he said.

"No," I whispered into his ear. "You have not finished it well, or badly. You have not finished it at all."

Then I let his head drop to the floor. He was dead.

Indeed, it was not finished. Many things happened very quickly. I have never been able to fully account for all of them, even after many centuries of meditation.

I was blind again. I heard the priests come running, shouting in alarm. I was afraid, ridiculously, that my assassination would be discovered and I would be punished.

Quickly I groped around for the mask, found it, and put it on. Then I could see through eyes of silver.

The face of the dead man was first my father's, then my brother's, then face after face of countless strangers, the features running together, blurring, melting like wax. I stripped off the King's robes and put them on, then sat on the throne.

When the priests arrived, their masks glowing like little moons in the darkness, there was a King seated before them, and a corpse on the ground which had no face at all, merely a blank oval of flesh.

As Voinos had once remarked, *How do they know it's him?*

I leaned forward, indicating the corpse and the bloody dagger.

"Take that away," I said. "It has served its purpose."

They took the corpse but left the dagger, and it lies there still among the pebbles at my feet. I have regarded it often.

Even then I had not come to the end of my wanderings. I thought I had, but I was mistaken.

Through the mask, many things were revealed to me. I looked out into the world and I knew the flight of birds and the ambitions of kings and the words of lovers. I beheld armies in the night and grain ripening slowly in the summer sun, and I heard the songs of the leviathans in the depths of the midnight seas.

I sought my brother Voinos, and found him standing in a dank cell, his wrists chained to the wall. I manifested myself to him, and the cell was alight with the glory of the silver mask.

He started when he saw me, rattling his chains.

"So you do exist," he said. "I was never sure of that."

"Voinos —"

He let out a shriek of hysterical laughter, and dropped down limp in his chains. "That's *very funny*," he said. "You have the voice of a child I knew once. I'd always intended to throttle him, but I never got around to it. I don't know why." He banged his head against the wall, first gently, then harder, and laughed some more. There was only pain in his laughter.

"Voinos, it is I, Evad, your brother," I said, and I told him some of the things that had happened to me.

"That's the funny part," he said, sobbing gently now. "The Faceless King shaped us like a pair of clay pots. For all the good it did him. Or us. Now, as you will be glad to hear, my celebrated crimes have caught up with me. I shall die tomorrow. What a pleasure to spend the last night of my life with you, dearest brother. But then, what choice did I ever have?"

"I think you could have have set your foot in another direction. You could have turned aside."

He screamed again and leapt up, straining at his chains. "You say I can *turn aside*. Well let me do it, now. Work a miracle for me and I'll be as wretchedly virtuous as you, snivelling brother —"

I saw then that even I could not bring him peace, not yet, while he still raged at the terrors within his own heart, and I left him.

I found him again later, hanging from a gibbet, black birds pecking out his eyes, and a third time in the grey dawn mists, wandering aimlessly among the trees near the ruined altar of the Faceless King. That third time I bore his poor ghost in my arms and placed him at the feet of the gods, not to be judged, but to be unmade.

All these things are as one to me, for I know the secrets of the dark forest, and of dreams, and of the grave.

For I am the Faceless King, the Blessed of Verunnos-Kemad; and I am also the hero of old, the slayer of dragons; and I am a man called Genimer who dwelt in a land far to the south and once designed a clock to measure eternity (but it did not work, for he has outlived it); and I am, further, En-Riose, the foolish one who longed for and actually believed he could achieve death by the shaping of the life of that Evad who dwelt down by the river.

I contain multitudes. En-Riose should have known that no one who has been the Faceless King ever dies, though their bodies might perish. All of them join together in the next, each newcomer changing the rest, like a new color stirred into a mixture of paints.

I am still Evad, who did not want to turn back, lest all his sufferings be for naught. So we go on — I go on — until we find the final mystery, and our empty bag is filled and we might rest.

I am Evad, who caused the eyes of En-Riose to be opened, so that he too might understand.

I am Evad, who granted to Voinos the only release he could ever have.

Somehow, I was worthy.

For the mind of Verunnos-Kemad is my mind and the splendors of the worlds are before me — as new gods awaken by the hundreds and make themselves known, and the Earth is filled up with magic, and the holy powers thunder in the night like great storms. I sit on the throne in the dark temple, yet I am everywhere, year into year, even as the signs in the heavens are slowly rewritten.

This is my path. I will not turn from it. ∎

WHAT CAN A CHILD DO?

by Chet Williamson

She saw the boy the first day she moved in. It was close to eight o'clock, and she had just stepped from the shower, when she saw him standing naked by the bathroom closet. For a split second the thought that the boy was real was strong in her exhausted mind, but almost immediately she realized that he was a ghost.

His pale pink body was translucent, and she could just make out the brass hinges of the closet door through the child's shallow chest. She noticed dark blotches on the arms and legs, grayish-blue marks, like bruises. And she knew it was the Bradley boy.

What was his name? The real estate agent had said. Tom? No, Timothy. Yes, that was it. "Timothy," she called softly, her own nakedness forgotten, "Timmy?"

The boy slowly disappeared, like a Polaroid print in reverse, she thought. He hadn't moved. He had just stood there, as if waiting for someone (his mother? *Not* his father, surely) to lift him into the tub.

Linda hadn't been frightened while it was happening, but now she trembled uncontrollably, whipped the towel from the rack she had put up that afternoon, and wrapped it around her shivering body. She sat on the toilet bowl and ran her hand through the salt-wet tendrils of hair that stuck to her forehead. The bathroom was warm from the electric heater, but she felt chilled.

It seemed so real that not for a moment did she think it was her imagination. She had seen him, she was

certain. Timothy Bradley. She had read the stories in the papers last year when it had happened. The boy was four years old. His father had been abusing him, and evidently the mother did nothing to stop it. The child was finally taken to a hospital with a concussion. He went into a coma and died a few days later. The father was sentenced to eight years in prison, the mother to three years for complicity. A small enough payment, Linda had thought at the time, for stealing seventy years of a person's life.

He'd been so thin, so brittle looking. The bruises had stood out so clearly. His father must have been brutal.

She stepped back into the shower for a minute to wash the sweat away. The water swept into her face and hair, cold at first, then growing hotter. She closed her eyes and let the steam wrap around her like a shroud. She thought about the boy.

Paul above her, towering like the giant in Jack and the Beanstalk, his big red-knuckled hand coming down again, and the red before her eyes — not blood but rage, stop, stop won't you stop, and crying harder until the wet tears ran

The pipes started banging, and she wiggled the faucet handles until they stopped. She slid back the shower door, half expecting to see him again, but there was nothing more than the light of the fluorescents and the mist that hung in the air and settled like dew on the mirror and tiles. The rough towel felt good on her skin. When she was

105

dry, she put on her bathrobe and went into the kitchen.

All the papers were there. She'd have to take them to the bank and rent a lockbox tomorrow. As she picked up the mortgage she smiled. Even at the high interest rate the house had been a great buy. It must have been small for the Bradleys, she thought, but for a single woman who wanted a little equity, it was perfect. After the boy's death and the arrest of the mother and father, the house had been vacant for over a year while the price went lower and lower. It was due, the real estate woman had told her, simply to the fact that most people were leery of a house in which (technically at least) a murder had taken place. Linda had scarcely thought about that. She liked the house, it was the right size for her, and the price was low enough for her to handle on her new salary. The fact that it had once had sorrow and pain within its brick walls was irrelevant to Linda, who had had those things within her heart. She didn't fear the ghosts of past acts, didn't believe in them until tonight, when she accepted the existence of ghosts — or a ghost — as easily as she accepted and believed in the neighbors' laundry hanging on the line next door. She had seen the boy. That was a fact.

And now as she looked up from the papers on the kitchen table she saw him again. He was standing by the refrigerator, his face and hands smeared with something purple, or maybe red — it was hard to be sure because of the light coming through his body. She read fear in the wide eyes, and as she watched tears started to roll down his cheeks and his tiny mouth opened in a wail she could barely hear, as if he were calling from outside, and the doors and windows of the house were shut tight against him.

Again she felt no terror, no sudden thrill of fright, but a pity so deep it gripped her bowels, and something like love that urged her to reach out to that frail insubstantial thing across the kitchen.

As if in a dream she rose and walked toward the boy, and as she drew nearer his fear seemed to increase, and he raised his shadowy arms in a defensive gesture and drew back from her. "No," she whispered, "no, it's all right." And at her words his face changed into a mask of outrage and hate whose force stunned her. She stopped and watched as he faded away once more, and the warm hand of pity became a cold claw of fear around her spine.

But *what* frightened her, she asked herself. Was she scared of the little boy, a weak four year old? No, even less, a *shadow* of a four year old with no substance, no solidity with which to harm her. A *wraith* (her mind tingled at the word) bound here by past hurts, a sad little thing caught between death and life — was she scared of *this*?

Or was she scared of the look in the child's face, the look that her own face still remembered how to wear, the futile gesture of defense she too had made a hundred times?

The belt snaking through the trouser loops, like a python uncurling from around a tree branch in the Tarzan movies, and the sound of it, that soft shhhhh as it whispered around his waist, always so slow, so slow, and she could feel the pressure of her bladder, feel the wispy hairs on the back of her neck nearly pull away from the skin as he came closer, finally flinging her over his bony knees, his rough hands pushing her skirt above her waist, pulling down her cotton panties so she felt the autumn chill on her buttocks, and then the pain that murdered the cold, the redness that seeped up her belly, over her chest, and onto her cheeks, her forehead, her ears and her eyes until everything was red and she could only think kill me, kill me, I'll kill you, I will, just kill me and be done, and it would stop and Paul would push her onto the floor and leave her there, saying that'll teach you, little bitch, and she would lay there alone in the red darkness and the stale smell of beer, and the sound of her mother crying downstairs only made the red hurt more

The refrigerator motor kicked on, and she lost the memory in a mechanical whir of hidden fans. Dear God, she thought, is this what it's going to be like to live here, that boy showing up every few minutes? What would she do, what *could* she? The thought occurred to her to call someone, but she was new in the town and had made no friends in whom she could confide a crazy ghost story. She thought of calling her mother, but the difference in time zones made it certain that she'd be asleep by now. Besides, since Linda's stepfather had left her mother a few years before, she'd been withdrawn and strange in Linda's presence.

She gave up the phone idea and suddenly realized that she felt hungry. She'd had no dinner, and a sandwich would taste good, maybe some Tab too. The breadbox door squeaked as she opened it, and she made a mental note to get some 3-in-1 tomorrow when she bought paint. She pulled open the refrigerator and saw Timothy Bradley inside, staring up at her.

She shrieked and leaped back. The door swung slowly shut with a muffled thud and she screamed again. The sight was etched with steel on her mind's crystal surface. He'd been huddled, shivering, on the flat enamel of the bottom, his body occupying the same space as the groceries Linda had bought earlier that day. The boy's form passed through the wire rack next to the bottom, but seemed pressed against the second one up, as if he'd been jammed in there for . . . for what? Punishment?

Yes. She'd seen the marks again, this time on his face, and some blood on his lips, which were turning blue with the cold.

Christ, she thought, *monsters, monsters!* and her heart beat fast and her stomach churned until she was afraid she would throw up. She sat down heavily in the kitchen chair and moaned softly. Then it struck her. *He's in there. He or his ghost or whatever I'm seeing is still in there,* and she leaped up and swung the door open again. This time she didn't step back or scream, but held the door open for the whimpering child to crawl out. He was still there, and the sounds of his sobbing seemed far away as before. As if underwater, he fumbled his way out of the refrigerator, his hands touching and then going through the floor, until his whole body disappeared beneath the house. She had noticed his eyes again before they passed from sight. There was something primal in them, a fear and an urge she cocould not quite read, and then he was gone.

She would not stay. She would not be a noble idiot and stay in that house. She would go to a motel and think about this and maybe call the real estate agent in the morning. There were still three days to get this straightened out before she started her new job, and if there was a problem she would leave and live somewhere else. But she would not stay here tonight.

She got dressed, threw some underwear and some toilet things in her flight bag, and grabbed her purse. She locked the door, thinking as she did that if a burglar *did* go in, the boy would probably scare the living bejeesus out of him. Then she shuddered, took out her car keys, and wished for the first time in her life that she had a dog.

She found a motel three miles down the road, one of those places that manage to stay open with only three cars at the most in front of the U of brick compartments. But it was cheap, it was warm, and it was private. There was no little boy to pose for her nightmares, no boy bound to the bed, no boy locked in the closet, no boy forced to kneel in the shower as cold water beat down upon him, or whatever else they had done to him.

The bed was too soft, but she sank into its embrace thankfully, and fell asleep fully clothed. She awoke the next morning around seven, amazed that she hadn't dreamed, or, if she had, hadn't remembered it. In retrospect, she thought her night should have been filled with lurking terrors, but in reality she could not recall when she had slept more soundly.

She made some instant coffee on the wall-mounted machine, sat at the desk, and thought about the previous evening. In the hatchwork of bright sunlight coming through the opened venetian blind, her experience softened, became almost romantic — not the boy's maltreatment, not that, but the idea of his remaining in the house. She thought she knew why.

All the ghost stories — true or false — that she had ever heard had given the ghost a reason for remaining on the earthly plane. Perhaps it was to show where buried treasure was hidden, perhaps for revenge to right a wrong, perhaps to find something the ghost didn't have in life.

Could that be it? Could the little boy, who had lived with fear and madness and torment all his young life, could he be looking for that which he had never had? A kind word, a touch, a gesture of loving concern?

It could be just that simple, she thought. If she ran away from him, if no one would live in the house because of the haunting, then he would remain chained there forever.

But if she tried to comfort him, perhaps she could free him.

She shook her head to clear it of doubts and sentimental illusions. First of all, she would go back to the house — now, in the clean unshadowed light of the sun. It was her home, and today she would do what she had planned to do — clean it, fix it, rearrange it until it was hers even more. And when . . . *if* the boy came . . . well, she would do what she thought was right, that's all.

He was waiting for her as she came up the driveway. He had on a powder blue snowsuit that was too small for him, and she could see his bare ankles above the rubber boottops. The air was cold, and the brisk wind seemed to ruffle his hair and make him shiver. She stopped the car, opened the door, and got out slowly. When she held out her hand and started to walk toward him, he turned and ran through the back yard to the hedge, into which he merged and disappeared.

The look had been there again; she had seen it just before he had bolted. Panic, fright . . . outrage.

She went inside. He didn't reappear that morning at all, and she did what she had planned. The house was terribly dusty, and she made cleaning her first priority, reaching high up on door sills and cupboard tops with the vacuum cleaner extension until no more thick streamers of dust clung to her exploring fingertips. The loud roar of the Hoover pounded her ears all morning, and at last she gratefully turned it off and made a light lunch of soup and plain yogurt. When she opened the refrigerator door, she felt a chill that was not due to the escaping cold air, but she saw nothing, and reached into the back for a Tab with only a slight shiver.

After lunch she mixed some powdered cleanser in water and started on the woodwork. On the back of the door of the smaller bedroom, which she planned to turn into a study/sewing room, she found some penciled marks that she could not bring herself to wipe off. The first was a short horizontal line with the notation, "Mar 84," beside it. The next was a few inches up, marked "Aug 84." There were six in all, the last and highest marked "Dec 85," about three feet off the floor.

Linda half expected to see Timothy suddenly appear before her, looking up in fear and expectation as he must have looked at *them* to see whether they would use the ruler to mark his height or to strike him again. She made a bitter face, closed her eyes in pain, and suddenly felt very tired.

No one was coming to see her today — the telephone man was due next week, and the washer and dryer were being delivered tomorrow. There was no reason for her not to lie down for a few minutes, and the floor with its deep carpeting seemed so comfortable that she lowered herself down onto her side and rested her head on her arm, the rich muskiness of her sweat bearing her on an onyx cloud down into sleep.

And in her sleep and in her dream the smell of sweat grew stronger until Paul stood over her, and the belt came off, and he took her over his knees, but now she was bigger and stronger and *no* he would not whip her again, and she bit his leg hard until she heard him gasp in pain and surprise. Then the hand with the belt curled around her head and wrenched it away from his leg, and she heard his heavy breathing turn ragged, and felt something beneath her stir and press into the softness of her stomach. There was no transition. One second she was over his lap and the next he was on top of her, pinning both her arms with one of his own while his other hand roughly guided himself into her.

But she was no longer there. Instead she hovered over the bed like a ghost, watching herself struggle beneath Paul's massive body, feeling the pain dully through the anesthesia of disembodied memory.

The eyes of the girl on the bed grew wide, and as they stared into hers as she hung suspended in the air the terror in them faded and was replaced by a hot flame of lust, not for the grunting that aped passion on that bed, but lust for the blood of the defiler, the blood of those who rob the innocent of innocence, who turn childhood into nightmare.

Then the face beneath her changed again; the brown eyes turned a pale blue, the dark hair lightened, the thin nose flattened, until the face of the twelve year old girl was that of a four year old boy, and the look of savage vengeance on that face was the one she had seen him wear before. The raw power of it frightened her, and she rose higher and higher until the face was only a dot and the bed a red smear in a black void.

She awoke with the slanting rays of the late afternoon sun in her eyes, her blouse soaked with perspiration, her heart tripping over its beats. When she staggered to her feet, the boy was standing in the doorway. She could not see through him now.

There was something else. He had changed subtly in some other way. He still seemed small, frail, but there was a power around him that she could feel, that drove her slowly backward into the corner of the room. And now the reddish rays of the falling sun shone full on his young face as he stood there glaring at her, every bruise and mark on his body a living thing that screamed out its agony in a voice she heard only in her soul.

She could not think of extending her hand to the thing that wielded that power. She could not feel compassion, or pity, or sympathy. She could only feel terror and the need to escape from the force that surged out from that demonic face.

She knew now that he had not come back for love.

And as the boy drifted across to her with the speed of a thought, her head flew back in astonishment, and his right hand sheared across her exposed throat, showering petals of blood that sparkled in the sun, and ran from her throat like a penitent's tears.

■

HAD I APPROACHED MY DISCOVERY IN A MORE NOBLE SPIRIT

The other Mr. Hyde
Was like the first:
Short and young, being only a little
Of a life,
Stronger and hairier than gentlefolk,
Skin dark with being out
In weathers
Muscles ropey with exertion,
Step light and eager,
A drain on Dr. Jekyll's checkbook.

Hyde stood and ranted
In Hyde Park
Bellowing the needs of people
In satanic London:
Work and space to play
Air, food, water,
Light.
He gave to charities
And to reform societies
More than the doctor could afford
And threatened all the doctor's friends
With loss of income,
And a world ruled
By matchgirls.

Dwarfish and dark and a nuisance
The other Mr. Hyde
Gave to all who saw him
The impression of
Deformity.

— Ruth Berman

110

WELL-CONNECTED

by T.E.D. Klein

His first mistake, Philip later realized, had been in choosing a room without a bath. Years before, honeymooning in England while still on a junior law clerk's salary, he and his first wife had had great luck with such rooms, readily agreeing to "a bathroom down the hall" whenever the option was offered; they'd gotten unusual bargains that way, often finding themselves in the oldest, largest, and most charming room in the hotel for a third less than other guests were paying. Now, even though saving money was no longer an issue, some youthful habit had made him ask for just such a room, here in this rambling New England guesthouse. Or maybe his choice had been meant as a kind of test, one that might help determine if the young woman he'd brought with him this weekend was too intent on a luxury-class ride with him, or if she was the sort of person who remained unfazed by life's small inconveniences — the sort who might become, in the end, his second wife.

This time, however, it seemed he had guessed wrong; for here at The Birches, the rooms without a bath faced the front lawn, still pitted from last winter's snows, a smooth expanse of newly tarred road that ended in a parking lot behind a line of shrubs, and a large, rather charmless white sign declaring **VACANCY** and **SINCE 1810**, beside which stood the woebegone little clump of birch trees that, presumably, had given the place its name; while it was the bigger, more expensive rooms just across the hall that looked out upon the wooded slopes of Romney Mountain, rising like a massive green wall somewhere beyond the back garden. Disappointingly, too, while their room boasted such amenities as genuine oak beams and a working fireplace, it had no telephone, at a time when, with young Tony precariously installed at a private school near Hanover less than thirty miles away, he'd have liked one handy. He envied whichever guest was staying in the room opposite theirs; when he and Margaret had passed it last night as they'd brought their bags upstairs, they'd heard its unseen occupant talking animatedly on the phone, embroiled in some urgent conversation.

It was the off-season, too late for even the most dedicated of skiers, too early for the annual onslaught of hikers, and the inn, from all appearances, was barely half full. It would have been a simple thing to request a different room. Still, some perverse sense of obligation to his youthful self kept Philip from speaking up. He had made his choice, and, vacancies or not, he was not about to pack up and move elsewhere. Anyway, it was only for two more nights.

Today was Friday, the first Friday all year that he'd taken off, though when he'd quit the firm last summer to set up his own practice, he'd vowed there'd be many such weekends. Maybe now, with Margaret, there would be. The two of them had driven from Boston last night, speeding up Route 93 past the

111

brightly lit ring roads curving round the city like lines of defense, through the lowlands of southeastern New Hampshire, and finally, long after darkness had fallen, past the dim shapes of starlit hills and a range of distant mountains, Sunapee and the Monadnocks looming far to the southwest. Their destination lay twelve miles off the highway, down a series of roads of ever-diminishing width, in a part of the state more settled a century ago than it was today, when men no longer worked the land and once-prosperous farms had been reclaimed by forest. The region around Romney Mountain, with its caves and scenic gorges, had known even grander days, having seen, in the century's opening decades, the construction of at least two lavish hotels; a scattering of summer homes for the well-to-do of Boston; and, it was said, even one clandestine casino. The hotels and casino were long gone, and only recently had the effects of the postwar real estate boom been felt here. The glistening black road that wound through the valley to The Birches had been dirt less than a year ago.

They had spent most of the morning in the king-size fourposter that dominated their little room, snuggled under a patchwork quilt that made up in atmosphere what it lacked in warmth, and didn't come down to the dining room till long after the tables had been cleared. Fortunately the proprietress, Mrs. Hartley, still had enough Westchester in her soul to sympathize with late risers; and she'd kept a pot of coffee warm for them, along with extra helpings of that morning's blueberry pancakes. She and her husband had purchased The Birches only last spring; before that her only connection to hotelkeeping had been as a part-time pastry chef, and his as a salesman of advertising space to an occasional resort. It was obvious from the look of the

place that, with more zeal than knowledge, the Hartleys were trying to restore the inn to something approximating its original appearance, or, failing that, to something approximating a house out of Currier and Ives — a row of whose prints, in matched maple frames, decorated the dining room wall.

While Margaret slipped back upstairs to change, Philip checked the time; Tony would already be finished with his morning classes. In the alcove off the bar he found an old-fashioned wall phone and, through the unit in the office, obtained an outside line. He dialed Tony's school.

Summoned from lunch, the boy sounded distracted. "I didn't think you'd call until tomorrow," he said, breathless as if from running. "Braddon's giving us a multiple-choice quiz in half an hour, and then I've got to try out for the play."

Philip wished him good luck, pleased that the boy was keeping so busy, and asked what time tomorrow would be best to visit. Spending a day with his son was the primary purpose of his trip; relations between them had been strained these past years.

"Is somebody coming with you?" asked Tony warily.

"You know very well I'm here with Margaret," said Philip. "I thought I explained all that in my letter." He immediately regretted the impatience in his voice. "Look, son, if you'd rather I came alone, I'm sure she can find something to do for an hour or two."

"Tomorrow's no good anyway," said Tony, having maneuvered his father into this concession. "We're supposed to have a track meet with Cobb Hill, and it's away. They told us last week, but I forgot." He added, apologetically, "They'll really be mad if I miss it. I'm one of the two best in the relay."

"How would Sunday be then?" asked

Philip. "I'd have to leave by three."

"Sunday'd be great. You could take me into Hanover for a decent meal. And Dad . . ."

Philip waited. "Yes?"

"Do you think you'd have time to tell me a story?"

Philip felt an unexpected rush of affection so strong it embarrassed him. "Of course," he said. "I'll always have time for that." It had been years since Tony had asked for a story; once it had been their favorite pastime.

The day passed quickly. It was too cold for swimming — the new semicircular pool at the end of the garden stood empty, in fact — but Margaret, it turned out, was a nature enthusiast, and one thing The Birches had aplenty was nature trails. It was all Philip could do to keep up with her. Still, this Girl Scout aspect appealed to him; till now he'd only seen Margaret's urban side, the tall, studious-looking girl he'd secretly lusted after at his former office, and who'd seemed far too smart for the routine secretarial tasks required of her. Clutching glossy new guidebooks provided by the Hartleys, the two of them trudged along the base of the mountain, dutifully peering at fungi in their various disquieting shapes, admiring the newly blooming wildflowers, and searching — in vain, as it turned out — for identifiable animal tracks, all the while snacking on the sausage, bread, and cheese which Mrs. Hartley had packed for them. They discovered, nonetheless, that by dinner time their appetites were quite unimpaired; they shared a bottle of cabernet with their meal, chosen from the inn's small but adequate wine list, and still found room for dessert. Glowing rosily, as much from the wine as from the bayberry candles that flickered at each table, they staggered into the lounge.

The room, high-ceilinged and handsome, was already occupied by several guests, who themselves were occupied over after-dinner drinks and conversation. Flames danced and sizzled in the obligatory fieldstone fireplace covering most of one wall. Before it, taking up more than his share of a bench by the fire, sat a large, barrel-shaped man, his bald head gleaming in the firelight, eyes sunken in wrinkles like an elephant's. He was wearing loose-fitting white pants and a somewhat threadbare cardigan. They had seen him in the other room, devouring Mrs. Hartley's rack of lamb with considerable gusto. Aside from one wizened old lady who, from her own table, had stared at him throughout the meal with apparent fascination, he was the only guest who'd dined alone. It was impossible to tell his age.

"Am I blocking you from the fire?" he asked. He flashed a smile at Margaret. "Here, you young people, have a seat. April nights are chilly in this part of the world." There was a trace of accent in his voice, a hint of Old World frostfires and battlements. He eased himself sideways and patted the bench beside him. Margaret politely sat; Philip, with no room for himself, pulled up a wooden chair.

"I trust that you two are enjoying your stay." He spoke as one who expected an answer.

"So far," said Philip. "Actually, we came up to visit my son. He's at prep school a bit north of here."

"And, of course, to relax," Margaret added.

"Of course!" The man grinned again. His teeth were long and widely spaced, like tree roots blanched by water. "And have you found your relaxation?"

Philip nodded. "Of a sort. Today we took a hike around the base of the mountain, and tomorrow we may go for a drive, maybe look for some antiques."

"Ah, a fellow antique-lover!" He turned to Margaret. "And you?"

"I'm more of a swimmer myself. Unfortunately, this isn't the weather for it."

The other cocked his head and seemed to study her a moment. "Odd you should say that, because I happen to know where there's an excellent heated pool not half an hour's stroll from here. All indoors, with antique brass steps in each corner and a well-stocked bar right beside it, so close you can reach for your wine while standing in the water. The bar stools are covered in leather from, if the lady will pardon me —" He regarded her almost coyly for a moment. "— the testicles of a sperm whale." Philip and Margaret exchanged a wary glance, then a smile. "It's true," the older man was saying, "I assure you! No expense was spared. The pool has its own underground oil tank which keeps it at exactly seventy degrees. You'll find a painting of Bacchus on the ceiling, best appreciated while floating on your back, and heart-shaped tiles on the floor shipped specially from Florence."

"I've never heard of such a place," said Philip. "There's certainly nothing like it listed in the guidebooks."

"Oh, you won't find it in a guidebook, my friend. It isn't open to the public." His voice was low, conspiratorial. "It's in the private home of a certain Mr. Hagendorn, on the other side of the mountain."

"Sounds like he must be worth a fortune."

The other shrugged. "You've heard of the Great Northern Railroad? One of Mr. Hagendorn's ancestors owned nine million shares. So as you might imagine, Mr. Hagendorn has always been accustomed to getting what he wants. The bed he sleeps in once belonged to an Italian prince, and the house itself is modeled on a Tuscan villa. It has its own greenhouse, a billiard room with six imported stained

glass windows, and a sun porch with a magnificient view of the gorge."

"You seem to know the place pretty well," said Philip.

A shadow crossed the other's face. "I used to live there," he said softly.

"You mean you once owned it?"

"No, not at all. I merely worked there. I was young when I started, and new to this area, but by the time I was twenty I was Mr. Hagendorn's personal aide. Wine for the cellar, an antique painting, a new maid — whatever he required, I obtained. I served him well for many years, and we remain in close touch. He asks me often to his home. I'm always welcome there." He sighed. "So while I'm not a rich man, I suppose you'd have to say I'm well-connected."

"It sounds," said Margaret, "like a fabulous place."

The old man brightened. "Would you care to see it? I'm sure Mr. Hagendorn would love to have you as his guests. You could come for a swim, say tomorrow afternoon. Stay for an early dinner, and I'd have you back here just after dark. I know the trail by heart." Leaning toward them as if afraid the other guests would hear, he added, "You've never had dinner till you've had it in the great hall, overlooking the valley. The new people who've taken over this place —" His hand swept the room. "— they cook a meal fit for a peasant like me. But Mr. Hagendorn has employed the finest chefs in Europe."

"But why," said Philip, "would this fellow want to put himself out for two complete strangers?"

"The truth is, my friend, he's somewhat lonely. He doesn't get many visitors these days, and I know he'd want to make the acquaintance of two young people like you."

"But we didn't bring bathing suits," said Philip, hoping, somehow, that the matter might rest there.

"Speak for yourself," said Margaret

brightly. "I brought mine."

The man turned to Philip with what looked disconcertingly like a wink, but it may just have been smoke in his eyes. "I assure you Mr. Hagendorn has plenty — for men, women, boys, girls. Though you may find them a little out of style!"

Margaret clasped her hands. "Oh, I love old-fashioned things. It sounds like fun." She turned to Philip. "Can we go, honey?"

He swallowed. "Well, I still don't like just barging in on the man. I mean, what if he's not in the mood for visitors?"

The older man stood, a surprisingly rapid movement for one so large and so seemingly advanced in years. "No need to worry," he said. "I'll simply ask him. I'll be speaking with him tonight anyway." Excusing himself with a courtly bow, he made his way from the room, picking his way among the other guests.

It was only after he'd left that Philip realized they had failed to exchange names, and that their entire conversation had been watched — with, it appeared, an almost indecent curiosity — by the wizened old lady of the dining room, who now sat regarding him and Margaret from the depths of a wing-back chair in the corner, dark eyes glittering.

"Maybe she's just got a crush on him," said Margaret later, as they moved about the little room preparing for bed. "He looks like he's nearly as old as she is, and men that age are scarce."

"I'll bet that by tomorrow he changes his mind about the pool," said Philip, with a curious feeling of hope. "I'll bet he was talking through his hat about how chummy he is with his boss. He probably won't even bother to phone the guy."

But shortly afterward, when Margaret returned from the bathroom at the end of the hall, she closed the door behind her and whispered, "You're wrong, honey. He's telling him about us right now — about how he met us in the lounge tonight."

"How do you know?"

"I heard him," said Margaret. "He has the room across from us."

Gathering his toothbrush and towel, Philip stepped gingerly into the hall. Sure enough, he could hear a man's low voice coming from the room opposite theirs, and recognized it now as belonging to their companion from the lounge. Still half turned toward the bathroom as if that innocent goal were all he had in mind, he tiptoed closer.

"Yes, they're both coming . . . What's that?" There was a pause. "No, not at all. They both seem quite well-bred. . . . Yes, she's charming. You're going to like her." Another pause. "It's agreed, then. Tomorrow, by three."

A door rattled somewhere down the hall. Philip whirled and hurried to the bathroom. By the time he emerged, the hall was silent. He thought he could hear, faintly, a snoring from the old man's room.

Margaret was already in bed when he returned. She looked up expectantly. "So? Hear anything?"

He planted a kiss on her lips. "He says you're charming."

She laughed and pulled him down beside her. "How in the world did he find out?"

Later, as they lay beside one another in the darkness, she stirred and said sleepily, "I hope I don't dream again tonight."

"Had a bad one last night? You didn't tell me."

"I can't remember it." She pressed her face deeper into the pillow. "All I know is, it was scary. Leave your arm around me, will you?"

"It'll fall asleep in three minutes."

"Leave it around me for three minutes."

He himself was asleep in less than that. Some time later — it must have been near dawn, for beyond the lace curtains the sky had grown pale — he felt himself awakened by a tugging at his arm, and heard Margaret whisper his name.

"Whatsamatter?" he mumbled.

"Is it really you?"

The idiocy of her question seemed, to his sleep-befogged brain, too enormous to contemplate. "Yes," he said, "it is." In a moment he was once again asleep.

"I got frightened," she explained the next morning, sunlight flooding the room. "I somehow got it into my head that there was someone else in bed with us."

"You mean, like threezies?"

"Like another man lying between us, pressing up against us both. And you know, I think he was black — a little black man."

"Maybe it was that guy from the mailroom."

She seemed not to hear. "What's so weird is, I'm sure it's the same dream I had the night before."

Philip yawned and rubbed his eyes. "Well, you know what they say about dreams. Wish-fulfillment."

She poked him in the ribs. "Honestly, Philip, you're so trite!" Frowning, she looked about the room — the cloud pattern in the wallpaper, a spiderlike crack in the ceiling, a row of dark pines in the painting above the dresser. "You don't suppose this place is haunted, do you?"

"Talk about trite . . ."

"I mean," she went on, "inns *have* been known to be haunted."

"Sure," he said, "they all are. Or claim to be. The ghost of some long-lost sea captain comes back every hundred and twelve years, or a serving wench who hanged herself appears at each full moon. Here it's probably Daniel Web

ster's brother-in-law. All part of the charm."

"Just the same, will you ask the Hartleys? Ask them if there's a ghost."

"Why don't you?"

"I'm too embarrassed."

Embarrassed himself, Philip asked Mr. Hartley in the office downstairs while Margaret finished getting dressed.

"No ghosts that I know of," the man said, scratching his thinning hair. Suddenly he grinned. "But golly, I sure would like to have one. It'd help business."

Their stout companion was waiting for them in the lounge by the time they had finished breakfast. "It's all agreed," he said genially. "Mr. Hagendorn would love to meet you both."

"It certainly looks like a beautiful day," said Margaret.

He nodded, beaming. "Magnificent. You'll be able to see clear to the Monadnocks." He seemed, on this sunny morning, the soul of jollity. "By the way, I didn't introduce myself last night. My name is Laszlo." His grip was like iron as they shook hands and arranged to leave after lunch.

When lunchtime arrived, however, a call came for Philip on the phone by the bar. "Sorry, Dad," said Tony, with a babble of youthful voices in the background. "I got it wrong. The track meet's tomorrow. Can you come see me today?"

"Hell," said Philip, "we've already made plans. I can't just —" He caught himself. "Yeah, sure, I guess. No problem. What time's good?"

"That's just it. I don't know yet. Jimmy and I are getting a lift into town, and we need you to pick us up." There followed a dismayingly complicated series of adolescent proposals and provisos, the upshot of which was that Philip was to wait for Tony's call "sometime in the early afternoon," whereupon further directions would be supplied.

Dinner with the reclusive Mr. Hagendorn was clearly out of the question. Laszlo, waiting for them at the bottom of the garden where the trail began, agreed to take Margaret up to the villa for a swim alone, and promised he would have her back by nightfall, in time for Philip's return. Far from being put out, he seemed to take the last-minute change of plans with surprising nonchalance.

"Mr. Hagendorn will of course be disappointed," he said. "He told me how much he looked forward to meeting you both. But at least I am bringing the young lady."

He was dressed in the same loose-fitting white pants, like some ancient man of medicine — they even had a drawstring, Philip noticed — but he'd added, over his white shirt, a warm alpine jacket, and his bald head was covered by an old-fashioned homburg. Far from being unfit for a protracted uphill walk, he looked younger and more powerful than he had by the fireside last night. It was clear he belonged on the mountain.

Margaret carried her bathing suit wrapped in a towel. A camera dangled from a strap around her neck. "I'll bet the view's wonderful from up there," she said, kissing Philip goodbye. She blew him a second goodbye kiss as she and her companion started gaily up the trail.

The air had grown chillier as they climbed, but their exertions kept them warm. The walk was proving more arduous than Margaret had expected. "How in the world did your boss ever manage to build a house up here?" she had asked half an hour ago, as they'd pushed their way up a steep section of path near the foot of the mountain.

"There's a narrow road that winds around the other side," Laszlo had said, pausing to tilt back his hat and wipe the sweat from his bald head. "We're going up the back way. You'll find, however, that it's faster."

He had sounded friendly enough, but since then they'd exchanged barely a word. As the day had grown colder, so had his mood; he'd become silent, preoccupied, as if listening for voices from the mountain, and when she'd asked him how much farther it was, he'd simply nodded toward the north and said, "Soon."

They had been on the trail for nearly an hour, following a zigzag course up the densely wooded slope. It was plain that Laszlo had misled her — or perhaps he had misled himself as well: though he continued, even now, to walk steadily and purposefully, with no sign of hesitation, she was beginning to wonder if he really knew the way as well as he'd claimed.

By the time the trail grew level, the trees had begun to thin out, and when she turned to look behind her she could see, in the spaces between them, the distance they had come. Below them spread the undulating green of the valley, though the inn and its grounds were lost from sight around the other side of the mountain. They were midway up the slope now, following a circular route toward the northern face. Ahead of her Laszlo paused, staring uphill past a faraway outcropping of rocks, and said, "We're nearly there. It's just past that curve of land."

Shielding her eyes, she searched the horizon for a glimpse of rooftops. Suddenly she quinted. "Who's that?"

"Where?"

"Up among those rocks." She pointed, then felt foolish; for a second she'd thought she'd seen a small black figure merge with the shadow of a boulder as it fell upon the uneven ground. But now, as she looked more closely, she could see that the ground lay covered in ragged clumps of undergrowth, and that it was this, tossed by the wind, that had moved.

"Come," said Laszlo, "the house is just ahead, and we will want to be back down before dark."

Philip sat impatiently on the back porch, leafing through one of the previous winter's ski magazines while waiting for the phone inside to ring. The potted geraniums blew softly in the breeze from off the mountain. He found it absurdly unnecessary to keep assuring himself that Margaret would be all right with Laszlo, but he continued to assure himself of that just the same.

He looked up to find himself no longer alone. The elderly woman from last night had seated herself in a chair nearby and had taken out some knitting. She nodded to him. "First time here?"

"Yes," he said, automatically raising his voice on the assumption that she might be hard of hearing. "Just a weekend vacation."

"I've been coming here for more than fifty years," she said. "My husband and I first came here in the summer of 1935. He passed on in '64, but I keep coming back. I've seen this inn change hands seven times." She gave a little cackle. "Seven times!"

Philip laid aside the magazine. "And does the place look different now?" he asked politely.

"The inn, no. The area is different. There've been a lot of new people coming in, and a lot of the old ones gone." She looked as if she were about to enumerate them, but at that moment the screen door opened and Mrs. Hartley emerged, an account book in her hand. She saw Philip and smiled.

"Still waiting for your call?"

"Yes," he said. "I don't know what's keeping that kid. I'll hear the phone out here, won't I?"

"Sure, but somebody's on it now, and it looks like they may take a while. I'll try to hurry 'em up."

Philip frowned. "How about the phone in the office?"

"Well, my husband's using it right now. He's going over the orders with our supplier down in Concord. But don't worry, it won't take long."

"The problem is," said Philip, with growing impatience, "my son may be trying to reach me at this very moment. Couldn't you transfer his call to a phone upstairs? I could wait in one of the vacant rooms."

She shook her head. "There aren't any phones up there. The two down here are the only ones we've got."

"But that's impossible," said Philip. He could feel his heart beginning to beat faster. "*Impossible!* That big fellow, Laszlo, has a phone in his room. I heard him just last night, and the night before. He was talking with someone named Hagendorn. I *heard* him." Yet even as the words rushed from his lips, he knew that what he'd said was false; that it was not impossible at all; that the only voice he'd heard had been Laszlo's. For all he knew, the man might have been speaking to the walls, the air, the empty room.

They had a word for people like that, people who talked to themselves. Psychos.

"*That's* where I know him from!" the old woman was saying. "He was Hagendorn's man. I knew I recognized him." She turned to Philip. "The person you were talking to last night, he used to be a kind of — oh, I don't know what you'd call him. A kind of valet. He worked for some dreadful man who lived up on the mountain. Bringing women up there for him, and I don't know what else. There were all kinds of stories."

"That's right," said Philip, eagerly grasping at any confirmation of the facts, however unsavory. "This guy Hagendorn. He's apparently got some sort of opulent villa up there."

The woman's eyes widened. "But that house burned down in 1939. I remember it — some kind of terrible explosion. Something to do with an oil tank. That man Hagendorn was burned to death, I remember distinctly, and everyone said it was just as well." She shook her head. "There's nothing up there now. There hasn't been a house there for years."

"Honestly, Laszlo," called Margaret, "are you sure we haven't come too far? This can't be the way."

They had passed the outcropping of rocks and had wandered out onto a narrow tableland overgrown by scrub pine and weeds. Ahead of them, curving against the mountain's face, stood what looked like a low broken-down stone wall half concealed by vegetation. Beyond it the pines appeared to be anchored in nothing but blue sky, for at their base the land dropped away into a haphazard tumble of boulders a thousand feet below, as if giant hands had sheared away part of the mountain.

Laszlo was well in front of her, his pace here grown more eager, while she, fearful of the drop, walked slowly now, eyes wary. With an impatient wave of his hand he motioned for her to join him.

"Laszlo," she said breathlessly, as she caught up with him, "where *are* we? Where is Mr. Hagendorn's house?"

"What's that? The house?" He pursed his lips and looked blank for a moment. Absently he gazed around him, like one seeing this place for the first time. Suddenly his gaze grew fixed; she noticed that he was staring past her feet. "Why, here's the house," he said in a small voice, as if explaining to a child. "It's right here."

She followed his gaze. He was point-ing directly into the gorge.

She stepped back in confusion. *He's only joking*, she told herself, but her stomach refused to believe her. She felt his hand fall lightly on her shoulder.

"I suppose," he said, "that first you'll want to see the pool."

"Oh, yes," she said, trying vainly to twist away. "Yes, show me the pool, Laszlo."

For a moment his arm dropped from her shoulder and she was free; but already he had seized her hand and was dragging her implacably forward.

"Come," he said. "There's so much to see." Smiling, he gestured at what lay before them, a vast cavity in the rock, deep as a pit, cut sharply as the lip of a monstrous pitcher into the precipice's edge. Laszlo tugged her closer. With a gasp she realized that its three stony sides were squared off, as regular as the walls of some enormous dungeon, but cracked and weathered now, patch-worked with lichen and moss — ancient. The bottom was a mass of weed-grown rubble opening onto the sky.

"And here," he said, "we have the pool."

Her wrist ached as he urged her to its brink. The ground seemed to shift beneath her as an edge of cloud swept past the sun. She took an unsteady step backward.

"No," he said in a chiding voice, "you can't leave now. You'll have to stay the night."

Drawn forward, she peered into the shadowy depths. Within them, as the light changed, something stirred, black as soot, like a stick of charred wood.

"The tiles are imported," he was saying. "No expense was spared."

She felt his free hand close tightly on her shoulder. The ground was spinning beneath her feet, the shadows rising to claim her.

"And now," he said, "it is time to meet Mr. Hagendorn."

Neither of the Hartleys had been of any help, beyond locating, in one of their local guidebooks, a map of the hiking trails that crisscrossed the mountain; but the old lady, lips quivering with concentration, had been able to make an educated guess where the villa had stood, just above a jagged grey line identified on the map as Romney Gorge. Judging by the map, it seemed, despite Laszlo's claim, the climb of at least an hour; but Philip made it in half

that — in time to see a burly figure in hospital whites struggling with a young woman at the top of the trail, by the edge of a cleft cut deep into the rock and opening onto the sky.

He raced toward them with what little strength remained, knowing that, days later and far away, he'd be able to tell his son the story of how one of the pair was snatched back from the abyss, while the other went to meet his master alone. ∎

OLD GODS PROWL

A bloated moon.
Corpses hang from trees.
In gelid air the smell of burning
Pumpkins.

It is the festival of death,
And lurid images grin from windows.
In darkness, revelers
Rap on doors,
Practicing an ancient blackmail,
Dressed in semblance
Of the demon gods.
You god of corpses,
This night we salute you,
You god of the ghastly
And livid god of gore.
Make sacrifice, householders,
Or bear the penalty.
Vestigial fires burn on porches,
Warding off the peril of visitors
From the other world.

Enshrined on lawns
Stand plaster Maries,
Skeletons hanging
By their bowers.
Old gods prowl
The night of the bloated
Moon.

— Nancy Springer

SISTER ABIGAIL'S COLLECTION

by Lloyd Arthur Esbach

Rob Moreland had walked past the pawnship countless times over the years and he knew it was there, of course; but ordinarily for him its dirty windows, screened by a heavy steel latticework, simply did not exist.

Except today.

It was the skull that caught his attention, impinging on the very edge of his perception. He halted, faced the window and peered through the dinginess. He moved closer for a better view. Unusual. A time-browned human skull skillfully encrusted with carefully fitted fragments of polished turquoise. Mexican, probably, and centuries old. Or possibly Mayan. Amazing, the skill of the primitive lapidaries; and strange to find this, a museum piece, in a pawnshop window.

He appreciated good gem work. Gem polishing and silver smithing — jewelry making — was his hobby.

He half turned away — spun back, staring. As he gazed, it seemed as though a hand had clutched his throat, cutting off his breath. His eyes widened in unbelief. It — couldn't be!

There on a strip of black felt amid a disordered spread of all sorts of jewelry was a beautiful oval pendant of pierced silver about three inches long. Set in its center was a large opal, flashing its vari-colored beauty even through the smudged glass, encircled by small, evenly spaced cabochons of alternating bright green and lavender jade. Moreland stared at the pendant with total incredulity. It was beautiful — and he knew every stone, every construction detail — for he had made it himself — but it simply could not be there!

Eight months ago he had buried his wife — and that pendant, her favorite jewel, on a Sterling chain and resting on her breast, had been buried with her.

With features set in grim lines Rob Moreland entered the pawnshop, pausing momentarily inside the door. With a single glance he took in the crowded confusion of merchandise covering walls and filling cases, then strode up to the store's single occupant, a short, heavy, dark-haired man standing behind a counter.

"That opal pendant in the window — where did it come from?"

Heavy brows lowered and the professional smile vanished. "That's information we never give out. Are you interested — ?"

"Mister, that happens to be stolen goods." Moreland's tones were icy. "And don't tell me I'm wrong. I *made* that piece and there's not another like it in existence."

The pawnbroker forced a smile. "My friend, you must be wrong. The lady who brought it in is known to us — and she wouldn't be the kind —"

"Get it out of the window," Moreland cut in. "Engraved on the back you'll find the words, 'For Ann — with all my love — Rob.'"

The man hesitated on the verge of protesting, then shrugged, opened the little door leading into the window and slid inside. Moreland's thoughts raced.

What was his next move? If he called the police what could he say? The implication would be dishonesty on the part of someone at the funeral home, the most respected in the city, and he really had no proof. One thing was certain. No matter what developed, he wouldn't leave the piece here. He'd buy it if he had to — but he'd insist on getting the name and address of the woman who had brought it to the pawnshop. She must be the key. And he *had* to learn the answer to this impossible affair.

The short man reappeared, his gaze fixed on the pendant cradled in one heavy hand. He nodded grudgingly. "That's what it says," then added defensively, "but that doesn't prove it was stolen." He changed the subject. "You do nice work, my friend."

Moreland's eyes narrowed and he spoke slowly, enunciating every word. "Mister, that pendant was buried with my wife in Pleasant View Memorial Park eight months ago!"

The pawnbroker gasped, his eyes widening. Carefully he placed the jewel on a square of black velvet on the countertop. He pursed his heavy lips, obviously weighing the situation, then finally spoke.

"My friend, I don't want any trouble. I don't know what this is all about — and I don't want to know. But first, who are you?"

Moreland produced a business card. "I'm a lawyer. So what's next?"

The pawnbroker grimaced, then nodded. "All I want is to get my investment back. The woman sold it outright — she always does — and I gave her a hundred. I've been asking three but you can have it for the hundred."

Moreland grinned sardonically. "I'll believe fifty. And I want the name and address of the woman. Otherwise I'll call the police. Probably should anyway."

Discussion followed; it ended with Rob Moreland leaving with the silver pendant, a signed receipt, and an address: Amelia Lowry, 818 Waverley — a tree-lined street in the oldest and most respected part of town.

As he continued on his interrupted way to his office, Moreland's mind was in a turmoil. The several blocks' walk did nothing to bring order to his thoughts. He greeted his secretary absently and entered his private office, closing the door behind him.

He placed the opal-and-jade pendant on his desk and stared at it intently, as though to solve its secret by his concentration. His thoughts moved back to the funeral, eight months ago. Tears blurred his vision as he again felt his loss — the end of almost thirty years of happy companionship. He visualized the last moments in the funeral home — saw again the pendant on Ann's breast, almost flamboyant in its vivid coloring, but her wish.

And then, sudden as a bell sounding he recalled Ann's cousin taking pictures — ghoulish, he had thought at the time. She had sent him a set of color prints; he remembered tossing them into a drawer. After a brief search he found the envelope and the picture that clearly showed the jewel. Sternly repressing any emotional reaction, he placed the single photograph in an envelope and slid it into an inside jacket pocket. Over the intercom he spoke to his secretary.

"Miss Connell, get me Lane Stafford of the Stafford Funeral Home."

"Yes, Mr. Moreland."

In moments the phone rang. "Mr. Stafford — Attorney Moreland. Will you be free any time this morning? . . . Good. I'll be there within the hour." He stood up, moved briskly into the outer office.

"Miss Connell," he said, "I'll be gone for the rest of the day, and I may not be in tomorrow. So far as I know, there's nothing pressing, but if you need to reach me, I expect to be home after four." He saw the curious look in her eyes but did nothing about it.

Outside, he retraced the twenty minute walk to his home. He'd need his car. Passing the pawnshop he could not resist another look at the turquoise-covered skull, an involuntary "Damn you!" flashing to his mind.

The part-time maid had already arrived and was busy with her chores. Too big a place for one man, he thought, as he had done many times before. Some day he'd sell and move into a bachelor apartment.

He drove across town to the funeral home, a structure of genteel opulence, typical of all of its kind. An attendant opened his car door and ushered him into the hushed interior where he was greeted by the somberly-clad Stafford himself. As the mortician led the way into his office, he said in professionally subdued tones, "Our paths haven't crossed in quite some time, Mr. Moreland. I trust that you have no need of my services."

Moreland shook his head impatiently. "No — but I do have a problem which I hope you can solve." After they were seated he drew out the photograph. "I suppose you'll recall my wife's funeral eight months ago. This picture was taken by her cousin — atrocious taste, I thought it." He indicated the pendant. "Remember the jewelry?"

Stafford frowned, obviously puzzled. "I do indeed remember."

"You may also remember that I made the piece; I do this as a hobby. This was the reason my wife valued it so highly." Without waiting for a response Moreland brought out the pendant and laid it on Stafford's desk.

"Less than two hours ago I found this in a pawnshop on Cumberland Street. It's the jewel I made which was sup-posedly buried with my wife. I'd appreciate an explanation."

Stafford gasped, his cloak of quiet dignity vanishing in a breath. "But — that's impossible! There — there's just no way that could have happened." In his agitation he stood up. "Do you realize what this means?"

Moreland nodded grimly. "I know very well what it means to you professionally. But there's the pendant."

The mortician dropped back into his chair, groping for words. "But — it's — it's impossible! You yourself — you drew the coverlet over your wife's face before we closed the casket. The floral blanket was placed on top — and after the pall-bearers, your friends, carried the bier to the hearse they stood by while the flowers were brought out and placed around the coffin. Then they went to their cars."

Again he stood up, suddenly remembering. "At the cemetery, I believe, you did not leave until the casket was lowered into the grave and the steel lid placed on the vault. Mr. Moreland — there just was no opportunity for anyone to open that casket!"

Rob Moreland nodded slowly. "I have to agree — but we still have the pendant."

Silently both men stared at the silver oval, the stillness broken only by the soft, all-pervading music in the background.

"Could it be," Stafford ventured hesitantly, "that someone made a copy of the piece without your knowledge? I mean during the years your wife wore it."

Moreland shook his head impatiently and exposed the engraved inscription. "Obviously it wouldn't make sense for anyone else to reproduce those words, and besides, the opal is distinctive. No two are exactly alike. And I *know* I cut and polished that particular stone. There can be no question about it." A sudden

123

thought returned.

"Do you have anyone on your staff named Lowry?"

"Lowry? No — and I haven't had as long as I can recall. Why?"

"That's the name of the woman who sold the pendant to the pawnbroker."

Eagerly Stafford seized the thought. "Then there's your answer."

Moreland rose to leave, a wry grimace on his face. "My answer to an impossibility."

As he drove away from the funeral home Moreland headed north to Pleasant View Memorial Park. It was absurd, he knew — grave robbers existed only in fiction and among archeologists — but he had to be sure. The park — nonetheless a cemetery — lay in the midst of a sweep of rolling hills, with second-growth forest as background and an expanse of well-kept farmland falling away from it to meet the horizon. The parklike fiction was sustained by an occasional fountain, well-trimmed hedges and randomly spaced trees, and with bronze grave markers flush with the thick turf, as carefully cut as a golf-course fairway.

He found the grave — and felt momentary embarrassment as he noted the smooth lawn covering it, only the marker indicating what lay beneath. He stood there in silent contemplation, aware of the inner emptiness that only time — much more time — could erase. He looked at the plate — Ann Moreland and the dates — and his own name beside hers, awaiting completion. He became aware of a caretaker working nearby and called out a greeting to break the somber spell.

As he drove back to town, no nearer an answer to his problem, he decided on a quick lunch, then a visit to Amelia Lowry.

Rob Moreland approached Number 818 Waverley Street with some uncer-

tainty. He had no idea what to expect, nor had he any plan of approach. There was no phone listing for Amelia Lowry, nor any other Lowry for that matter; probably a visit without warning would be best anyway.

The Lowry house, of white clapboard with gray trim and a gray slate gable roof, was set well back from the street in the middle of a well-kept lawn, not differing greatly from its neighbors. Somewhat austere and somehow aloof, he thought — the latter impression probably suggested by the tightly drawn shades. A closed-for-the-summer appearance.

He moved up a gray flagstone walk to a gray door flanked by two square white pillars supporting a narrow protecting roof. He grasped the weathered brass knocker, rapped sharply several times, then waited. After an interminable period he rapped again, more sharply. Finally after a third insistent rapping the door opened narrowly and a pair of faded blue eyes peered through the crack. As a precaution Moreland braced one foot firmly against the door, but a moment later it opened wider and a little old woman was framed against the dark interior.

"Oh," she exclaimed in a high, querulous voice, "I don't know you. I thought it was Henry who mows the lawn." Moreland noticed that she was breathing rapidly, almost panting, perhaps indicating excitement or the result of hurrying. "Who are you and what do you want?"

Moreland held out a calling card. "I'm Robert Moreland, an attorney, and I've come to see you about some jewelry. Mr. Rothstein of the pawnshop gave me your name. You are Amelia Lowry?"

"Y-yes," she answered uncertainly. "Mr. Rothstein? I suppose if he sent you it's all right." She hesitated, wavering. "Sister Abigail says I should never let strangers come into the house." She

125

looked at him intently through silver-rimmed glasses, then inspected his card. "A lawyer, you say? But they're mostly rascals. Are you a rascal?"

Moreland smiled ingratiatingly. "I hope not. I try to be honest. May I come in? It's really quite important."

While Amelia Lowry thought things over he got a quick impression of a figure out of the eighteen-nineties. Her dress was gray, of fine-spun cotton he judged, long-sleeved, full cut, with a narrow waist, the skirt reaching to the tops of her black shoes. Gray lace, supported by stays, completely covered her neck. Her face, finely featured, was deeply lined with wrinkles and was topped by thin, gray-white hair gathered in a small coil on the top of her head.

She made up her mind, opening the door and stepping aside. "I suppose it's all right. We never get company, you know. Not since father went away. We'll go into the parlor."

As Moreland followed the slowly moving and faintly wheezing figure through the shadowed hallway, he became aware of the mustiness and chill that permeated the place. Outside, it was a warm summer day. Within, the air was damp and stale, as though too long confined and reused and forever barred from sunshine. The mustiness, he thought, of a cellar with moist walls and an earthen floor.

No wonder the poor creature was short of breath.

The corridor was thickly carpeted, deadening sound. He followed the woman past two doorways, tightly closed, and through a third which she opened. The room was almost as dark as the hallway, the light of two windows kept out by heavy, tightly drawn drapes. His eyes had grown somewhat accustomed to the gloom and he was able to find the chair Amelia Lowry indicated.

"I don't need much light," she said half apologetically, "but I guess you'll appreciate a little more." She opened a drawer in a small square table beside his chair, drew out a box of matches and lit a kerosene lamp on the table top. Seating herself she said, "We used to have electricity but after Aunt Rebecca's house burned from the wiring we had it taken out.

"Now what have you in mind?"

Moreland's fascinated gaze had been circling the room. It was crowded with antiques, including companions to the horsehair seat on which he sat. Now he fixed his eyes on Amelia Lowry.

"Miss Lowry, I'm simply seeking information." He brought out the silver pendant. "I bought this from Mr. Rothstein, and I *must* find out where it came from."

The faded blue eyes glanced at the jewel, then a quick smile wreathed the pale lips, emphasizing the parchment-like texture of her face.

"Oh, yes — that is one of the last pieces I sold to Mr. Rothstein. It's from Sister Abigail's collection. You see — when we run low in funds I sell a piece or two. We must live, you know. I have her permission."

"But — where does your sister get the things?" Moreland persisted. "Where did she get this?"

Amelia Lowry shook her head regretfully. "I can't say — she never tells me — not that I want to know. But she travels a lot. All over the world. And she brings back things for her collection. Father started it many years ago." She glanced from side to side, then leaned forward with a show of secrecy. "I don't like some of her things, opals for instance. They are bad luck and she should know it. That's why I got rid of that piece." She added with a trace of pride, "I always felt I had better taste than Abigail."

Moreland frowned. This was no help

at all. Returning the pendant to his pocket he asked impatiently, "Is your sister here — may I talk with her?"

She cocked her head to one side as though listening. "No — she's not here just now. She comes and goes. She travels a lot. She always was one for traveling. Traveled with father even when she was a little girl. I never wanted to."

"When can I talk with your sister? Can she get in touch with me? I must find out how she got that pendant!"

Amelia Lowry stood up, spoke as though brushing his question aside. "I'll tell her what you said. She'll find you." A suddenly gleeful, almost impish expression transfixed the old face. As suddenly Moreland sensed the truth, and in spite of himself he felt a chill that was not induced by the musty damp of the room. There was senility here, but there was also a wilder insanity.

"Would you want to see Sister Abigail's collection?"

Better humor her and leave.

"If you wish," he said, "and then I must go."

Amelia Lowry drew a deep breath and started for the doorway, then glanced back. "You bring the lamp."

Holding the flickering, now slightly smoking lamp aloft, Moreland followed to a room at the end of the hall. As the door swung noisily open on dry hinges, his guide reached for the lamp.

"I'll take it in so you can see. I'm sorry," she added, "but you won't be able to go in. I can because I know how. Sister Abigail fixed it like this — doors and windows. Burglars, you know," she added brightly, bobbing her gray topknot. She moved slowly into the room.

As the weak light penetrated the darkness, casting grotesquely moving shadows, Rob Moreland caught his breath and his heart raced, his mind refusing to accept the testimony of his eyes. The room was lined with shelves and filled with tables — and all overflowed with an incredible assortment of jewelry and artifacts, like the plunder of the world's museums or a pirate's treasure. The dim glow was cast back by cups and armlets and chains of smoldering yellow gold. There was the flash of innumerable gems, kaleidoscopic in color and brilliance. He saw carved Chinese jade — a gold headdress that could only have come from an Egyptian tomb — ropes of pearls. And all in chaotic disorder. An utterly impossible display in an impossible place.

Moreland took an involuntary step forward — and struck an unseen barrier, an invisible wall as solid as the oak door itself. And suddenly he shivered.

This must be hallucination. This was the twentieth century, in a city where he'd lived all his life. On a street where dogs barked and children played and bacon fried in the morning. But he had to get out of here!

"Thank you, Miss Lowry," he said in a voice that sounded strange in his ears. "A remarkable collection. But I must be going. I can find my way out." Turning, carefully controlling every step, denying the urge to run, he moved through the dark hallway, opened the door and stepped out into a world of sanity and warm sunlight. Quietly he closed the door behind him. Only then, he realized, did he start breathing again.

The rest of that incredible day passed without incident. Rob Moreland drove into the country, trying not to think of his visit to Amelia Lowry, not daring to consider the implications of that treasure room, particularly in light of the jewel in his jacket pocket. It was a beautiful day for a drive. The blue sky with an occasional wisp of cloud, the green fields, placid cows browsing in meadows — the sights and sounds and odors of the country — had a soothing effect, freeing his mind of the pressures of all that had happened.

Reaching home about four o'clock, he called his office to learn that nothing had come up which needed his immediate attention. Then, feeling he could survey the day with some degree of detachment, he got out a writing pad and pen, slumped into a reclining chair in his library-den and with his lawyer's mind ran through the day, making notes.

When he had finished he read what he had written. Problems? Plenty. Answers? None. Except that things were happening which had no natural explanation. Especially that utterly unbelievable collection, and that doorway through which he couldn't pass. He glanced at his watch. Krebs might still be in. He dialled a number — Marvin Krebs, Private Investigator.

"Marv? Moreland. I have a little job for you. Should be no trouble — I'd do it myself but I'd rather pay for the legwork. I want everything I can get on a Lowry family. L-o-w-r-y. Start with Amelia Lowry, 818 Waverley. . . . Yes, they're local. Father, mother, siblings. Relatives — history. You know what I'm looking for. I'm particularly interested in Abigail Lowry. Got it? Get back to me as soon as you can — here at home or at the office."

He left his den and descended to his basement workshop, taking the pendant with him. Selecting a masculine-looking stainless steel chain from among a dozen reels, he cut off a length and prepared it to receive the opal-and-jade pendant. He'd wear it himself, until this mystery was resolved — under his shirt, of course. He wasn't risking possible loss.

For the rest of the day he followed his usual routine — a shower, reading, an early dinner at a favorite restaurant — not greatly enjoyed — more reading, on which he couldn't concentrate; a bit of television which he found boring, then bed. A restless and seemingly endless night followed.

About eleven the next morning Marvin Krebs appeared at Moreland's office. A little man, quiet, self-effacing, expert in his line.

"No difficulty whatever, Mr. Moreland." He handed him a typewritten report, several pages in length. "Amelia Lowry is the last of her direct line. There's one surviving relative, a distant cousin living in Sellersville. Amelia's father was a rather prominent archeologist who died in the nineteen fifties, probably old age. Amelia had a twin sister named Abigail who died of a heart attack ten years ago. You said you were especially interested in Abigail, but that's the only one I could find. But it's all there in the report. Anything else, Mr. Moreland?"

Mechanically the attorney answered, "No, Marv — that's all. Give your bill to Miss Connell."

Alone, Moreland stared blankly into vacancy. The words kept echoing in his ears: "Amelia had a twin sister named Abigail . . . died of a heart attack ten years ago."

He read the report. Krebs as always had been thorough. Every detail was there. Ancestors. Dates of births and deaths. Interment of the last three deceased in Pleasant View. Only one new item of information that Krebs hadn't told him — Abigail had also been an archeologist, had been Dr. Lowry's assistant and had continued in the field until her death.

But what did this contribute to the solution of his problem? Nothing — only more unanswered questions. He felt the unfamiliar weight of the pendant on his chest and thought savagely, "Why — *why* did I stop to look at that double-damned skull!" He'd be wise to forget the whole matter — but he couldn't. He'd have no peace of mind until he had the answer.

A few legal matters — some letters to dictate — these filled Moreland's morning. When the secretary left for lunch he told her he'd be out for the afternoon. He had made a decision. Distasteful though it was, he'd have to make a second visit to Amelia Lowry.

After lunch he drove to the old house on Waverley Street. He had to bang repeatedly before an answer came. This time he did not receive even the semi-welcome of his first call. The door opened about six inches; and there was obvious hostility in the little gray woman's thin voice.

"So it's you again! Abigail told me you'd be back — and I wasn't to let you in under any conditions. I shouldn't have let you in yesterday. Go away!"

Moreland forced a smile. "I'll go in a few moments, Miss Lowry. I just want to know why you insist on saying that your collection belongs to your sister Abigail — and that she continues to speak to you. You know, as I know, that she died ten years ago."

The woman's reaction was startling. She fell back as sharply as though he had struck her. Her pallid face became even more parchment-like, and she grimaced with utter fury.

"Don't you *dare* say that! She's more alive than you are! And it *is* her collection — she adds to it constantly. Why must you come here to make trouble?" Her voice grew shrill and her breath came in great gasps. "She doesn't harm anyone. These things are buried in the ground and she finds them. That's what archeologists do. Why did you come? Go — go —"

The worlds trailed off and an expression of sharp pain contorted Amelia Lowry's face. Her hands fluttered to her breast — and abruptly she collapsed in a gray heap.

In consternation Moreland froze. A heart attack! He should have known

with her troubled breathing. He had triggered this. He looked about wildly — saw a neighbor a half block away brooming her walk.

Cupping his hands he shouted, "Call an ambulance! Miss Lowry has had an attack!" He saw the woman hurry into her house, then he bent over the pathetic figure, pressing his ear to her breast. He detected a heart-beat, faint and irregular. Mouth-to-mouth resuscitation — it was all he could do. His fault — his fault! When the ambulance arrived there still was life in the frail body.

As the medics drove away with Amelia Lowry, Moreland made sure that the door was locked and followed in his own car. At the hospital he signed the woman in, since there was no one else to do so. To his relief he learned that she had been there before with a cardiac problem, so her physician was known. Assured that everything possible was being done, he drove to Police Headquarters and reported what had happened, minimizing his own part in the incident.

Deeply troubled, Rob Moreland returned to the Good Samaritan Hospital and inquired about her condition. He was able to speak with her physician. She was in the intensive care section, of course, and she was conscious. She was in stable condition, but her advanced years and congenital heart trouble made recovery very unlikely. When he asked to see her he was told only immediate family was permitted in intensive care. He told them there was no family and he was her attorney, and reluctantly permission for a brief visit was granted, with the admonition that he avoid any excitement.

He found the little gray woman awake, but very weak, equipped with all the wiring and tubing associated with emergency cardiac care. He spoke quiet words of regret, and apparently her earlier wrath had dissipated for she smiled faintly and weakly shook her head. He gained the impression that she wanted to speak, so he leaned over with an ear close to her mouth.

Her words came in a faint whisper. "Sister Abigail tells me — I'll soon join her. We'll be — closer than ever. And we've decided — what to do — with — the collection."

"Why not leave it to the Cumberland Museum in memory of your father?" Moreland suggested. "And you still have one living relative, you know — Greta Lowry."

Her reply came haltingly. "The museum — for some larger things — the things that were father's. But other things — we wouldn't want to — give up. The house — to Greta. You're a lawyer. Would you write — a will?"

"Of course." Moreland drew a note pad from an inner pocket. "Now you relax. It won't take long."

The language was as familiar as the back of his hand. He wrote rapidly, keeping it simple. The house and furnishings with the land to the distant cousin. The contents of the artifact room at the rear of the first floor, "consisting of archeological specimens and gems, as designated by my attorney, Robert Moreland, to the Cumberland Museum as a memorial to my father, Jonathan Lowry." There was more, to make everything clear, but it was confined to the bare essentials.

Slowly he read it to Amelia Lowry, asking if she understood and approved. She nodded. Moreland then rang for a nurse and when she responded explained what was wanted. She left and returned immediately with an associate. Very shakily and faintly, assisted by a nurse, Amelia Lowry signed the impromptu will and the nurses witnessed the signature. Moments later, with the document in an inner pocket, after words of encouragement, and after

leaving his home address and phone number, Moreland headed for the parking lot.

He had barely reached his den, dropping into the desk chair, when Amelia Lowry's physician phoned to tell him she had died. Mechanically he gave instructions that her body be sent to the Stafford Funeral Home; as mechanically called his secretary with the directive that she notify Greta Lowry in Sellersville about her relative's death, and that she notify Lane Stafford. He'd see him the next day to make the funeral arrangements.

As he cradled the phone Moreland wearily leaned back in his desk chair, scowling in self disgust. He certainly had made a complete mess of things today. He had brought on Amelia Lowry's heart attack and death — no amount of rationalizing would change the fact. He had displayed the finesse of a gorilla. As he thought of the tirade which led up to the tragedy, one statement rang in his memory.

"These things were buried in the ground and she finds them. That's what archeologists do."

He fingered the pendant through his shirt. "Buried in the ground." Found by a twin sister dead ten years! A ghostly grave robber. An archeologist plying her trade after her death! His frown deepened. The occult was one area about which he knew almost nothing, had no interest. There was little in his library that would shed light on the subject — probably the *Encyclopedia Britannica* was his best bet. Starting with "apparition" he began his research. He found little of interest until he reached "poltergeist."

There were almost three pages of comment, the writer citing instances of various objects moving without apparent cause, of things from a second storey room crashing to the floor in a room directly below. The reported occurrences were world wide. This brought to mind something he had read somewhere. A well-known Methodist — or was it Episcopalian — bishop receiving communications from his dead son. The son supposedly had transmitted objects halfway around the world, had transferred things from one closed drawer to another. Would this be called a poltergeist? But what matter a name!

One thing was evident. Now he'd never know the answer to mystery of the jewel that refused to remain buried. He was conscious of its weight against his chest. He could conjecture, but that was not knowledge. He thought of the invisible barrier that had blocked his entry into that incredible treasure room. Had it been real, and if so, had it vanished with Amelia Lowry's death? In any event, the local museum would get an amazing windfall bequest.

A sound overhead interrupted his thoughts, brought him stiffly erect. It was a dull, metallic thud, as though a heavy object had been dropped. It appeared to come from the rear of the second floor, a little used storage area. Instantly it was followed by a distinctly metallic clang.

He started to his feet, half crouching, the hair on his body bristling with instinctive dread. He stood erect — halted, waiting, scarcely breathing, listening for a repetition of the sound. It came with other noises of moving things. Stealthily he slid from behind his desk.

Then stopped.

He felt a sudden rush of frigid air, miasmic, lingering, passing within inches of his face, As though something invisible had brushed against him. A hint of motion in the corner of his eye drew his unwinking gaze to a hazy something forming above his desk. He held his breath, his body rigid.

It solidified — became the familiar age-browned human skull encrusted with turquoise. It dropped with a dull thud to the desk top.

The cold touched him, drawing a suppressed cry to his lips, sending an icicle of fear up his spine. And suddenly beside the skull materialized the opal-and-jade pendant on its chain, its pressure gone from his chest.

Overhead the clanging and thudding sounds continued unabated. Rob Moreland's thoughts whirled insanely, bits and pieces tumbling over each other. Amelia Lowry saying, "We've decided what to do with the collection." That will — in his handwriting, witnessed — giving him disposal of the jewelry and artifacts. And dominating everything, pounding in his brain, the single thought, the certainty that at that very moment, piece by piece, his storage room was being filled with Sister Abigail's collection. ■

Deathdances

by Tanith Lee

© G. Barr – 1987

Death came to Idradrud at suns' rise. She had appointments to keep.

The city lay along the banks of its river, a river green as jade and thick as soup, sprinkled with garbage, rotting hulks, and slave-powered quinqueremes like floating towers. The tiered towers on the banks kept still, save in the occasional spring earthquakes, which revived religion in the city as only the plague could do otherwise. Domes and minarets and steeples stood against the Great Sun and the Sun-Star on the yellow-green sky. But closer to the earth, the slums that were the truth of Idradrud, and the cut-throat alleys which bisected them, huddled in the warming sludge and muck. Diseased-looking steps piled into the water. There were those who got their living from the river in an immemorial way. Not by plying goods or hauling sail, not by catching the slightly-poisonous fish or the now-and-then-lethal oysters, but by detaining the corpses to be found in the water, stripping them of valuables, clothes, bones, and hair even — to be sold later for wigs. This trade was carried on by boat, or sometimes it was performed by those who, holding breath a long while, swam deep down into the jade broth, down to the bottom, and searched about there in the smoking mud.

* * *

Along among the quays, there was a gaudy stretch or two. Tenements dressed with balconies, awnings, birdcages, and evil exotic flowers. Here was a narrow house with its skirt in the river, pink plaster and ornate scrolling — all battered and peeling from sun and wet.

Bitza, as she gazed forth from a window, saw all those other buildings, hers and the rest, upside down in the water, one with a young woman gazing out of a window, and an eel snaking by through her hair. *But she is free*, thought Bitza on reflection, of her reflection.

Bitza, the Harlot in the Pink House, was not beautiful; but she had learned to give the impression of enormous and indefinable beauty, and was much desired. Even lords came to her slum palace to visit her. She might have been rich, but was not entirely honest. Certain enemies of her youth had died in mysterious circumstances. But she was concerned for the poor and gave most of her fortune away in the interests of caring for them — namelessly. Once, she had been poor herself, and dreaded the idea of it. Now her fine dark hair was curled and streaked with gilt. Her large eyes were perfectly shaped, the primeval colour of the river, but crystal clean as the river never was. Her body was strong and graceful, honey's hue in summer.

As she was putting loops of gold through her charming ears, Bitza's maid came fleeting in.

"Madam, a messenger-runner brought this."

Bitza took the slip of parchment. It had an unfamiliar look and texture, and a strong smell of incense. The wax was black, without a seal. Bitza imagined one of the more-than-usually eccentric lords of Idradrud was about to seek her out. (Her clients, to a man, exacerbated her.) There was one who liked to be chained and whipped by a

Bitza masked like a silver eagle, and another who liked to make love while semi-drowning in a bath of wine. . . . But Bitza broke the wax and opened the parchment, and it said: "As arranged, tonight I will be with you. *Death*."

In one of the blacker alleys, in an overhanging storey that seemed, with every creak of winter winds and capricious shift of spring quakes, ever more likely to fall smack in the six-foot-wide street below, Kreet was lying late abed, having kicked out his boy companion several hours before. Kreet of the dark soul and the light fingers, popularly called Golden Hands — Kreet the Thief.

He had stolen monumental treasures, they said. Then been robbed of them by others, whom he had later paid by various means, without recovering the prize, or else he used the loot to bribe the city authorities to be obliging, or he had gambled the proceeds away. Then, too, despite the squalor of his lodging, he was said to own the whole alley and half the streets and crumbling edifices around. While in the apartment of dirty, nasty rooms were there not chests full of money guarded by his ruffians, and bed-curtains sewn with rubies over a bed whose sheets were seldom changed? There were.

Kreet, the Thief with Golden Hands, was not a kind man. Swarthy of skin, foxy of face and eyes — though without a fox's good-looks — his bush of long black hair was washed once a year, while his beard bathed daily in his meals. All this had become a trademark. On the back of rivals he sometimes personally tattooed these words: *Kreet dislikes me*. And others, discovering the phrase, tended to shun the bearer of it.

But Kreet loved no one, not the fair boys he misused in his bed, not his gang of robbers, who admired him. Not even the chests of ill-gettings. Kreet stole because he was good at stealing. He liked the thrill of *taking*, and the violence — Then, the skeins of jewels in his golden mitts, Kreet scowled, dissatisfied. While the violence had repercussions that were beginning to worry him.

Yet, one thing Kreet did love and like, and now he summoned it to him off the bedpost.

"Come, my tatty joy!"

And down flapped a brown chicken, and nested in his arms, crooning peaceably and pecking scraps of grain from his hand that only last night had barbered a couple of noses, while Kreet crooned back in perfect communion.

But there was a scratch on the door. One of Kreet's gang came sidling in.

"A messenger-runner left this at the tavern."

Kreet looked at the parchment and the black wax seal. He squinted at his robberling and instructed, "Open and recite."

The robber, who had his letters as Kreet did not, obeyed. In an incredulous and quavering croak, therefore, he presently read out these words: " 'As arranged, tonight I will be with you. *Death.*' "

Where the bank rose away from the river, up terraces, up a hill, a domed temple stood, lifting its stone head clear of the slums. Between the temple's pillars, cool shapes went drifting; and the murmur of chants came and went, continually, and the purr of doves. The wings of these doves were clipped, for fear they should fly too far and meet the river gulls, which would tear them in pieces. But the priests and priestesses passed in and out carelessly, protected by their pale azure robes. The slums were superstitious. Idradrud did not rob or murder its priesthoods.

High up in the temple, just under the dome, was a round chamber with an altar of marble. From the altar ascended a hollow silver cup, in which there burned eternally a pastel blue flame. This flame, or Flame, was the spirit of the temple. Even in the earth-shocks, though it had faltered and smouldered, it had not gone out. It was said to be the result of a pulse of subterranean gas, which had breached the ground before the city's birth. Later, holy men saw in the gas — which could be made to catch bluely alight — a manifestation of the Infinite. So the temple was built, and the gas channelled up via pipes from cellar to altar and so into the hollow cup, where the flash of flint and tinder brought it alive once and for all.

There was always, it went without saying, a guardian for the Flame. It was the task of a year. With every new year, a new guardian was elected. To the esoteric creatures of the temple, this task, which shut them more or less all one year in the round chamber and its adjacent annexe and gallery, was considered a wonderful privilege.

Sume had now tended the Flame for seven months, and had therefore seven further months of the Idradrudian year to tend it.

White and slender as a wand, from aesthetics, incarceration, dedication, Sume wore the azure robes of her order, the sapphire rings; and her hair was bleached and tinted faintest blue, as was the hair of all the priests and priestesses. Sume, as she glided about her duties, at prayer, feeding the doves, moving along the gallery like a ghost, Sume was no different from every other inhabitant of that place. She seemed, as they all seemed, to have no life but the expression of the temple.

Yet, to such as drew close and glanced at her directly, there might come a check of surprise. For Sume's narrow delicate face hinted a curious passion that had nothing to do with solitude or the Infinite, and her dark eyes burned in a way that did not speak of sacred fire. The less reverent who had noticed this had said, *Here's one ripe for something.* But they were unsure what — mischief, mayhem, or only sensuality and sexual fall.

Now Sume poised before the Flame, straight and slim and upright, the Flame itself in human female guise. She had been repeating the morning orison, but as she concluded, a bell sounded outside at the annexe door. Someone wished to speak to her, or to bring her some news. Sume, who had no family but the temple, having been left an orphan on its steps, went quietly and without alarm to receive the visitor.

A young novice bowed low to Sume, the Priestess of the Flame. He held out a piece of parchment sealed in black.

"The High Priest sent me to you with this. A messenger-runner brought it to the porch."

Sume took the parchment with a slight astonishment. Once or twice, men of the congregation had importuned her, having seen her at her offices and become infatuate with her spirituality — or her promise of the spiritually profane. Was this another such note?

It was not. It read: "As arranged, tonight I will be with you. *Death.*"

It was now midmorning, and the two suns shone high above the city, putting gold-leaf on every crease of the river and every slate of every lurching roof. While along the spires and parapets of fine mansions and palaces, the suns unctiously poured, in dazzling bad taste.

Uphill, in a high-class inn on one of the nicer streets, a young army captain, raising his eyes, was promptly blinded by three golden statues positioned atop some lord's house across the way. So that, looking back at what he had been writing, he saw only their three black

after-images stuck there over his words.

It was tradition among the lower circles of the upper echelons of Idradrud, that third sons enter the army. Here they soared as fame, war, cash, and influence permitted. In seasons of conflict they fought the battles of Idradrud; or, as now, in peace, they strutted, idled, or slothed away the time at home. Mhiglay, a captain of three companies — sixty men — a soldier, but also a scholar, had eschewed both barracks and family and put up at the inn. Poet also, he had been employed all night with that. He could not sleep, felt he would never sleep again. He had seen too much of friends who died, and enemies he did not hate yet must kill. And recently, a man who was very nearly his brother in everything but blood, had turned out to be a traitor; and it had fallen to Mhiglay to attend the military scaffold. Please for mercy for this man as Mhiglay had done, mercy had been omitted. The near-brother had spat on him and died in agony, screaming. A scene often recaptured in dreams, which caused Mhiglay to turn slumber out of the room whenever possible.

Though duty-bound to be a clever and able soldier, and dutifully being all the rôle demanded, it did not fit him. He had always half suspected, and now was sure. Blond of hair, handsome, and thoroughly haggard and hollow-eyed from lack of sleep and sleep's scourge when he accepted it, he looked the poet and scholar he surely was, and also somewhat the haunted murderer he seemed to himself to be. None would or could console him. Least of all his family of puffed uncles and irksome brothers.

No hope, no help, Mhiglay, the Captain of Three Twenties, had written on the page. *No cure, for the sickness is my life.*

And just then, even as the after-images of the statues faded out of his sad, distraught, and sleepless eyes, someone rapped on the door. An inn-girl entered, flirtatiously, (he did not see), to tell him a messenger-runner had brought something, and to hand him a leaf of parchment sealed in black.

Mhiglay opened and read the parchment. He gave a contemptuous laugh.

"As arranged, tonight I will be with you. *Death*."

There is a saying in Idradrud of the green river, *Life will dance with some, and some Life will refuse. Yet Death dances with every man.*

When Bitza, the Harlot in the Pink House, read the message, she said, boldly, "Some kink-full suitor is playing a trick. I had better get ready."

When Kreet, the Thief with Golden Hands, read the message, he said, nervously, "Some filth-laden foe is after my hide. I had better get ready."

But when Sume, the Priestess of the Flame, read the message, she said, stilly, "Can this be so? Well, I am here."

And when Mhiglay, the Captain of Three Twenties, read the message, he said, coldly, "Then let her arrive. I am waiting."

It was suns' set. First the Great Sun sank down behind the western bank of the river, in a murky glory of red, russet, and amber. The Sun-Star followed like a lover. The sky turned to walnut brown, resembling an expanse of highly-polished table, then went black. The stars appeared, in complex patterns, such as the Sphynx, the Lion, the Lyre. The most intricate of all was that of the Winged Woman, which stretched for a quarter of the night across most of the easern horizon, and was easily discernable, even by a child — body, limbs, wings, hair, drawn in blots of diamond. The air over Idradrud was thickly crusted with stars. So many that, even

lacking a moon, which it always did, night was always also very nearly bright as day, except if there should be overcast.

Darkness being present then, punctually Death knocked at Bitza's door.

Bitza reclined in or upon a black couch like a coffin. The room was hung with black cerements and had generally been made to imitate a tomb. Bitza herself wore a translucent shroud, and bone combs in her hair.

"It is a woman," hissed Bitza's maid.

Bitza raised her brows. "Very well."

And so Death was shown up to the tomb-room, and Bitza looked at her with disfavour.

"I do not as a rule deal with women," said Bitza. "But if you will meet my price, I will consider your desires."

Death smiled. When she did so, Bitza realized she had been mistaken. "Then," she said, "it is a fact?"

Death nodded.

Soon after, Death approached the door of Kreet's lodging.

A hundred butcheroos stood ready with drawn knives, but Death naturally walked through the knives and came to Kreet's door, and the bars and bolts crumbled at her touch.

"Kill me, would you!" yelled Kreet, standing on his unclean bed. The chicken flapped his feathers and tried to take a peck at Death, but Death said, "Hush," and the chicken went to Kreet and sat on his boot. And then Kreet himself said, after a medley of oaths and cries, "Spare me! Spare me! Or at least, you damnable fiend, spare this innocent chicken —"

"The chicken," said Death, "is not inevitably my business."

Not long after, Death met Sume as she glided along the gallery of the Flame-chamber.

Sume paused. "Is it you?" she asked.

Death waited.

Sume meekly bowed her head in assent, though her dark eyes flamed more fiercely than the Flame.

And next Death came through the door of Mhiglay's room at the inn, which door had been left open, and Mhiglay seized Death in his arms and kissed her passionately on the lips.

As everyone understands, Death too plies a Boat along a River. Small shock then to behold the slim sable craft with its sickle of sail, going like a sombre thought between the two-banked landscape of the city and its lights, and over the lighted stars in the air, with only one lamp at the prow to let down a glistening green tail into the water. Now and then, one of the afloat tower-tiers of a quinquereme is passed, at rest for the hours of night, and going up twenty-nine feet, rigging folded and oars drawn in, and slaves lying in swoon-sleep, and masters getting drunk. Or some other river thing goes by, and perhaps hails the dark boat, getting no answer. Death herself stands for'ard, guiding the vessel, remote. There has never been, and is not now, any requirement to describe Death. Who cannot picture and has not pictured her? All know her and how she seems.

But amidships the four passengers sit. Fascinating Bitza is twisting her necklaces, trying to fashion some trick. Ugly Kreet scowls, and sweats, wondering if Death is bribable. And on his shoulder the chicken broods, having refused to leave him. Fey Sume is immaculate, eyes cast down. And handsome Mhiglay, his head thrown back, is bitterly enjoying the wretched romance of it all, glad to be going away.

Finally Kreet erupts.

"I complain!" he shouts, and the chicken applauds. "I complain at the bloody and stenchful injustice. Who is in charge here?" No one replies, though Bitza looks at him and Sume ignores him, and Mhiglay laughs ironically and

insultingly. Kreet lapses into invective.

At that, "Do not offend her," cautions Bitza. And bites her manicured nails.

Sume whispers, "What is life? I have had no life." Her eyes burn holes in the night.

Mhiglay says, "Be thankful."

At this point, however, all four perceive a new area of darkness on the dark, a sort of archway rising up out of the river, higher even than the quinqueremes, the distant towers on the banks: The entry to some chasm. It was never on the river before, this chasm, this tall black arch. And Bitza screams, and Kreet curses and grovels — and the chicken hides in his collar — and Sume again lowers her gaze, and Mhiglay sighs.

And the boat of Death creeps nearer and nearer toward the massive black hump where no lights show and no stars are. Only the green tail in the water flickers before them, and against it, the remote figure of Death, who suddenly speaks.

"Remember," says Death, to each and to all, "that my message to you read *as arranged*." (Then there is a silence, as the four in the boat consider, reject, revile, puzzle on, these words, not essentially in that order, while the black archway comes closer and fills the world and is surely about to swallow them.) "I am," Death then announces, "myself. Not necessarily what you think me." (And they are, surely, swallowed whole.)

It was from the most peculiar dream that the Harlot woke. In the dream there was a boat, which had passed around a wide dark loop inside some cavern, and come out at length on the spangled lime-jade water of Idradrud's river. At which the Harlot opened his eyes and looked about him, and found the familiar cosy coarse splendour of his Pink House. Soon, joking off the dream, he rose, called his maid, and toyed with her in a luxuriating bath. She washed his hair, streaked it with gilt at his somewhat coy request, and shaved him. When once he was clothed, (in elegant leathers), his eyes drawn round with kohl, and the gold rings in his ears, the Harlot took breakfast. Then he called, "Come, my tatty angel!" and a brown chicken jumped into his lap, and they clucked pleasantly to one another.

The Thief, meanwhile, had woken from a similar dream, up in a dirty flea-tip, and at once, in a cruel clear voice that was not to be denied, exclaimed that linen must instantly be changed, floors scrubbed, and an unaccountable quantity of chicken feathers removed from the hangings.

Ruffians and knife-boys leapt to obey with alacrity. One crouched fawningly at the Thief's blue slippers. He asked if he was needed to read her anything.

"Read?" she kicked him flying. Her pale face was flushed and her black eyes shone with relaxed malevolence. "I can read quite well for myself, you damnable ant. Was I not temple-trained?"

The kicked cut-throat beat a retreat. How could he have been so aberrant? The whole slum quarter sang of her learning, yearningly.

While the Priest who guarded the Flame had been writing poetry to it all night, adrift in intellectual space. Or so it seemed he had, only once contrastingly drifting into a peculiar dream, doubtless of vast psychic import, when he could be bothered to interpret it — but he had cast it aside on waking with a rather military shrug.

Now, standing over it, he regarded the sacred Flame, just immortalised in his verse, with eyes that matched the fire and blond hair which did not. Eventually, leaning forward, he blew the Flame out.

"Yes," said the Priest, with gentle satisfaction. "And *there* you have it." And striking flint and tinder, he lit the Flame again, nodded at it, and walked from the chamber.

Outside, he found a novice on duty, waiting to take up the poet-Priest's guardianship whenever he felt inclined to abscond. This often happened, as the novice would explain. This one Priest was noted for such behaviour. And for other actions. For example, exactly to-day, striding to the temple treasury with an idle yet undeniable salute at its sentries, he flung open the coffers. Going out on the street he began to distribute largesse to the deserving, (and sometimes, to the beautiful). "Every temple, even ours, should have its oddity, its wayward matter," the High Priestess had declared in glowing defence of the poet. "We are admired for our tolerance. Besides, his writings and verses are nonpareil." They were rather captivated, too, by his lack of guilt over anything.

And last of all, the Captainess of Three Twenties, which she already had some plans to increase to Six Twenties before high summer, had left her inn and gone home. Home to that family of hers so rich it was ludicrous. They were somewhat in awe of her. It was not very usual to have one's daughter enlist in the armies of Idradrud, and then to become celebrated and successful there. But she had a way with men, the Captainess. Riding into battle, with her dark hair under helmet and war-plumes, her green eyes feral, and her sword-hand rock steady, she had inspired an exceptional sort of fright in many an adversary.

Her kindred welcomed her this morning with uneasy open arms, almost as if they had expected someone else, and were bruised by the medals clanking on her delightful breast. (It was said, the last enemy general she had whipped across seven hills.) But now she only seemed inclined to push her brothers in the lily-pond. And there they went, splish-splash.

Those who got their living in an immemorial way along the river of Idradrud, these had had a busy night. What a catch — gems, cutlasses, military insigniae . . . and — *chicken feathers?*

It would appear a harlot had been murdered by a mad client and pushed in the water from her balcony. It turned out a thief had been attacked by rivals and dumped there, with a hole in his back, and a little fowl clinging to his collar. It seemed a priestess had grown insane and run from her temple to suicide in the unsavoury depths. It transpired an army captain had done likewise.

And yet, is there not something not quite right with the bodies the traders in death have fished from the river? Brought in by net and oar alongside the narrow boat, or raised up by the hair through panting divers bursting the surface, muddy from the river's bottom, and with shells in their beards — cadavers, such as one expects, but skins unsolid, faces washed *too* expressionless — "Just take the jewels, the coins and knives, the rings, the medals, and sword — Why philosophise? Why quibble? The river does that to corpses. But quick — strip them quick — before they melt away altogether and are gone."

And over there in the Pink House, Kreet bangs open the door and roars at his visitor: "Late again, you dog of a lord!" And thrashes a truly grisly whip, (to loud approving cackles from some-

where), and the lord — in startled, horrified misgiving and ecstacy — flops on his face to get his money's worth — and never did he recall such *enthusiasm* in his treatment formerly —

And along there, in an alley two feet wide, Sume, who has recently tattooed on the ankle of an enemy: *Sume* likes *me*, Sume picks the pockets of sozzled merchants as she asks them the hour, or the way to the blue temple of the Flame, to which she has no intention of going. And presently points out an exquisite boy, who blushes, at which Sume says to her loving homicides: "Bring me that one, for later," and smiles, oh-so-softly-eyed —

And up there, in the blue temple a moment ago mentioned, Mhiglay is sitting with his feet on the High Priest's inlaid table, oblivious to duty, the table, and the High Priest, writing nonpareil poetry on an orange skin, proudly and fondly watched on every side —

And in the topmost lower mansion of Idradrud, where gold statuary crowds the roofs, Bitza is having a 'mock' duel with an opinionated uncle, and he is in grave fear of his life —

And it is of no use asking what goes on. Asking what arrangement, precisely, led to this. Or if perhaps we are not all involved in it and simply do not recollect, or have been, or will be . . .

Ask Death. There she is, down in the groves just beyond the city, where the myrtles grow with snakes around their boughs. Death, pretty as a picture, in between the wild white trees. Look, you can see what she does. Death dances, with her shadow — and why should she not have one? — and all the stars in her hair. ∎

Reviews

by John Gregory Betancourt

Opening Shots, and Policy of Sorts

Welcome to review section of the first issue of the new *Weird Tales*™! For those who aren't aware of my qualifications to pontificate on books & other subjects, I'll state them briefly: I've been reviewing science fiction and fantasy professionally for about three years, first in *Amazing Stories*, then in *Fantasy Book*; I've also been reading bad (and good) fiction editorially for almost five years now, for both magazines and book publishers. I tend to select less-obvious books, rather than best-sellers: Diana Wynne Joneses rather than Stephen Kings. Please use my comments and reviews as a gauge to your own book-reading habits. If you find our opinions in complete agreement, terrific! If not, well, tough. You'll just have to enjoy the books I pan.

Mostly, though, we're here to have a good time. So sit back, and enjoy.

Books, Obscure and Not

The Legacy of Lehr, by Katherine Kurtz
Walker Books, 235pp., $15.95

Technically, I suppose, this book is science fiction — but it has vampires and giant blue cats, so what more could you want?

Seriously, this is a murder mystery in a science-fiction setting, and it works as both SF and a mystery, which I imagine is pretty hard to do. The luxury spaceliner *Valkyrie* has been detoured to an out-of-the-way planet to pick up four captive, catlike animals — the Lehr of the title — for transport back to civilization. But then people start dying, and it looks like the cats are doing it. It's up to Mather Seton and his wife to prove otherwise.

The book ably showcases Kurtz's strengths as a writer. Her characters are briefly sketched, partly (I imagine) because of length restrictions in Walker's Millenium series, but even so they are real people whom one can care about. Even the Lehr-cats come alive as characters: each has its own personality. The action is non-stop, in the finest pulp action-adventure tradition, and there is genuine thought behind the ideas in the story. Recommended.

The Model, by Robert Aickman
Arbor House, 138pp., $14.95

Aickman was a masterful writer of horror stories, and his death in 1981 marked a great loss to the field. Now this very short novel has been found in his papers and pub-

AUTHOR OF THE BESTSELLING SERIES
THE CHRONICLES OF THE DERYNI

KATHERINE KURTZ

THE LEGACY OF LEHR

lished by Arbor House.

Alas, I found it a disappointment. While the tale is beautifully, even poignantly written, it seemed to be building to an ending that just wasn't quite satisfying enough: imagine reading a classic like THE LORD OF THE RINGS where it all turns out to have been a figment of Frodo's imagination; and when he returns home, only he is changed, not the world. There are elements in The Model, like Lexi, the wandering revolutionary, which lead one to expect Elena Andreievna's personal oddysey will end with a rebirth or reawakening of her old world.

Briefly, Elena Andreievna is the daughter of a country lawyer in Czarist Russia. When family fortunes begin to decline, she takes refuge in a fantasy world revolving around the model of a stage she has constructed. Gradually she falls away from the world and becomes a ballerina in a dreamworld populated by all manner of odd folk. It is essentialy a journey through life, mainstream rather than genre fantasy. Recommended if you like Aickman's work.

Voodoo Dawn, by John Russo
Imagine, Inc., 190 pp., $9.95

John Russo is probably best known as the co-author of Night of the Living Dead, which has become a cult classic among movie buffs. He has also written a number of other screenplays and books. It should be of no surprise to anyone that his latest, Voodoo Dawn reads like a movie — from pacing to characterization. Which is not to say it's bad; it's certainly not! It has a pulp vitality which makes it hard to put down.

The story: In Haiti, the voodoo king Changa (a living incarnation of the god of death), is finally driven out of the country by police pursuit. (It seems he's been kidnapping children and eating them. Being a god, he feels no moral qualms about it.) Like so many Haitian refugees, he and six of his disciples travel to Florida by boat. Unfortunately the boat sinks and they're all drowned. Changa, of course, rises from the grave and sets about massacring innocent tourists to raise his disciples and make them zombies, and it's up to the U.S. police to stop him.

The multiple viewpoint is used effectively. Except for a couple of minor but nagging flaws with the writing — like a tendency to drop out of viewpoint and foreshadow people's deaths, and the over-use of bookisms (teased, jibed, snapped, acknowledged, gasped) instead of "said" in places — it's a solid, well-crafted novel. My main reservation is the price: ten bucks for a trade paperback with large type seems a bit high. There is also a hardcover edition which is limited to 1000 copies. You can order either one it directly from the publisher: Imagine, Inc., PO Box 9674, Pittsburgh, PA 25226. Add $2.50 for postage/handling

Archer's Goon, by Diana Wynne Jones
Berkley Books, 241 pp., $2.95

Now here's a real bargain: a witty little urban fantasy from a popular British writer. When young Howard Sykes comes home from school, he finds the house in a turmoil. There is a very large, very stupid person — a self-proclaimed Goon — taking up most of the kitchen. It seems Quentin, Howard's father, hasn't sent in his latest two thousand . . . words, not dollars (or pounds), as it turns out. Quentin is a writer and (it de-

REVIEWS

velops) his writings have been restricting seven Superior Beings — magicians with vast powers — to town. These Superior Beings would all rather be out ruling the world, and to this end most of them become involved in a power play for Quentin's work. Of course it falls to Howard, his little sister Awful, and his best friend Fifi to try and get to the root of the matter.

It's a delight to read this kind of ageless fantasy. I wish there were more of it around. Recommended.

The Jaguar Hunter, by Lucius Shepard
Arkham House, 404pp., $21.95
This is Shepard's first collection, and it contains: "The Jaguar Hunter," "The Night of the White Bhairab," "Salvador," "How the Wind Spoke at Madaket," "Black Coral," "R&R," "The End of Life as We Know It," "A Traveler's Tale," "Mengele," "The Man who Painted the Dragon Griaule," "A Spanish Lesson," and a foreword by Michael Bishop — essentially the best of Shepard's

short fiction. If you've never read his elegant fantasies, this is certainly the place to start; if you're familiar with his work, this is the place to pick up the stories you missed. And, of course, Arkham House does its usual splendid job of production, with cover and illustrations by J.K. Potter. Recommended.

Sight Seen: In Brief
Since *WT*'s primary retail distribution is to comic-book stores, I thought I'd review some of the graphic novels that have been coming my way. The following are, in essence, one-shot comic-books with adult themes, perfect-bound, on good paper, and at rather hefty prices.

Michael Moorcock's Elric of Melnibone, by Thomas, Gilbert, Russell, and Orzechowski
First Comics, $14.95
It took me a while to get used to Russell's drawings of Elric, but once I did I was thoroughly hooked. The images are striking, the

text faithful to the novel, the lettering easy to read. In all, it's a classy job. Kudos to all involved. For Moorcock completists, there is an interesting two-page foreword by Moorcock himself. Recommended.

Robert Bloch's Hell on Earth, by Keith Griffen and Robert Loren Fleming
DC Comics, $7.95

This slender comic is an adaptation of a short story by Robert Bloch, who is surely no stranger to all *WT* fans! In fact, "Hell on Earth" originally appeared in *Weird Tales*™ in 1942. Briefly, it's a deal-with-the-devil story with a twist: two scientists and a horror writer accidentally summon the devil and restrain him in a glass cage. Of course, when the devil begins influencing the characters' minds, bad things happen. It's fun, but the drawings are mundane; for $7.95 I'd expect more.

Mage: The Hero Discovered, by Matt Wagner
Starblaze Graphics, $12.95

This one is entirely the author/artist's own work; it's slight on words, but has some neat pictures. The plot's a bit old, too: good guy who doesn't know he has super-powers is suddenly thrust into a cosmic battle between good and bad. Wagner has a light touch; it kept me reading. Note: the story is not complete in this volume; it ends with

a "To Be Continued." Recommended if you like graphic novels.

Sight Heard: Also in brief

Ursula K. LeGuin's The Word for World is Forest, read by Lawrence Ballard
Book of the Road, 2 cassettes (3 hours), price unknown

I picked up this nifty little 2-tape package at the American Booksellers Association Convention in Washington, DC. Book of the Road certainly has a winner here: Ballard's reading is terrific. The story is well crafted, too. (Well, it *did* win a Hugo . . .) If you have a cassette player in your car, this is something that would be very helpful in whiling away the hours on a long trip. It would also make a good present for someone who has trouble seeing or reading. Recommended. If your local bookstore doesn't carry tapes, you might write to: Book of the Road, 7175 SW 47th St., Suite 202, Miami, FL 33155. Ask for a catalog.

Bradbury 13, Brigham Young University Media Production Studios
The Mind's Eye, 6 cassettes (12 hours), price unknown

Here is something you really should look for: a package of 6 tapes of dramatizations of Bradbury stories. About half of the dramatizations are first-rate; two are uninten-

tionally humorous; the rest are fair. I'd say that's a good percentage.

These 13 episodes (12 come in the box; you send $1.00 for the final cassette, which also contains an interview with Bradbury) were originally produced for National Public Radio, the PBS of the air-waves. A list: "A Sound of Thunder," "The Screaming Woman," "The Fox and the Forest," "The Happiness Machine," "Night Call, Collect," "The Ravine," "Kaleidoscope," "Here, There Be Tygers," "The Veldt," "There Was an Old Woman," "The Wind," "Dark They Were, And Golden-Eyed." All the episodes are quality productions, with good actors, good special effects, and appropriate music. Recommended. (If your local store doesn't stock The Mind's Eye's tapes, I know they have a catalog and do mail order business; I've ordered quite a few old radio shows from them. Address: The Mind's Eye, Box 6727, San Francisco, CA 94101.)

Small Press: Unknown Worlds

Weirdbook 22, edited by W. Paul Ganley Weirdbook Press, 64pp., $6.00 (+ $1.00 p&h)

One of the most under-appreciated small-press fantasy magazines around is W. Paul Ganley's *Weirdbook*. In its two decades of existence, it's published major fantasy works by everyone from L. Sprague de Camp to H. Warner Munn. This latest issue contains new material by Brian Lumley, Darrell Schweitzer, Gerald W. Page, Janet Fox, and Charles R. Saunders. Cover is by Stephen Fabian. Order from: W. Paul Ganley, Publisher; Box 149, Amherst Branch; Buffalo, NY 14226.

Odds & Endnotes

Materials for review should be sent to: John Betancourt, 410 Chester Ave., Moorestown, NJ 08057. Copies should also be sent to the editorial offices. ∎